DARE TO LOVE

BOOK YOUR PLACE ON OUR WEBSITE AND MAKE THE ARABESQUE ROMANCE CONNECTION!

We've created a customized website just for our very special Arabesque readers, where you can get the inside scoop on everything that's going on with Arabesque romance novels.

When you come online, you'll have the exciting opportunity to:

- View covers of upcoming books

- Learn about our future publishing schedule (listed by publication month and author)

- Find out when your favorite authors will be visiting a city near you

- Search for and order backlist books

- Check out author bios and background information

- Send e-mail to your favorite authors

- Join us in weekly chats with authors, readers and other guests

- Get writing guidelines

- AND MUCH MORE!

Visit our website at
http://www.arabesquebooks.com

DARE TO LOVE

YAHRAH ST. JOHN

ARABESQUE

★BET BOOKS™

BET Publications, LLC
http://www.bet.com
http://www.arabesquebooks.com

First Printing: July 2005
10 9 8 7 6 5 4 3 2 1

Printed in the United States of America

*To my uncle Marvin Smith for being a rock,
a tower of strength and a surrogate father
when I needed one.*

ACKNOWLEDGMENTS

I've survived the roller coaster of writing this second connecting novel with the help of some truly incredible people.

To my mother, Naariah Yisrael, who religiously read every draft and provided her valuable wisdom as an avid reader: thank you. You've been not only my best friend, but a confidence booster, too!

To my loyal best friends: Therolyn Rodgers, Tiffany Harris, Dimitra Astwood, and Tonya Mitchell: thank you for all your support. I am truly blessed to have such wonderful women like you in my life, who know when to allow me to write and when to tell me to take a break. You rock ladies!

To my dear cousins, Gita Bishop, Herschel Smith, and Ronetta Smith, it's because of you that I've had such a wonderful resurgence of family in the last year, and I'm the better for it. Thanks guys.

To the entire Mitchell family, thank you for your support, encouragement, and tremendous spirit in helping promote my first book. You're simply the best!

Most of all, I would like to thank my father, Austin

Mitchell: you've been amazing! A daughter couldn't have a better publicist in her corner. Thank you so much for making my journey to becoming a published author *One Magic Moment*.

CHAPTER ONE

"Adrian and I are through," Lexie declared as she stormed into her mother's catering shop on Main Street in Highland Park, Illinois. Lexie was livid. She'd just come from an embarrassing interlude with her ex-boyfriend Adrian Turner, in which he'd begged and pleaded for her take him back, all because her mother had set up an ambush date.

How dare the woman interfere in her private affairs? Tossing her purse and suede Dolce & Gabbana jacket on a nearby chair, Lexie strode to the counter. The jacket missed and fell to the floor instead. Oblivious, Lexie nearly stepped on it as she prepared for a face-off.

"Listen up, mother." Lexie spoke firmly and prayed her message got through. "I live my life according to *my* terms. And I will not be told how to live it. Especially not by you."

"Who's doing that?" Isabel Thompson fired back. Leaning down, she picked up Lexie's jacket and placed it on the back of the chair.

"You are!" Lexie huffed with arms folded across her chest. "You seem to think you know what's best for me, better than I do." She reached out and snatched one of her mother's freshly baked goodies. "Well, I'm telling you, Mom, the days of you telling me who I can and cannot date have come and gone."

"Don't you think I know that?" Isabel handed her a napkin to prevent crumbs from falling. "All I'm saying is that Adrian was the perfect man. He's everything a woman your age should be looking for: good-looking, intelligent, charming, and stable. Girl, he was exactly the kind of man you need."

Lexie rolled her eyes in frustration. At twenty-eight, she already knew exactly the kind of man she needed and wanted. Her mother was using her breakup with Adrian as an excuse to focus on a larger issue: her job as a junior fashion buyer for Bentley's department store. Isabel had a problem with the choices Lexie had made, including those about her daughter's career. But that wouldn't change the fact that Adrian was not Lexie's soul mate.

Boring was what he was. She should have never brought him to dinner because in a few short months, Adrian Turner had managed to endear himself to the entire Thompson family. He always showed up with flowers for her mother or brought his wealthy investment and developer buddies to her brother Sebastian's showings. His cronies alone helped keep Sebastian's photography studio afloat. Her family loved the man. So what was the problem?

Plain old chemistry.

There were no sparks between her and Adrian. When they'd made love, Lexie tried hard not to think of other more exciting lovers. She'd had her share of men who knew how to please a woman in the bedroom. And Adrian wasn't one of them. Several times, she'd had to fake an orgasm just to get him off her.

The more she thought about it, the more she realized that she was just too much woman for him.

Blessed with smooth mahogany skin, almond-shaped brown eyes, exotically high cheekbones, and a size-six body, Lexie could easily pass as a model. At five-foot-ten with killer long legs, she was strikingly beautiful; with her sex appeal, many men lined up at her door. And Adrian knew it, which could explain why he'd piled on the charm and the gifts. He knew she was way out of his league.

"Mother," Lexie replied, with a mouthful of one of her mini cakes, "I know how much you like Adrian, but we were not meant to be and you're just going to have to accept that."

"I don't have to *do* anything, young lady." Isabel stood her ground, all the while rolling delicate pieces of crust together for one of her French pastries. "You best remember who you're talking to."

A mere five feet with long black hair in an updo twist, her mother was a force to be reckoned with. Barely a wrinkle touched her fifty-four-year-old, nutmeg-colored skin, and she still retained a size-ten figure by eating right and living well. Isabel Thompson was the model of success, whether she was in the kitchen baking pastries or out selling clients on Sunset Catering.

Dressed in capri plants and a peasant shirt, her mother was more sophisticated than anyone Lexie had ever met. Lexie rarely went toe-to-toe with her.

"Oh, I remember," Lexie muttered underneath her breath.

"You could stand to learn a lesson from Nia, Lexie Rose Thompson. That girl has a good head on her shoulders. She's found a good man to settle down and have a couple of babies with." Isabel patted her daughter on the back. "I would sure like a couple of grandchildren before I die, you know."

"Don't wish some little crumb-snatchers on me just yet. Kids will come eventually. All in due time."

Isabel laughed at the comment. "Time's a-wasting."

"Oh, Mom, please. Women my age are having kids later and later. Right now I am focusing on my career. I don't want to be tied down."

Isabel shook her head in amazement. "Why did both my children have to inherit their father's creative gene?"

"Thanks a lot." *Which parent is the one in the kitchen coloring pastries?* she wanted to ask. Sometimes Lexie couldn't believe her mother could be so cruel. Isabel had to know how much Lexie's design career meant.

Besides, she wouldn't be a fashion buyer forever. Someday she would see her designs on a Paris runway.

Hours later, Lexie sashayed into the Park Avenue Cafe along Chicago's Magnificent Mile for lunch. Nestled among Chicago's elite department stores, the café served a great lunch or brunch and was one of Lexie's favorite places. Plopping down in a wrought-iron chair on the patio, Lexie waited for the arrival of her best friend, Nia Taylor. Recently engaged, Nia had a laundry list of details for Lexie to complete to launch the wedding of the season.

Wearing the latest Bentley's suede skirt, with a chocolate crocheted sweater and matching suede fringed boots, Lexie looked every bit the fashion queen. She had to; her job required her to look the part. A five-day regime in the gym with a trainer on cardio and weights, a brisk swim three times a week, and her staple diet filled with salads and no carbs assured that Lexie maintained a size six.

She couldn't remember the last time she'd indulged in a juicy cheeseburger; she couldn't afford it. She might gain weight. The fashion business was a tough, take-no-prisoners game and Lexie would not be left at the back of the pack.

Nia joined her several minutes later on the patio.

Five-feet-four with a curvaceous shape, short curly hair—her new look—and a vibrant smile, Nia was as cute as a button. And she finally knew it. Suddenly Lexie's once-shy best friend was showing off her fabulous, voluptuous, God-given shape in form-fitting designs, and giving Lexie tips on how to keep a man. How could that be? Meeting Damon Bradley, a wealthy banker, had been the best thing to ever happen to Nia.

After giving the waiter her order of mandarin chicken salad, Lexie turned to face her best friend. "So, tell me, sister girl," Lexie asked, "what do I have to do in my role of maid of honor besides throw you an off-the-chain bachelorette party and bridal shower?"

"Well . . ." Nia twirled her napkin around in her hand. "There's nothing to it, really. You just have to help me pick out my wedding dress and finalize the invitations, the hall, the food, the photographer, flowers, and the guest list."

"Wait a second!" Lexie exclaimed, holding up her hand. "What have I signed up for?"

"Girl, I need all your support and fashion sense. This is going to be quite an affair if Damon's parents have anything to say about it."

"Don't worry." Lexie leaned over to give Nia's shoulders a firm squeeze. "I won't let you down. You know I'll hook you up and design you the most fabulous dress you've ever seen. Look no further for your photographer because Sebastian is by far the best around and my mom would be more than happy to cater your big day. See, girl," she said as she patted Nia's hand, "the Thompson family has got this whole wedding sewn up."

"What would I do without you?"

Lexie raised her shoulders. "I wouldn't know. Some of us aren't so lucky to meet our Mr. Handsome, Rich, and Successful right off the bat. Some of us have to work at it."

The waiter returned with their salad plates and set them in front of the women.

"I'm sorry, Lexie. I didn't mean to monopolize our lunch conversation with all this talk of weddings and the like, especially since you just broke up with Adrian."

"Ain't nothing but a thing, Nia." Lexie put a forkful of mandarin chicken salad in her mouth and munched. "On paper, Adrian was perfect. But he just didn't thrill me. You know how you get butterflies in your stomach with the right man? How you light up when you're around them? Well, Adrian had the opposite effect on me. When he came around, I cooled off. I just need more man than him."

"You need a man that can challenge you," Nia volunteered, picking at her salad. She hated rabbit food, but she had to eat it. Maintaining her current weight was important if she wanted a killer wedding dress.

"Yes." Lexie nodded her head in agreement.

"Someone who you're compatible with intellectually as well as physically."

"Absolutely!"

"Someone who is confident and assertive, someone who's completely sure of himself."

"Hmmm . . ."

"Someone ambitious and successful in his career. Someone who's going places."

"Preach!"

"Someone who can thrill you, please you, tease you."

"Yes!" How did Nia know exactly the kind of man she wanted, but had yet to find? "Know anyone like that?"

"Maybe," Nia replied.

Lexie slapped her hand. "Spill the details. Have you been holding out on me? Who is he? And where have you been hiding him? Have you been keeping him on the side just in case things don't work out between you and Damon?"

Nia laughed. "Lexie, please. Damon is all the man I will ever need."

"Then who is he?"

"He is Damon's best friend, William Kennedy. Actually, he prefers to be called Will."

"Hmmm." Lexie scratched her chin. "Why haven't you mentioned him before?"

"I have. You guys just have never met before."

"I wonder why that is?" Lexie pondered, arching her eyebrow at Nia.

"Well, could it be that every time I've tried to set it up for you to meet, you're always busy with one of your new playthings?"

"Then maybe you should take a hint." Lexie sipped a glass of water. "Could be fate's way of telling you it's not meant to be."

"Oh, hogwash! I'm sure that once you meet Will, you'll be mesmerized."

Lexie sighed. "Nia, darling, it takes a lot to keep me *interested*, let alone mesmerized."

"That's because you're too hard on men."

"I'm not hard on them. I just know what I want and I refuse to settle."

"Trust me. You won't have to settle with Will."

Lexie looked at Nia mistrustfully. She knew Nia had the best of intentions—she just wasn't sure she wanted to be set up on a blind date. But would Nia really steer her wrong? She seemed to know exactly what Lexie was looking for: Mr. Right, who's perfectly well balanced!

"So you'll agree to meet him if I set everything up?"

"I don't know, Nia."

"Listen, if it'll take some of the pressure off, we could make this a double date. Damon and I could join you. How about that?"

Lexie's gaze rested on her best gal. Nia looked like a kid on Christmas morning who'd just come down the stairs and discovered a mound of gifts under the Christmas tree. Nia's eyes beseeched her pleadingly.

Lexie relented. "Okay, okay. But only if you guys come along to chaperone. That's the only way I'll be able to tolerate a blind date."

"Deal," Nia said. "I'll set everything up."

Famous last words, Lexie thought. What had she gotten herself into?

"Jerome, could you get me tonight's menu?"

Will's bartender left the bar, where he'd been wiping out glasses, and disappeared into the kitchen to consult the chef.

Will wanted Chef Gaultier to create spectacular culinary masterpieces for tonight's specials. Several important athletes planned on stopping by his nightclub, Millennium, and everything had to be perfect. Celebrities required a certain amount of finesse and hand-holding and Will was skilled at providing it. Whether he was talking social issues with a politician, smoking the finest cigars with a wealthy businessman, or dancing the night away with a new starlet, Will had it all under control.

Jerome reentered. "Will, Evan DuBois is on the line. He wants to confirm your dinner appointment. Do you want to take the call?"

"Absolutely." Will accepted the phone. "Evan, it's great to hear from you. Are we still on for dinner?"

"Yes, we are," Evan DuBois responded from the other end. "David and I are looking forward to hearing more on your ideas for a second club."

"And I look forward to presenting them," Will replied.

"See you then."

Hanging up the receiver, Will let out a resounding "Yes!" He was finally on his way.

Later that day, Will got ready to shower and dress for the evening in his loft above the club. The loft was a great investment. It provided him a low overhead as well as all essentials: stainless-steel kitchen, living room, bedroom and adjoining bathroom, and a separate entrance for all those late-night rendezvous. *Wouldn't do to have people in my business,* Will surmised.

The loft was minimally decorated, as was the case with most bachelor pads. His living room housed a padded leather sofa, lounge chair, and of course the typical entertainment media setup: a media cabinet held a fifty-inch plasma screen TV, a home stereo system with surround sound, and a PlayStation.

Will's favorite room was the step-up bedroom with king-size platform bed and royal-blue satin sheets. Will loved the feel of those on his skin. But his most prized possession was the mahogany-stained wine bar he'd ordered from Pottery Barn. It held more than fifty wine bottles and allowed him time to slowly build his collection of chardonnays, merlots, Rieslings, pinot noirs, and cabernet sauvignons.

The loft's best feature was the hidden window in the living room. It gave him a bird's-eye of the club and from what he could tell, it already was filled to capacity. The warm weather in Chicago always caused natives to get restless after a long, cold winter.

When Will turned on the shower and then went to call downstairs to his bouncer to confirm, Lawrence indicated that folks were already lined up around the block, eager to be one of the select few allowed entry into one of the hottest clubs on Chicago's North Side.

A mixture of high-end supper club and hot dance club, Will always wondered what kept people coming back for more. Was it the food all handselected by the best chef in Chicago, Jean Paul Gaultier, or the music on the high-quality sound system, or the ambience from the fine interior lighting, or the crowd of beautiful people that frequented? Whatever the reason, Millennium was one hundred percent class. And Will would continue to keep it that way by trying out new entertainment avenues, be it poets or new comedians.

Will smiled inwardly. He'd come a long way from the rough-and-tough South Side. Raised by a single mother, he could easily have become a product of his environment and ended up in a gang, jail, or worse. He chose not to end up another statistic. Instead, he graduated from high school and even went on to Harvard with a scholarship. Majoring in finance, he'd earned his bachelor's and made his mom proud. But being a Wall Street type wasn't in the cards for him.

Sure, he'd tried the nine-to-five routine, but found it completely unfulfilling. After two years, he'd chucked his career in the fast-paced world of trading to head out on his own. And as luck would have it, he had a little bit of business acumen.

The club had fallen into Will's lap after the previous owner defaulted. He got the place at an auction and never looked back. In a short time, Millennium had become a major success and was still going strong. Will couldn't be prouder of his little baby.

After the shower, Will stepped out and passed a mirror on the way to his bedroom, pausing to admire himself.

Tall and lean, he wasn't too bad to look at. The free weights and five hundred crunches every day helped. Turning side to side, he didn't see an inch of flab on his slim waist and tight abs. And the face—Will gave himself a wink as he stared in the mirror—was perfection. The ladies loved the dark eyes, roguish goatee, and stylishly short haircut.

Walking naked to his bedroom closet, Will allowed himself to air-dry. When he stepped inside he immediately found what he was looking for: tailored black slacks, a black silk shirt with diamond cuff links, and his Armani watch. The finishing touch of cologne would have the women panting.

Checking the time, Will decided to grab a bite to eat downstairs. He rarely cooked unless he was preparing something special for his mother and kid brother Ryan—which reminded him, he needed to keep an eye on that boy. Although Will was financially secure enough to move the two of them somewhere else, his mother steadfastly refused to move from the South Side. "I want to be near my church and all my friends," she said, so he relented, although personally he wished she and Ryan were right up in Country Club Hills with the Bradleys and all the other preppy black folks.

The phone rang on the nearby countertop. Rushing over, Will leaned down to pick it up. He hoped it wasn't something at the club. He was grooming the new manager to take over his daily responsibilities so he could focus his attentions on expansion.

Will reached the phone seconds before the answering machine kicked on. "Hello?"

"Hey, buddy, where ya at?"

It was his best friend, Damon Bradley, whom he'd known since they were probably both in the womb. Their mothers were best friends as well, both having gotten pregnant around the same time when they were in high school. The only difference was that Damon was a month older than Will. At six-foot-two, with pecan-colored skin and light brown eyes, Damon was Will's partner in crime, but after meeting Ms. Fine Nia Taylor last year, Damon had abandoned the single life in favor of a wife and family.

"Sorry, man, I was getting ready." Time had gotten away from him. He'd invited Damon to Millennium for the VIP party with the Chicago Bulls players.

"Well, stop primping and get your pretty butt down here. I've already started on my second beer."

"All right, all right. I'll been downstairs shortly."

"Now, Will—you know how much you love staring at yourself in the mirror." Damon laughed at his own joke.

"Ha, ha, ha," Will said sarcastically. He couldn't help it if he liked to look good. In his business, appearance was everything. "I'll be down in a few."

Will found his buddies congregated at the bar having Heinekens and the fat Cuban cigars he kept at the bar solely for their benefit.

"Gentlemen." He came alongside Damon and shook his hand. "How are you, man?"

"This brother is on cloud nine," his friend Julian Masters proclaimed, pointing to Damon. Six-foot-three with tawny-colored skin and a pencil-thin mustache, Julian was what they called yellow and proud of it. "He's about to marry his little princess."

"That's right!" Damon smiled. "Nia is everything I've ever wanted."

Will laughed at Julian's comment. Having all met in Harvard, everyone was close friends. While Damon and Julian continued their education—Damon in business school and Julian in law school—Will had struck out on his own after college. He'd known an advanced college degree was important, but he couldn't bear anymore schooling.

Meanwhile he'd maintained his friendship with both Damon and Julian, who was now a junior partner at his father's law firm.

"We all can't be as lucky as you," Julian commented. "Look at me, I have a woman like Whitney and I still can't commit. The thought of marriage scares the living daylights out of me."

"Ain't that the truth," Will agreed.

Julian had given a new meaning to the word *commitment phobe*. He'd been in a serious relationship with his girlfriend Whitney for nearly seven years and had yet to propose. From the outside looking in, Julian had it all. With close-cut hair, the body of a quarterback, and sizzling green eyes, Julian dazzled many a woman. "I can't imagine there is a woman who could capture my heart," Julian admitted freely.

"You just wait, Will," Damon said. "One day you're going to meet the one."

"This I would have to see," Maxwell Armstrong declared. Maxwell was the husband of Paige, Will's longtime nemesis. Although they loved each other, neither Paige nor Will could stand to be in the same room for long without arguing. "You know Will's got a block of ice where his heart is."

"Well, you would know, wouldn't you, being married to the original ice queen," Will returned.

"Easy, boys," Damon reprimanded.

"I'm not the one who's had one too many drinks," Will replied.

"Let's not start tonight." Julian had a Whitney-free weekend ahead of him and he intended to have fun.

Will looked at Maxwell, whose chest was puffed out several miles wide, and laughed it off. It wasn't worth the drama. "All right, let's squash it. Listen, I've got a great little-girl group singing on stage later tonight. I'm sure they'll set the mood."

"Now that's what I'm talking about." Julian took a swig of beer. "Let the games begin."

The night was a success. The music vibed, the wine flowed, and the food was out of this world. The Chicago Bulls VIPs left feeling like they were still the salt of the earth despite not having won a championship since Jordan retired.

Only Damon remained and helped Will close up shop. He'd had to call a cab for both Julian and Maxwell. Both of those brothers had had a little too much to drink. Will was sure he would hear from Paige in the morning, giving him hell for getting her husband drunk. As long as they'd known each other, Paige loved to give him grief. Maybe she thought he remembered how she looked when they were in diapers running around in the playpen.

"That was some party," Damon remarked as he pushed in the chairs scattered across the floor. "Those brothers can't hold their liquor worth a damn."

"So true, so true."

Damon grinned. "What's up with you, anyway? You seem more subdued than usual." Damon had noticed that Will hadn't actively sought out any of the women roaming the club that evening.

"Did you notice most of them? They probably couldn't hold a conversation if their life depended on it."

"Sounds like you're bored with the women you've encountered. Perhaps it's time you looked for a woman of substance."

"I have. They just have to understand that I'm not ready for marriage and all that."

"Hmmm." Damon grabbed some beer bottles from a nearby cocktail table and threw them in the trash. "So these women want more of a commitment than your standard fare."

"Yeah, dawg. Once I've kicked it with a woman for a while, all of sudden they get clingy, wanting to spend all their free time with me. And you know I like my space."

Damon nodded. "This I know. But eventually you're going to have to open yourself up to the right woman."

"As if such a woman ever existed." Will laughed from behind the bar as he counted up the night's tally.

"Trust me, it's possible." Damon was a firm believer in true love. "You never know, Will. Sometimes love strikes when you least expect it."

"Yeah, well, I'm not the lovey-dovey type."

"You might be." Damon rubbed his chin. "Matter of fact, I think I have the perfect woman for you."

"Damon, does it look like I need to be hooked up?" Will asked, throwing the bank bag in the safe behind the bar. He would make a deposit tomorrow morning.

"No, but then again . . . you haven't met Lexie Thompson."

"And what's so special about Lexie Thompson?"

"Besides from being absolutely gorgeous, with a

goddess body, she's smart, quick-witted, and viva-
cious?"

"She's all that, huh?"

"And then some. You should let me hook the two of
you up."

"Why is this the first I'm hearing about this Lexie?"

"No reason," Damon said. "She's a friend of Nia's.
And finally after all these months, it looks like you
might be available, playa."

"I don't do blind dates."

"Yes, I know, but Lexie is different. She's a chal-
lenge. And don't tell me you don't like a challenge!
Come to dinner and then you can decide from there.
Nia and I will be there as buffers."

"I don't know."

"What can it hurt? The evening is on me."

Reluctantly, Will agreed. "You know I would never
do this for anyone but you."

"And you won't regret it," Damon countered.

CHAPTER TWO

The overhead lights blinked, indicating guests should take their seats, when Lexie arrived at the Athenaeum Theatre foyer the following Friday. Searching the crowd inside, she found Nia waiting near the cocktail bar.

Nia waved the moment she saw Lexie and motioned her over. Rushing through the crowd, Lexie joined her at the bar.

Lexie gave Nia a gentle squeeze and kissed both cheeks. "Sorry I'm late."

Nia glanced down at her watch. "Lex, do you know what time it is?"

"Please don't chastise me, Nia. Everything that could go wrong went wrong. My panty hose got a run at the last minute. My cab didn't show up on time. It's been one fiasco after another. So where is this paragon?" Lexie inquired.

"He isn't here yet either. Oh, wait, here he comes right now." Nia pointed to the man walking toward them.

Nia hadn't needed to point him out—he was pretty hard to miss. Nia hadn't been joking when she'd said he was tall and sexy, Lexie thought. Dressed in a black tuxedo and silver bow tie, William Kennedy was arresting.

Even from across the room, Lexie felt drawn to the sexual aura emanating from his every pore, and as his powerfully muscled body moved with precision and grace across the room, her tummy did a gigantic flip-flop as she envisioned that very same hard body pressed up against hers.

As he drew near, Lexie gave him a thorough appraisal, raking his athletic physique from his broad shoulders to his lean torso. She glimpsed a view of very large hands. Was it true what they said about men with large hands? Lexie wondered. Then there was the face. And what a face it was. Smooth toffee-colored skin stretched over high cheekbones, deeply set jet-black eyes, and a sexy trimmed mustache and goatee all made for one compelling combination.

Putting on her best smile, Lexie waited for Nia to make the introductions, when all of a sudden her throat became dry and constricted and her skin hot and prickly. Fighting her attraction, Lexie attempted to regain her composure.

Will, on the other hand, was momentarily speechless at Lexie's beauty, but quickly recovered. "Miss Nia, you are looking as gorgeous as ever." Will gave Nia a kiss on the cheek and took a step back to survey her in an emerald-green dress with a sweetheart neckline that revealed her ample bosom. "Hmmm, and looking sexy as hell. Damon is a lucky man."

"Thank you, Will." Nia blushed at the comment while Lexie stood fuming. Was he purposely ignoring her presence? This was not good. Lexie could only hope it was not a sign of the evening to come.

"Where's Damon?" Will asked, ignoring Lexie's

sexy pout and looking over his shoulder for his way-ward friend.

"He's picking up the tickets." Lexie jumped into the conversation and gave Will her best smile and hair flip. There was no way she was going to let Mr. William Kennedy ignore her.

"Oh, I'm sorry, Lex," Nia said. "Will, this is my best friend, Lexie Thompson. Lex, this is William Kennedy, Damon's closest friend."

"Forgive my rudeness, Lexie," Will said smoothly. He brought one of Lexie's hands to his lips and kissed it softly. "It's a pleasure to meet you. Nia speaks very highly of you."

When Lexie's stomach fluttered again, she withdrew her hand quickly. Will's sensuously thick eyebrows rose inquiringly.

"Hmmm, it's a pity I can't say the same. Nia's hardly mentioned you at all," Lexie remarked.

Lexie heard Nia's sharp intake of breath, but didn't care. She was pleased she sounded nonchalant. She was nobody's doormat and that included Mr. Kennedy.

"Well, perhaps we can rectify that," Will suggested in a low, sexy voice.

"That's highly dependent upon you, now, isn't it?"

Will laughed richly. He appreciated Lexie's air of self-confidence. She was a wildcat. He'd encountered a few in his time. Thinking he could tame them, he had gotten his pride stomped on enough to know that you couldn't change a woman like that. They thought they owned the world, and any man lucky enough to enter their orbit better be grateful. No, no, no. Will preferred his women much more docile. And after his ex-girlfriend Carly Matthews, he didn't need any more drama. A nice casual affair was strictly on his agenda.

"Here comes Damon with the tickets," Nia interjected.

Turning back around, Lexie caught Will's sideways glance at her. Her instincts told her Will was not nearly as unaffected by her as he was leading her to believe. So he wanted to play smooth, did he? Well, there were plenty of tricks in her arsenal and she hadn't even begun to use them.

Damon strutted toward them and handed each of them a ticket to Blue Man Group. Apparently Damon had paid top dollar for the seats because the tickets were in the front row for the notoriously sold-out show.

Ever the gentleman, Will escorted Lexie into the theater. Reluctantly, Lexie allowed him to lead her by the elbow, all the while promising herself that she would not be swayed by his smoldering eyes and sexy grin.

After the show, Lexie excused herself to go to the restroom, with Nia nipping at her heels. Lexie had wiggled in her seat next to Will for nearly two and a half hours, soaking in his delicious smoky masculine scent and nearly going mad. She couldn't remember the last time she had been this aroused just *sitting* next to a man.

"So, what do you think?" Nia asked, breaking into her thoughts. Instead of answering, Lexie stared dumbfounded into the mirror in front of her.

Should she tell her friend that she wanted to take Will to bed and ravish his body all night long? Lexie doubted Nia wanted to hear her sexual cravings. Once during the show when Will's hard, taut thigh accidentally touched hers, Lexie thought she would jump out of her skin. All her senses were heightened just being near him; now she understood the saying about feeling like a cat on a hot tin roof. She definitely felt like Maggie the cat, perched atop the roof looking down at Will, ready to pounce on him at the slightest opportunity.

"Lexie, did you hear anything I just said?"

"Of course I did." Lexie grinned. "I think Mr. William Kennedy is very intriguing, but dinner will tell if he's more than a pretty face." Lexie snapped her purse shut and swung the door open, leaving a stunned Nia staring after her.

Seconds later, Lexie attached her arm to Will's. She couldn't tell if he appreciated the gesture, but she knew what moves to make to grab a man's attention. Her favorite fragrance would be enough to lure him her way.

Will noticed Lexie link their arms together. As much as he wanted to keep her at arm's length, he had to admit he was impressed. When Damon first suggested a blind date, Will vetoed the idea. Did he look like he had trouble finding a woman? But his natural curiosity got the better of him. His best friend knew him better than most and if he thought this Lexie Thompson was worthy of his time, then that was good enough for him.

Admittedly, Lexie Thompson was a fine-looking woman, but she hardly looked the type to need a date either, Will thought. She was a wealth of black wavy hair, long legs, a small waist, and high-perched breasts. High, exotic cheekbones on a delicate face and dainty nose only fueled the fire. The woman carried herself with an air of confidence. The slip dress she wore draped over her delectable slender frame very nicely and Will's groin tightened in recognition. Lexie was one helluva knockout. He wondered why she was alone. Was she one of those man-eaters that swallowed men up and spit them out?

"Well, that was most entertaining," Lexie commented.

"More like strange." Will said. Although he appreciated the arts, a bunch of men painted with blue faces throwing toilet paper at the audience was hardly his idea of gripping entertainment.

"You didn't like it?" Lexie queried. "I thought it was awesome."

"Well, I'm sure in fashion you're used to the ridiculous." The moment he said the words, Will wished he could take them back. The murderous look in Lexie's eyes told him he'd overstepped.

"Excuse me?" Lexie couldn't believe the man had the audacity to demean her entire profession while she stood beside him.

"I'm sure he didn't mean any harm, did you, Will?" Damon asked, stepping in to smooth the waters.

"Of course he didn't," Nia said. "Girl, you know how over-the-top some of those fashions are."

Lexie's eye shot daggers at Will, but seeing Nia's pleading eyes, Lexie laughed it off. She knew how desperate Nia was to ensure the evening was an astounding success. And she sure could use a little loving. "At times, yes, designers can be outrageous. But it's all part of the allure of the fashion world."

"I'm sure it is," Will said. "Lexie, I apologize if I offended you. It truly wasn't my intention."

"Water under the bridge." Lexie took a sip of her champagne as a long silence ensued.

"On that note, let's head to dinner. I'm starved." Nia grabbed Lexie's hand and proceeded to walk toward the door.

"Smooth, Will, real smooth," Damon whispered under his breath.

Halfway through dinner at McCormick & Schmick's Seafood Restaurant, Lexie realized she'd made an error in judgment. Although sexy as hell, William Kennedy was an arrogant jerk.

Sure, he initially exhibited a smooth, almost dangerous charm, but Lexie preferred the strong and powerful type, with a bank account to boot. Thanks to her job, which kept her wardrobe stocked with Gucci and Versace, she'd grown accustomed to a certain type of lifestyle. And it just so happened that her men kept her jewelry box filled to capacity with tokens of their deep and undying affection for her.

Did she consider herself a gold digger? No. She never asked for any of these things. Men just loved to bestow them on her and she accepted. And now, of course, she was spoiled.

What would a brother like William Kennedy know about pampering a bourgeoisie princess like herself? It took skill, finesse, and a wad of cash. As the owner of a small time club, Will wasn't even in her ballpark. Lexie doubted Will could do more than keep himself in stylish suits.

Polished and sophisticated, her men were the counterpart of her. Having been raised in Manhattan, one of the premier fashion capitals of the world, before later moving to Chicago, she'd been exposed to a melting pot of different cultures and could easily assimilate wherever she was. She was comfortable with friends of all races.

She was the apple of her parents' and grandparents' eyes; her parents spared no expense on her education by sending her to the best Montessori, high school, and college in the country. She never had a want in her life her parents hadn't provided, even though her mother was struggling to get her catering business off the ground. If Lexie wanted something, she always got it, be it tap dancing, piano, ballet, or cheerleading. A trip to Europe with her high school class? No problem. A new pair of Jordaches? Her grandparents would most certainly supply it.

But it appeared she would not get what she wanted tonight. Will didn't offer much in the way of background. He'd remained rather closemouthed about his upbringing. She'd only gathered that he was raised on the South Side of Chicago by his single mother and had a younger brother named Ryan.

Lexie wondered how he could afford a nightclub. Perhaps he'd run into some good luck. How else to explain it? Where did he get the financing?

"How's Millennium?" Damon inquired.

"Going well," Will returned, swirling his decanter of Scotch in his hand. "I have an important meeting lined up with some investors at the end of the week."

"Is the club business really doing that well?" Lexie asked, picking at her food. Despite herself, she couldn't disguise the hint of haughtiness that accompanied the question.

Turning his head, Will answered, "Yes, it is, Lexie. I plan to expand Millennium to other locations."

"Excellent. Congratulations."

"Thank you, and I presume the fashion business is going well for you?" Will asked, sipping on his Scotch.

"Yes, it is. Though I'm sure that's surprising to you, considering you feel it's such a fickle business."

Will sucked in his breath and slammed another gulp down his throat. "I'm sure I didn't use those exact words, but if you choose to believe that, then who am I to stop you?"

Several looks passed between Nia and Damon as they assessed how to proceed. How had the conversation suddenly turned sour?

"You obviously have a problem with the fashion industry." Lexie jumped to the bait.

"I don't have a problem with the industry. I just have a problem with models. They've got beauty, but no brains, but then again that's their business. Fashion, cosmetics, it's all the same. Most times these women are of little substance and have very little to offer."

Lexie couldn't believe the generalization she'd heard. Her ears were ringing and her throat burned with outrage. "What makes you think you're all that, Will?" Lexie wondered aloud. "Perhaps it's you and not these dumb beautiful women that have little to offer." Sweeping up her wrap and clutch purse, Lexie stormed toward the front of the restaurant.

Nia jumped up from her seat and followed her dramatic friend outside. She met up with Lexie at the valet station. "Where are you going?" Nia whispered, trying to avoid a scene.

"I'm not staying where I'm obviously not wanted. You're friend is a bore and I'm going to seek out better company."

"Lexie, wait. Don't leave like this," Nia pleaded, grabbing her arm. "Let us drive you home, for God's sake,"

"That's quite all right, Nia. I'm perfectly capable of hailing a cab. This is Chicago, you know."

"Are you sure?"

Lexie saw the huge frown on Nia's face, but she didn't care. She refused to spend another minute in Will Kennedy's company. "Don't worry, Nia." Lexie squeezed her shoulder. "I'll be fine. But no more blind dates." Seconds later, Lexie was out the door and safely ensconced in a cab.

Nia walked slowly back to the table.

"So, the little princess left?" Will asked. He couldn't believe how spoiled she was.

"Will." Nia threw down her napkin in disgust. "I'm really mad at you. Your behavior tonight was insufferable, make that unbearable. Why did you let me set the two of them up?" Nia asked, turning her wrath on her fiancé.

Will intervened on his best friend's behalf. "Don't blame him. It was all my fault, Nia. I guess I wasn't ready to jump into a new relationship, especially with another new beauty queen."

After his ex-girlfriend Carly, the last thing he needed was another airhead. It was time he found someone with a little substance. Someone who didn't give two shakes about hair, cosmetics, and clothes. Someone he could have a real conversation with. Someone he could take to meet his mother.

"Will." Nia gave him a warning look. She would not let anyone talk bad about her best girl.

"Sorry." Will cocked his head to the side and looked at her sheepishly. Nia smiled and Will laughed to himself. That move worked every single time.

CHAPTER THREE

On Monday morning Lexie arrived at her weekly buyers meeting at Bentley's with moments to spare. She'd completely slept through her alarm. With a quick shower, a brush of the hair, and a strawberry yogurt on the run, she'd raced her red BMW down Lake Shore Drive, praying a cop didn't pull her over for speeding.

She couldn't afford to be late to her meeting. Her boss, Lauren Davis, was announcing who would spearhead Bentley's Annual Spring Fashion Show, and Lexie was praying it was her. Her department was the best by far and Lexie's selections had improved Bentley's sales over the last year. But Lexie also knew her competitor and nemesis Sydney Hamilton would be angling for the position. Although Sydney was merely Lauren's assistant, Lexie knew Sydney was biding her time until Lexie screwed up. And when she did, the barracuda would be right there to take Lexie's place.

Rushing past her cubicle, Lexie paused by her assistant Mina's desk. A pleasant twenty-four-year-old brunette, Mina had worked for Lexie for two years and was a great asset. If Lexie wasn't there, she could always depend on Mina to get things done. "Have they started yet?" Lexie asked.

"No, not yet, but you'd better hustle," Mina said.

Lexie entered the conference room. "Good morning." She smiled at several department heads before taking a seat, none of whom were as qualified as she to host this year's extravaganza. She'd paid her dues and now it was time to be recognized for it.

Several pair of eyes looked her way, sizing up her latest outfit. Lexie set the bar for high fashion and today was no exception. Pulling off her black leather jacket, Lexie saw several eyebrows rise at her off-the-shoulder sweater, but she didn't care. She knew what was current and if Bentley's expected her to sell it, she needed to look the part. Tossing her hair behind her back, Lexie gave Sydney a dazzling white smile and watched Sydney's eyes narrow in response.

"As you all know," Lauren began, "it is time to show our spring collection to a few of our most select customers."

Everyone in the room applauded in unison.

"And I know all of you are eager to know who will head up this year's show."

Lexie heart pumped wildly in her chest. *Please let it be me!*

"The person I've selected started at Bentley's at the tender age of sixteen as a sales clerk. She worked her way up the ranks, first as head of accessories, then lingerie, until finally taking over women's wear. I am pleased to hand the reins over to . . ." Lauren paused for effect. "Lexie Thompson."

Cheers erupted from the table. Maintaining her composure, Lexie stood and took a bow. Being selected as fashion-show director proved how much faith her superiors had in her abilities and she couldn't be more thrilled.

"Speech! Speech!" Her colleagues clapped eagerly in anticipation.

Lexie held up her hand to hold the applause. "I won't take up everyone's time with a speech, but thank you, Lauren, for the opportunity."

"No need for thanks, Lexie," Lauren countered. "You've done a fine job with the innovative buys and consulting you've brought to Bentley's. Our renewed reputation is a direct result of that, and I'm sure the fashion show will be an equal success."

Closing her folder, Lauren adjourned the meeting and the department heads began to file out. Some congratulated Lexie for the opportunity while others fled the room in disappointment.

Leaning toward the huge floor-to-ceiling window that overlooked State Street, Lexie felt on top of the world. Sensing a presence in the room, Lexie turned around and discovered she was not alone. Sydney was standing behind her with her hands on her hips.

"You may have won this round, Lexie, but don't count me out," Sydney sneered with ice in her cold blue eyes.

"That would be a foolhardy mistake." Lexie grinned. "And my mama didn't raise no fool."

"Touché. Well, I suggest you watch your back," Sydney warned, marching out the door.

Sydney's final comment wasn't lost on Lexie, but at the moment, Lexie could care less. The position was hers and she had already compiled a folder of ideas to present to Lauren. They all depended on the perfect venue, the perfect place to have the fashion tongues wagging.

Determinedly, Lexie pulled a nearby phone on the

conference table toward her and dialed her longtime friend Christian Blair. Christian answered almost immediately, sounding as chipper as ever.

"Christian, you'll never believe it." Lexie started.

"You got the fashion-show gig," Christian finished for her.

"How did you guess?"

"It's, like, the only thing you've talked about the last couple of weeks."

Lexie chuckled. He was probably right. She'd been on pins and needles waiting for word. And now that was no more. She was in charge. *She* controlled the outcome. "I guess you're right. I have been a little repetitious these days. Anyway, listen, I need every contact you've got for the Samba Room."

"Lex, are you for real? You know that place has got to be booked months in advance."

"I know, I know, but if anyone can work their magic, it would be you."

"Girl, you are looking for a miracle."

"And who better to supply it than you?"

"How you do go on."

"That's me, darling. Let's rendezvous at Sebastian's at seven for a rundown. Smooches." Lexie preferred Sebastian's loft as their meeting place. It always had the best ambience. And she knew he would always cook a tasty delight.

"Back at ya."

"Long time no see." Lexie ruffled her little brother Sebastian's new twists as she walked inside his apartment later that evening and handed him a bottle of Riesling white wine. Their mother hated the new hairstyle and constantly ragged that it wasn't appropriate for a man, but Lexie liked it. It fit her brother's image of a Renaissance man.

"Hey, watch it." Sebastian swatted her hand away and grabbed the wine.

Walking down the few steps into his parlor, casually dressed in Kenneth Cole slacks, a polo shirt, and Gucci loafers, Sebastian was a male version of her. Two years younger and several inches taller, he was equally as attractive and could turn heads when he walked into a room. The ladies loved his short twists, goatee, and diamond-studded ear. And with a personality to match, her brother made for one handsome catch.

"What's new?" Lexie asked, holding off on her news.

"Well, I just met this fine girl at a poetry reading," Sebastian answered, playing around with his camera. "We went out for coffee afterward and hit it off pretty well."

"That's great." Lexie smiled. "Are you going to see her again?"

"Yeah, we're going to hook up later for a drink."

"Well, you have to bring her over sometime so I can meet her."

"All in due time, all in due time," Sebastian replied. He liked to keep his private life on the down low until he was sure the relationship was worth having. "What about you? Did you get the director's gig?" At Lexie's ear-to-ear grin, Sebastian knew the truth. "Congratulations, sis. Now you can loan me a few hundred bucks."

"Didn't I just loan you some cash?" Lexie asked, kicking off her shoes and looking around for an empty place to sit. Sebastian's photography equipment—tripods, lens converters, flashes, and reflectors—were all over the room.

His photographs lined every available space on the textured walls while the rest of the studio was decorated with opulent fabrics, crown molding, and custom window treatments, courtesy of their good friend and interior designer Christian Blair. It was a place Lexie often came to get away from it all.

"Yeah, and your point?"

"What happened to it?"

"I have expenses. You know how hard it's been keeping the studio going."

"Has business really been that bad?" Lexie asked. Sebastian's photographs were edgy and symbolic. Not everyone could appreciate his work. But Lexie believed in him.

"Yes, it has. I'm considering going back to New York."

"New York! You can't go to New York. I'd miss you too much." Lexie pouted.

"Well, I wouldn't have to if you hadn't broken up with Mr. Moneybags Turner. I'd be rolling in the green stuff."

Lexie threw her hands in the air. "Christ! Not you, too." Lexie had heard enough about how perfect Adrian was. He'd even agreed to sponsor Sebastian's next showing, and as much as she appreciated the offer, Lexie couldn't let him do it. She would continue to support her brother's dream. Her mother had long since cut the cord, financially speaking, but Lexie just couldn't do it.

"Listen, Mom already catalogued Adrian's greatest features and I don't care to rehash it. So if this is the same old love song, then I'm leaving." Lexie headed toward the door.

"Slow your ropes, sis." Sebastian pulled his sister to a nearby couch and forced her down with him. "Consider the subject squashed. What's new, big sis?"

"Well, I had lunch with Nia and—"

"How is my love goddess?" Sebastian interrupted.

tian in the shoulder. "How was I to know? Nia raved about meeting Damon's best friend."

"So did you chew him up and spit him out?" Sebastian joked. He and Christian high-fived.

"More than that. I walked out on him."

"You're kidding!" Christian said with a hand across his chest. He was aghast at such a social faux paus.

"Will Kennedy was sexy, dangerous, and over-whelmingly *arrogant*. He told me people in my profession were airheads, so I had no choice but to show him who's boss."

"Sounds like this Will got under your skin," Sebastian commented from a stool nearby.

"No, he just proved what an absolute jerk he was. And made me sure that I want absolutely nothing to do with the likes of him!"

Sebastian and Christian exchanged knowing glances. Neither had seen Lexie all fired up about a man in years. Maybe this Will person was the right man and Lexie was just too blind to see it.

CHAPTER FOUR

The next morning Lexie was on the phone with every entertainment contact she'd ever made, with no luck. Every venue was booked. Lexie bit her pencil in frustration. It was imperative that whatever place she chose was high-class enough for the fashions but trendy enough to have everyone talking. But where could she go?

The shrill ring of the phone interrupted her thoughts. "Hello," Lexie answered gruffly.

"Meow!" Nia teased. "What's gotten into you?"

"Girl, you don't want to know."

"Try me out, maybe I can help."

Lexie paused for a minute. The last time her best friend helped her out, Lexie ended up with the blind date from hell. Just thinking of Will Kennedy got her blood boiling. Over the last few days, her thoughts had wandered to him. He who claimed to be a creative guy, but who had absolutely no sense of savoir faire. He who had a generously curved mouth just ripe for the tasting.

Lexie shook her head. Why did she even let the man

get to her? Could it be because he was the first man in years to set her heart afire? And not just her heart.

"I don't need any more of your advice, Nia."

"Hey, don't blame me if you don't know how to behave in front of a real man."

Lexie was speechless.

"I laid him right at your feet and what did you do but sabotage the whole thing. And you wonder why you're alone."

"Nia!" Lexie shrieked, attempting to sound outraged. Gone was the shy, quiet-mouse persona. Nia had finally gotten a backbone!

"I speak the truth and you know it. Will was interested in you, but you took the opportunity to blow a little comment completely out of proportion. And instead of letting it drop, you sulked the entire evening, killing any sparks between you two."

"Are you done with your psychological assessment now? Or can anyone jump in?"

"I'm sorry, Lexie. I happen to think Will is perfect for you."

"Well, I don't. The man was condescending to the entire fashion profession. If that's how he acts with someone he's likes, I'd hate to see the reverse."

"That's an excuse and you know it. You're just mad because the man got under your skin."

Lexie bit down on the pencil in her mouth. Did Nia sense what she'd tried so hard to disguise?

"As usual, Miss Thing, you have no idea what you're talking about. Matter of fact, I have far more important things on my mind than Mr. Kennedy."

"Oh, really? And what might that be?"

"Nia, I got the fashion-show gig."

"Congratulations, Lexie! I know how much the fashion show meant to you."

Despite her good news, Lexie was still at a loss. As much as she wanted to run the show, finding a location at the last minute was no easy feat. She needed reinforcements.

"So what's the problem?" Nia inquired, sensing the unspoken.

Lexie rose and paced her small cubicle on Bentley's top floor, which housed its corporate offices.

"I've called everyone in my phone book and still haven't found a venue."

"What about Dante's Corner?"

"Taken."

"And the Samba Room?"

"Taken. Any other bright ideas?"

"Frankly, yes," Nia answered, a little bit too quickly for Lexie's liking. "But I doubt you'll like my suggestion."

"Wait, don't tell me. Millennium."

"See? You already thought the same thing. Millennium is the perfect spot for the fashion show. Swallow your pride, girl, and ask the man if you can use his club."

"After my unceremonious exit the other night, I doubt Will would even allow me in the club, let alone give me permission to use it to host what he considers to be a brainless profession. There has to be another way, Nia."

"If you say so."

And Lexie would find it. There was no way she would go begging to Will Kennedy.

Will pulled into the parking space outside his mother's home in Chatham. He wished she were closer or in one of the northern suburbs but the woman refused to move from the South Side. Said she was born and raised there and that's where she was going die.

The one-story, red-bricked home with a finished basement was modest by most standards and nothing special to speak of, but his mother loved it. She'd kept the lawn well manicured by staying all over Will's little brother to keep it mowed and free of weeds. Eve Kennedy refused to have sorry-looking grass. Although she didn't have much, appearance was everything. Will wondered if she had become that way from years of hanging around the upper-crust Bradleys.

Jumping out of the car, Will glanced around and noticed some local riffraff hanging out at the end of the block. The young men were huddled together smoking cigarettes and looking real mischievous. They could easily be drug dealers. It was a good thing his kid brother's after-school activities kept him busy. From basketball to track, Ryan was quite the athlete, and if Will and his mother had anything to say about it, Ryan would be the next Michael Jordan.

With his key in the lock, Will turned around and stared at the group at the end of the block before going inside. "Mom, it's Will!" he yelled out.

"You're late," his mother stated as she walked into the foyer.

"I know, I'm sorry, Mom. I got held up at the club."

"As usual. That no-good club takes too much of your time when you should be here with family."

"Mother, that no-good club, as you like to call it, is my bread and butter and happens to put food on this table. Or had you forgotten that?" Will was annoyed at his mother's casual disregard of his business. A business he put his heart and soul into. A business that helped her when her salary fell short and she needed money for household expenses or to buy Ryan the latest pair of sneakers.

"Don't you get smart with me, young man—perhaps you forgot who you're talking to?"

"No, ma'am, I have not." Will maintained his composure. He would not disrespect her in her own home. "I'm sorry, Mom. But you know the club means everything to me."

"As I've told you before, William, a place like that will cause you nothing but trouble. Look at what happened to your father with his gambling and get-rich schemes. Brought this family nothing but heartache." With that comment, his mother turned away toward the kitchen.

"I've heard all this before. Do we have to have a repeat discussion?" Will asked, following behind her. He knew she disapproved of his going into the nightclub business; she used every possible occasion to tell him so. She was always advising him that he should be more like Damon. That he shouldn't waste his time and potential on a fickle business like nightclub-owning.

Countless times he'd heard how his father threw his life away getting involved with the wrong crowd. Did she think Will was blind? He was old enough to remember his father coming in with a black eye or having a sore belly from being punched in the gut. It was why Will was driven to succeed. There was no way he was ending up like his old man.

Throwing her hands up in the air, Eve went into another one of her bitter diatribes. "See, you're just like him. Your father liked to run the streets and you see where that got him. Dead and buried."

"I'm not my father!" Will yelled, his patience rapidly waning. "And I'm sick of you comparing me to him."

Stunned at his outburst, his mother began to cry.

"Why do you have to talk to me this way?" she said. "I only want the best for you."

"I know that, Mom. But your way is not the only way. You've got to trust that I'm doing what's right for me." Uncharacteristically, his mother stroked his cheek. Will couldn't recall the last time she'd shown him genuine affection.

"When we're sitting here like this, I can see so much of your father's good qualities in you. I just don't want you to end up like him. Can't you see that?"

"Look at me, Mom." Will's long fingers reached out to take her hand in his. "I'm a success. I own my own business. Aren't you proud of me?"

"Of course I am, Will, but you could be so much more."

"Enough, Mom." Will stood up. Why couldn't she believe in him?

"All right, all right." His mother gave up. "But I would only like to add that it would be wonderful if you settled down like Damon. Now there's a good boy. He's working for his father at the bank and getting married to that advertising girl. That's what you need to do."

"Do what? Get a job working at the bank?" Will played stupid. He knew exactly where his mother was heading with this.

"No, young man. You know where I'm going. I meant for you to meet some nice girl and get married. Make me a grandma while I can still move around to take care of my grandbabies."

"Don't for look for any of those anytime soon. I make sure to keep a helmet on my soldier."

"William!" His mother blushed.

"Don't worry, Mom. I'm sure Damon will let you be

a surrogate grandma to his kids. I'm sure he'll have ole Nia impregnated in no time."

His mother chuckled. "Boy, if you don't stop . . ."

"Where is that knuckleheaded brother of mine, anyway?"

"Probably out running the streets again with his friends." His mother shook her head in dismay. "I've tried to keep that boy in the house. Keep him from being led astray. But I fear for him, Will."

"Don't you worry, Mama. I'll have a word with Ryan. I gotta go. I'll see you on Sunday."

As the yellow school bus neared his neighborhood, Ryan's stomach rumbled uneasily. Ever since his brother had transferred him to a private high school, he'd taken heat from the neighborhood crew. They teased him so much about his uniform that he started changing when he got to school and changed back into his Sean John gear on the way home. The worst offender was J.T.

A high school dropout, J.T. was into all kinds of mess, from taking bets to selling a little marijuana on the side. Several times he'd asked if Ryan wanted to join in as he and his crew got high, but Ryan politely declined. Being an athlete, he didn't want to jeopardize his performance on the court. If the coach or principal found an athlete using drugs or steroids, or any other undue influences, it would be bye-bye college scholarship.

The bus came to a halt several blocks away from Ryan's home. Afraid of being hassled, he had long since requested that the bus driver not stop on his block. Exiting in a hurry, Ryan looked over his shoulder. Maybe he could make it home without any trouble. He was sure J.T. would want to hang out, play cards, or holler at the neighborhood hoochies as they walked by. Ryan was completely uninterested in any of these girls. He had his eye on one fine girl back at Lake Academy, a cheerleader named Arissa. The last thing he needed was to get caught up with one of those neighborhood girls who'd go off and get themselves pregnant. Then he would end up in the same predicament as the rest of the fellas hanging out on the corner. No way. He had a plan. B-ball was going to lead him out of the hood.

Once outside, Will's eyes searched the street for his brother. He didn't see Ryan, but he certainly saw that the same crew hanging out on the corner had moved a little closer to home. The young men were now a couple of doors down at old lady Jackson's house. Her fast granddaughter Monique was outside flirting with someone Will could only assume was the leader of the pack.

Short, bald, and tattooed, the kid had an air of authority about him. Wearing a T-shirt and baggy jeans and smoking a cigarette, he had all the boys huddled around him like he was some god or something. Will would definitely have a long talk with his brother about this young man.

Will glanced at his watch. The bus should have dropped Ryan off by now. Where was he?

Turning the corner to his block, Ryan sighed. J.T. and the rest of his followers were standing a few doors down from his house. And to make matters worse, he caught Will glaring at him from the porch.

With lead feet, Ryan trudged toward the crowd

outside Mrs. Jackson's. Stopping, he shook hands with a few of the guys.

"Hey, what's up?" J.T. inquired from his perch alongside Monique. Ryan couldn't believe a sweetheart like Monique would fall for J.T.'s bad-boy image.

"Nothing much, man," Ryan answered. "Just got out of b-ball practice." He looked over his shoulder and noticed Will pacing the sidewalk. He was going to hear it tonight.

"I swear this brotha always got a ball in his hands." J.T. sauntered down the stairs toward him. The guys all parted for him. "He gon' be the next Michael Jordan."

Ryan shook his hand. "I can only wish."

"So, when you gon' invite us to one of your games?" J.T. asked.

"Aw, man, I wish I could." Ryan fidgeted nervously. "But they only give tickets to students of Lake Academy."

"Well, aren't you special." J.T. snickered, blowing a puff of smoke directly in Ryan's face.

Ryan ignored the affront. He felt Will's eyes burning a hole in his back, and if he didn't get a move on it, there was going to be hell to pay. "Listen, J.T., I gotta go—my brother's over there waiting for me." Ryan pointed to Will, who had moved from the porch steps and was standing by the gate, ready to pull him away.

"Oh, yeah, so your brotha owns that sweet Lexus out front, huh? Man, what I wouldn't give for one of those."

"I'll see ya," Ryan said over his shoulder as he walked toward his very angry brother. Will did not like to be kept waiting.

Will watched his brother talking to those criminals and he didn't like it one bit. Ryan was so much better than this lot.

At six-foot-four, Ryan was tall and lanky and towered

over Will and many of the kids his age. With baby-fine hair, a smooth brown complexion, and big brown eyes, Ryan had truly turned into a fine-looking young man. And from what Will had heard, he also had a way with the ladies. Girls were always standing outside the locker room or waiting for him after a game. If he kept his head in the books and kept up the good grades, he was sure to get an athletic scholarship to an Ivy League university.

When Ryan finally made it to the gate, Will held it open for him to walk through. He would have his say inside the house. He wouldn't dream of embarrassing Ryan in front of the neighborhood thugs.

"Get in the house!" Will whispered in his ear.

Ryan heard the tone and knew his brother was about to give him hell.

When the front door was closed, Will wasted no time in letting Ryan have it.

"What the hell are you thinking associating with those fools?" Will grabbed Ryan by the arm and pushed him into the living room nearby. "And where the hell have you been? It's after six. Mom's been worried sick."

"That's right." Their mother joined in from the door. Hands on hips, she was ready to do battle. Ryan groaned at the thought. He was in no mood for two lectures.

Will held up his hand. "Mother, I can handle this. Please go in the kitchen and finish dinner."

After a long stare at her youngest son, Eve huffed and walked back toward the kitchen.

Ryan removed his coat jacket. "Before you get started, bro: basketball practice ran over."

"And you forgot to pick up a phone? What did I give you a cell phone for?"

"Please, Will, I don't need a sermon. I accidentally left it on the charge." Ryan pointed to his cell phone on the nearby side table, still in its holster.

"Well, don't do it again." Will's tone softened. "You nearly scared me half to death."

"Sorry, bro." Ryan sighed. He couldn't please everybody. "So, what's up?"

"Let's talk for a minute." Will sat down on the sofa. Ryan rolled his eyes. He already knew what was coming. Taking a seat beside Will, Ryan waited for the inevitable lecture.

"Listen, Ryan," Will firmly grasped the young man by the shoulder, "it's very easy for a boy your age to get caught up with the wrong crowd."

"You're not telling me something I don't already know."

"Good. I won't go on then. Just remember that Mama and I want you to be a success, which means you can't be hanging around the neighborhood crew. Enough said?"

"Got it."

Will gave him a bear hug. He could only hope that his short lecture hadn't gone in one ear and out the other.

CHAPTER FIVE

"Mom, I have fantastic news!" Lexie exclaimed as they set the Sunday dinner table at her parents' home in Highland Park. Her parents had lived in the four-bedroom, two-story house for more than twelve years.

"Oh, really," Isabel Thompson said with a huff.

"What is it, Mother?" Lexie heard the tone. Something was definitely up.

"Why does something have to be up?" her mother asked. "Just because my one and only daughter failed to inform me of a huge promotion . . ." Her mother sighed and continued fussing over the flower centerpiece. "Why should it matter to me that my children don't include me in their lives?"

"Oh, Mom, stop," Sebastian chastised his mother as he returned to the dining room carrying wineglasses. "Didn't I just tell you that I was seeing someone new? Why can't that be enough?"

Lexie shook her head in amazement. She appreciated Sebastian standing up for her, but nothing ever changed. Why did her mother always have to make a big deal out of everything?

She had come tonight to share her news with her

mother. And she needn't have bothered. It surprised her that even now, at twenty-eight years old, she still felt like a little girl begging for her mother's approval. It seemed that no matter how hard she tried to be the obedient daughter, she could never live up to Isabel's high expectations.

Valedictorian in high school: not enough. Graduating summa cum laude at a prestigious school like Northwestern: not enough. Snagging a fashion buyer's job straight out of school at Bentley's department store: still not enough.

Fashion buyer wasn't the profession her mother would have chosen for her. She had a business degree from Northwestern. Isabel expected her daughter to work at some huge corporation or continue her schooling and obtain her MBA. Instead, Lexie turned to retail and fashion, her true passions. If she'd had her way she would have ditched school long ago and become a designer from the start, but her mother would have had a coronary. And until recently she had dated boring Adrian Turner all to please her mother!

"You know your father and I aren't getting any younger. It would be nice if you both included us in your lives. But if that's too much trouble . . ." Isabel stormed off and left Lexie and Sebastian to stew on her dangling comment.

"I swear, sometimes I could strangle that woman," Lexie whispered under her breath.

"You and me both. But you've got to let it roll off your back, sis. You know she loves to guilt-trip us. And for some reason you fall for it every single time."

Lexie glared back at her brother. She couldn't be mad with Sebastian for speaking the truth.

"Are you two talking about me?" her mother inquired, returning to the dining room.

Did the woman have radar hearing?

"And if we were?" Sebastian rose to the bait.

"Then I would tell you you don't want to mess with the woman making dinner," Isabel replied with a smile, setting down the entrée platter.

"So what exactly is for dinner?" Wesley Thompson asked, strolling into the dining room with a beer in hand. After thirty years of marriage and a little gray at the temples, Lexie's father was smart enough to stay in his favorite recliner in the family room and wait out the bickering.

"I made my specialty, jerk chicken with rice and peas."

"Ah, woman, I don't know if my stomach can handle all that spice," Wesley replied.

"I've been slaving in the kitchen all day finishing up the Mathis' engagement party, so if you don't like what I've selected for dinner, tough. You don't have to eat. There'll be more leftovers for the rest of us."

"No need to get all in a huff, woman." Her father backed down from a confrontation and leaned across the table to give his wife a kiss, but Isabel angrily moved away.

"You kids, sit down and eat," Isabel ordered. To avoid any further confrontation, Lexie and Sebastian followed their mother's directive and took a seat on either side of the seven-piece mahogany dining table while her parents sat at the heads.

"So, tell me more about this promotion."

"Mom, it's not really a promotion. More like an opportunity toward a promotion."

"And what exactly does that mean?"

"Being given the responsibility to head the fashion

show is huge at Bentley's. Every junior buyer who's ever coordinated the show has gone on to become an assistant head buyer."

"And is that all you what to be, an assistant head buyer? I swear, Lexie, why do you always think small?" Her mother spooned a small portion of jerk chicken on her own plate before passing the entrée platter to Lexie. "Why don't you think big?"

Sebastian rolled his eyes at the comment. Taking bread from the breadbasket, he passed it to his father. A silent looked passed between the two men as they waited for World War II to break out.

"Well, Mother, I have to learn how to crawl before I can walk," Lexie returned, filling her plate with the spicy dish.

"Yes, dear," Isabel continued, "but you've always been this way. Even when you were cheerleading, *I* had to encourage you to run for the head position. And when you were thinking of running for class secretary, who was it that encouraged you to run for president? And did you not win?"

Throwing down her napkin, Lexie refused to listen to her mother catalog her faults or her lack of courage. "I'm so sorry you think so very little of your daughter. A Northwestern graduate, for goodness's sake! Why don't you ever pick on your college-dropout son?"

Lexie shot a quick apologetic look over at Sebastian.

"Don't go putting me in the middle of your troubles," Sebastian said. "Now listen up, the two of you. I didn't travel all this way from my cushy studio to listen to you bicker. So if this is how it's going to be, then I can just leave right now." He began to stand.

"Don't, son," Wesley spoke up pleadingly. "It's been so long since we last saw you." Wesley knew Sebastian stayed away because of Lexie and Isabel's constant arguing. "They'll behave. Won't you, Isabel?"

"Hmph." Her mother shrugged dispassionately.

"And Lexie?" Her father looked at her. Lexie hated when he gave her the puppy-dog eyes. He knew she was defenseless when it came to resisting them.

"Sure, Daddy, I'll behave." Lexie forced a smile. As much as she hated to admit the least bit of wrongdoing, Lexie turned to face her mother and apologized. "I'm sorry, Mother."

"Was that so hard?" Isabel inquired with a sardonic grin. Lexie knew the look; her mother had gotten her way. "All you children need to do is show me the proper respect."

"How about we start the conversation again?" Wesley suggested, passing Lexie a pitcher of iced tea. "Tell us more about the show, Lexie."

Pouring herself a glass, Lexie explained her new job. "Well, as fashion coordinator, I'll be handling the budget, production, the model selection, all the stylists, makeup artists, hairdressers, and of course all the publicity surrounding the event." Lexie sipped on her tumbler of iced tea.

"Wow!" her father exclaimed. "That's great, Lex. I'm really proud of you."

"Thanks, Dad. It's a real feather in my cap."

"I'm sure you'll do well, Lexie. You always do great at whatever you set your mind to."

Her mother remained suspiciously quiet throughout the interchange, but then spoke.

"Have you selected your staff yet?" Isabel inquired.

Bracing herself, Lexie answered truthfully. "Yes, I have."

"So, when do I start?" her mother asked. "When's

the date? What's the venue? I need to visualize the food setup."

Her mother rattled on and on. When Lexie didn't answer right away, her mother turned to stare directly in her eyes. "I'm waiting."

"Oh, crap," Sebastian murmured. A stalemate. Why was he not surprised? His father heard the remark and searched his face questioningly.

"And you'll be waiting, Mother." Lexie sat straight up in her seat and prepared for battle. "I have hired another caterer."

"Of all the . . ." Isabel stood up suddenly, sending her chair crashing to the floor. "I can't believe . . ." And with that her mother went running out of the room in tears. A few minutes later, a door slammed upstairs.

"Lexie." Wesley genuinely seemed stunned and hurt that Lexie would dare hire a caterer other than Isabel. He rushed out of the room after her, but not before laying one last disapproving look over his shoulder at Lexie.

"Damn her!" Lexie rose and stormed to the window. "Did you see her? Why do I always let her get to me?" She looked to Sebastian for approval.

"C'mon, sis, you had to see that coming. You didn't even let her bid on it."

"I couldn't. If I had, she would have completely taken over and wanted to do things her way. I had to take control." Lexie refused to feel bad. She would not let her mother run rampant over her fashion show. Still, a nagging feeling began to form in her stomach.

"You could have at least told her your theme, and if she'd didn't like your menu, then she could have at least turned you down."

"C'mon, Sebastian. You know she would never have

done things my way. I have a vision for the show. A
Mai Tai happy hour, light appetizers like coconut
shrimp skewers, baby quiche. You know she would
never have done it my way."

"I guess you'll never know, will you?" Sebastian
asked.

"You know what?" Lexie glanced around for her
purse. "I'm not going to stay here with her punishing
silence. I'm leaving. Are you coming with me?" She
tossed her Fendi over her shoulder.

"Of course I'm coming with you," Sebastian answered, throwing his napkin on the chair. "I'm not
going to stay here with her in this mood. We'll let our
father handle it. He's had years of experience."

Grabbing their coats, they headed for the door, but
not before Lexie threw a final glance up the staircase.

"All right, Lexie, you're up," Lauren barked at their
sales meeting the following week. "How's the show
coming along? Any success on finding a venue?"

"W—well, I . . ." Lexie stuttered. How could she tell
her boss that she'd come up empty? If she did, Lauren would lose faith in her abilities. This was a big
break and she couldn't blow it.

"Are you having a problem?" Sydney inquired. "If
so, I would be more than happy to assist." Sydney gave
her a smug smile.

Lexie shot daggers at Sydney. She was sure the little
witch would love for her to fall on her face, but she
would never let that happen.

"Although I appreciate your very generous offer,
Sydney," Lexie paused to give a reassuring smile to the
rest of the Bentley's staff, "I have everything under
control. Matter of fact, I have a meeting lined up with

a venue this afternoon that I'm sure would be perfect for the show."

"Care to give us any juicy hints?" Sydney asked, sensing Lexie was lying.

So you can sabotage it? No, thanks! "I will keep you informed, *Lauren,* once the deal is finalized," Lexie stated, closing her folder and effectively putting little Miss Sunshine in her place. Now all she had to do was make it happen.

Minutes later, Lexie returned to her desk. She had yet to finish selecting the moderate, sports, and evening wear designs from Dolce and Gabbana, Gucci, and Donna Karan's DKNY that she wanted for the fashion show.

There was just so much to do in so little time. To make matters worse, her budget was due on Lauren's desk along with the quarterly sales figures. Plus, her sales staff was awaiting her input on several displays in the department. Her buyer's job still went on despite her fashion-show duties.

Lauren stopped by her cubicle. "May I have a word?"

"Absolutely. Please sit down, Lauren." Lauren took the seat next to Lexie's desk.

"Let me be frank, Lexie. You know I don't like to beat around the bush.

"Yes, I know."

"I don't need to tell you this, but just in case you didn't know, you have a lot riding on the success of this venture." Lauren paused. "I've invested a lot of time in mentoring you. I hope you're up to the task."

"You don't have to worry, Lauren. I've got it covered."

"In this business," Lauren paused to lean over and stare Lexie dead in the eye, "if you falter, there is always someone waiting in the wings to take your place. Are we clear?"

"Crystal."

When she left, Lexie's head fell to her desk in despair.

The next afternoon, Lexie drove to Millennium. She'd run out of options. Christian had turned up empty, leaving her with her last hope. Lexie found Will sitting beside the bar looking over a stack of purchase orders. Head held high, Lexie marched toward him. Standing next to him with her hands on her hips, Lexie waited for Will to acknowledge her presence.

Will sensed Lexie the moment he heard the clicking of her heels against the hardwood floor or smelled the exotic scent of gardenia perfume, but he refused to be the first to speak. Miss High and Mighty had obviously come for a reason and he would let her stew in it.

He appeared to be very deep in paperwork, but Lexie would not be deterred. When Will didn't look up, Lexie coughed loudly to clear her throat. "Ahem. Excuse me." Lexie snapped her fingers in front of Will's face. Before she had a chance to pull away, Will's hand reached out and seized hers.

An electric charge ran through her veins like she'd been hit by lightning. Stunned, Lexie remained silent. Neither of them spoke or moved a muscle. Instead, they peered into one another's eyes. A long silence ensued before Lexie finally snatched her hand away.

"And to what do I owe the pleasure?" Will finally asked after several intense moments.

Lexie blinked and broke herself out of the daze she was in. Why was it that every time she was within five feet of this man, her heart flip-flopped?

"I—I, umm," she stuttered, trying to collect her thoughts. *Pull yourself together, Lexie, and put your ego on the shelf.* A promotion depended on the fashion-show success.

"I need to use your club," Lexie spit out unceremoniously.

"Oh, really?" Will greeted her harsh tone with sarcasm. "I don't recall your asking."

"Well, I'm here, aren't I?" Lexie asked, oddly annoyed at his manner.

"And?"

Biting her tongue, Lexie answered. "And I need your help."

After her diva routine on their blind date, Will soaked up every minute of Lexie's discomfort. Maybe it would bring her down a peg or two.

"I would like to use your club for Bentley's fashion show." Lexie managed to eke out her plans. "I would of course pay you handsomely for the use of your club."

"Of course." Will stood up. Even in three-inch-high Prada boots, Lexie was dwarfed by his stature.

Lexie watched him walk behind the bar and pour himself a glass of brandy as he thought about her offer. "You mind if I have one of those?" she asked. Will grabbed another glass from under the bar. Pouring some in a decanter, he pushed it toward her. Taking a sip, Lexie anxiously awaited his answer. "Well?"

"I don't think so."

"And why not?" Lexie replied haughtily. "I'll pay you double the fair market price."

"Why should I help the woman who thinks I'm a thug as well as a Neanderthal?" *She must think I've had a memory lapse,* Will thought. He hadn't forgotten her harsh words during their first encounter and he wasn't about to get into bed—no, make that business—with a shrew like Lexie Thompson.

Lexie blushed at the memory of her less-than-kind

words. Unfortunately, she needed this man. Hmmm, wrong choice of words. She needed the man's club and she would do anything to get it. Every avenue she'd checked came up empty. She had no choice but to cater to his oversize ego.

"Listen, Will," Lexie began, lowering her voice to a low, sultry whisper. She was hoping a little feminine charm might go a long way. Easing out of her leather jacket, Lexie leaned over the bar, giving Will a tantalizing view of her cleavage, elevated by one those push-up numbers. "I apologize for my behavior the other night. It truly wasn't one of my better moments."

"No, it wasn't. So why don't you tell me what's in this deal for me?" Will enjoyed watching Lexie's attempts to seduce him. Even better was the view of her full breasts from across the bar. He wondered what it would be like to mold those beautiful breasts in his hands. Would they be as soft and malleable as they appeared?

He hoped so. It took a lot of nerve for the little pampered princess to come to him. He liked chutzpah and Lexie Thompson had it in droves.

Lexie, on the other hand, was tied in knots. She hoped Will wouldn't automatically turn his nose at the idea of a fashion show because of her grand theatrics the other night. She needed a venue and Millennium was it. So if a little groveling was required, then by all means, she would suck it up.

"As I said, I will pay you a small fortune. And let's not forget the free publicity the show would provide for your club. It'll be advertised in all the fashion magazines and society pages. Imagine all those wealthy people coming to the club and spending all their money?"

CHAPTER SIX

"You have a deal." Will extended his hand.

Cautiously, Lexie accepted it. She was stunned. Had she heard correctly? Was he giving up that easy without fight? She'd expected a lot more resistance from him.

"Do you have a problem?" Will asked, observing Lexie's open mouth.

Disconcerted, she crossed her arms and pointedly looked away. "Of course not. I'm just surprised. I expected you would turn me down."

"Why? You presented your case and it sounds reasonable and quite profitable. There is one condition, though."

The moment the words were uttered, Lexie's sexy grin was replaced with a frown. She smelled a rat.

"I knew it. There had to be more to the story. What's your condition?"

"All items must be approved by me first," Will replied, taking a sip from his drink. What better way to get under the beautiful lady's skin?

"Have you lost your ever-loving mind?" Lexie jumped out of her seat. "This is my show."

"Actually, I haven't," Will answered wryly. "This is

my restaurant and I decide what goes on here and what doesn't. You can take it or leave it."

Lexie thought about it for a minute. She was all out of options and in desperate need of a venue. "I'll take it."

"Good. I think that was a wise move on your part."

"Ugh, why do you have to be patronizing?"

"And why do you always rise to the occasion?"

Did she enjoy sparring with him? Lexie was momentarily speechless and Will took her silence as a sign of triumph. "Why don't we seal this deal?" In one fluid motion, he'd moved from behind the bar and, with powerful hands, yanked her to her feet.

Instantly, Lexie stepped back, but Will closed the space between them until Lexie had no choice but to look into his onyx eyes. And when she did, he moved in for the kill.

Leaning forward, Will planted a long, searing kiss on her lips. Lexie stiffened in shock, but Will didn't waste any time bending her to his will. His tongue teased them open until Lexie allowed him access to explore the innermost caverns of her mouth. Once inside, his hot, wet tongue molded with hers, causing Lexie to moan out loud.

Never in a million years would she have dreamed that coming to the club would lead to this moment. After the initial spark between them, Lexie had banished all thoughts of Will Kennedy to the farthest recesses of her mind, but her body had a mind all its own and it was responding to his with equal fervor.

Instinctively, she moved her midriff closer, eager to feel his pulsating masculinity. And when she felt his growing manhood pressed up against her, every part of her felt alive and thrilled by this man with whom she had little in common.

Suddenly a door slammed and several people walked in, who Lexie could only assume were Will's staff. She pulled away, embarrassed not by her wanton behavior, but by the person she was engaging in it with. Lowering her head, she adjusted her blouse, which somehow had risen up during their encounter. Had he been about to touch her breasts? If so, his staff would have received quite an eyeful.

Lexie shook her head in amazement. What had gotten into her? Looking over at Will, she caught the sly, unashamed grin on his face. He didn't appear phased in the least bit by what had just happened between them. Instead, he looked oddly pleased with himself as if he had just proven a point.

"And why are you looking like the cat that just swallowed the canary?" Lexie asked. She hated that he stood there so smug and unaffected. Surely her kisses had caused him to get weak in the knees, too. Or had she lost her effect on men?

"Well, you proved my point—"

"And what theory might that be?"

"That as much as we might protest and claim to dislike one another, you and I are well suited physically."

"That's utterly ridiculous," Lexie said. "Of all the things, you just caught me off guard is all."

"Would you care to put it to the test again?" Will took a playful step toward her.

"No, I do not. Keep away!" Lexie warned, holding her hand up in defense. She doubted she could resist such a temptation and she refused to give him the satisfaction of being right. Things were getting out of hand; she had to leave now and clear her head so she could assess the situation.

"Well, if you're so immune, meet me at the club

later this evening. We'll have dinner, drinks, a little dancing, and settle this once and for all."

He was offering a challenge, but the more important question was should she take him up on it? "I have to go." Lexie searched around for her purse and jacket, which Will held up in his hands—big, strong hands that had cupped her bottom so deliciously a moment before. Stop it, Lexie told herself.

Snatching the items from him, Lexie strode out of the club, leaving Will smiling after her. *She'll be back*, Will thought.

"Hey, is that you, playa?" Ryan asked from behind him. He'd just come to pick up a check from Will for his class trip to Walt Disney World when he saw Lexie walk away. "'Cause if that's the kind of women that be rolling up in here, then this is definitely the place I want to be."

"First of all, where do you get off using that kind of language? Who have you been hanging with?"

Ryan laughed, smiling mischievously. "You know, I be hanging out with the fellas."

"You be," Will mocked, slapping him upside the head. "I am not sending you to that private school for you to come out sounding like some hood rat."

"But, Will, everyone talks like that."

"You're not everybody. Come here and let me talk to you for a minute." Will led Ryan by the arm to take a seat at the bar stool. "Do you know how lucky you are to have the kind of opportunities you have?" Will pointed to Ryan's Air Jordans and his Tommy Hilfiger outfit. Their mother's nursing income didn't allow for much so Will made sure Ryan had everything he needed. Whether it was a new pair of gym shoes or a new backpack, it was important to Will that Ryan didn't do without like he had.

Ryan was too young to remember being poor, as soon as Will was financially able, he'd provided him with everything he needed. But Will remembered the times he'd envied Damon's latest new toy or brand-name outfit or watched the Bradleys go on fancy vacations. Although they tried to include Will when they could, his mother didn't always allow him to impose.

"Not that same ole story again," Ryan replied, turning his back on Will.

"Yes, it's this same story again." Will grabbed Ryan by the shoulders and looked him dead in the eye. "And from now on, I don't want you hanging around those little hood rats on your block anymore, you hear me? Those guys are bad news. They're hoodlums, soon to be career criminals."

"Why you trying to mess me up like that?" Ryan turned away from Will. "It's bad enough they see me trotting off to that preppy school you've got me going to, and now this."

"That preppy school is going to get you into college." Will hoped he could get through to his little brother. "Promise me you're not going to hang around those guys anymore."

Ryan didn't respond. Instead, he sat looking sullen and despondent.

"Ryan? Promise me."

Sucking his teeth, Ryan gave Will the answer he wanted to hear. "All right, all right."

"Good, get out of here. I've got some work to do."

Pleased with himself and his parenting skills, Will returned to the stack of files he'd ignored from the moment sexy Lexie entered the club. He'd given her something to chew on and now the next move was hers.

* * *

A short while later, Lexie met up with Christian at Rhythm and Blues, a local martini bar on Rush Street, to discuss the day's events. An abandoned office-building-turned-club, Rhythm and Blues kept it simple with a tiny bar specializing in Cosmopolitans and Appletinis as well raspberry, lemonade, and chocolate martinis. It was one of Lexie's favorite spots to have a cocktail. In addition to its delicious drinks, it offered a selection of light snacks including buffalo wings, coconut shrimp, and assorted cheeses and veggies.

The bar was already jammed full of the nine-to-five set trying to mellow out after a hard day's work. She and Christian usually came in to make fun of everyone's wardrobe, but tonight Lexie had Will on the brain.

"Can you believe the gall of that man?" she asked from her seat at the bar. "Groping me and kissing me like that? He had absolutely no right." Her mouth still throbbed from Will's kisses.

Christian laughed. "Hmm, sounds like he had every right to me." He nibbled on R&B's scrumptious spinach and artichoke cheese dip. "Because women like you, my dear, need to be kissed. And often, if you ask me."

"Christian!" Lexie smacked his hand.

"You know I speak the truth." Christian scooted his bar stool closer to hers.

"I have no idea what you're referring to," Lexie replied, finishing her Cosmo and signaling the waiter for another. Frankly, she'd thought the man was rude and uncouth, but when he pulled her to him, she'd definitely felt something, and that she simply couldn't allow. In her past relationships, she was the one who set the rules, who outlined how things would go. But Will was different; he was truly an alpha male taking the bull by the horns and Lexie had to admit she found it exciting.

And then there was the fact that he hadn't held a grudge. He'd dismissed their first meeting as water under the bridge and allowed her to use the club. She couldn't have been more surprised at his generosity of spirit. Lexie wondered if she could have been so forgiving of a man who'd stormed out on their dinner date.

"Oh, yes, you do, missy." Christian was not going to let her off the hook. It was time for Lexie to stop hanging out with boys, grow up, and find herself a real man. And he intended to encourage her. "This Will fellow sounds like exactly what you need. Were you not complaining that you couldn't find a man that could fit your needs?"

"Well, he is definitely not it. In my two meetings with this man, I've gathered that he is an arrogant, obnoxious, womanizing playboy who owns a bar, for goodness's sake."

The waiter brought her cocktail and Lexie took a liberal sip.

"Okay, so he's not Mr. Universe like Adrian, who was educated at Dartmouth, lives on Lake Shore Drive, and drives a Mercedes-Benz, but he sure did get your juices flowing, didn't he?"

"Christian, have you heard a word I've said?" Lexie grabbed his shoulder and shook him.

"No. You better grab him while you can because I am sure with his sexy good looks, Mr. Kennedy won't be alone for long."

"You're probably right. Dozens of little twits probably line up every night at his club, hoping to be one of the few to wind up in his bed the next morning."

"And would that be such a bad thing?" Christian inquired.

Lexie smiled. "I won't be one of them. And if he thinks that I am, he's got another think coming."

"So you are going to take him up on his offer for a date tonight?"

"Maybe," Lexie replied coquettishly.

"Honey, I think your choice is clear." Christian snapped his fingers.

Feeling confident and assured, Lexie wore one of her own creations to Millennium later that evening, a slinky halter dress made of silky black satin that fit her like a glove and went well with her high stilettos and Fendi baguette purse.

She'd come to prove to Will that she was up for a challenge, and to discuss a little business. There would be no more manhandling her like this afternoon. He would have to appreciate her beauty, but from a distance.

Walking seductively around the club, Lexie perused the inside, taking an inventory. On her earlier visit, she'd hardly had time to assess how the place would fit into her vision. But now that she saw it, it was perfect. Although only eleven o'clock, Millennium was already filled up as patrons got ready to get their party on. Moving her way through the crowd, Lexie stopped in front of the dance floor. She glanced around and saw good lighting, a great sound system, a huge bar, and a large stage; her boss would be blown away.

"Looking for someone?" a deep masculine voice asked from her side.

Before she turned her head, Lexie already knew who it was. The rich timbre of his voice was enough to make the hairs on her neck stand up in recognition. "Hmmm, yes, I was." Trying to appear unaffected, Lexie whirled around to greet Will. "You."

"Oh. And to what do I owe the pleasure?"

Lexie stared back at the source of her consternation throughout the day. If it was possible, he looked even better than he had earlier. Closely cropped hair, a nicely trimmed mustache and connecting goatee, high chiseled cheekbones, and sexy, dark bedroom eyes, Will was one attractive package. And Lexie couldn't help but notice the tailored black trousers that fit his generous behind like a glove. Or the hard broad chest that was clearly visible through the black silk shirt he'd casually opened at the top. The glow of the recessed lighting only added to his allure.

Her heart rate sped up being near the raw, sexual energy Will exuded. Lexie willed herself to take control of the situation. He would not have all the power. *She* would set the terms of their little arrangement. Pulling him by the arm, Lexie moved to a quiet corner. She didn't want everyone in the world hearing their business.

"I thought we could start discussing ideas," Lexie said, offering Will a sexy smile. "Especially considering that I have to run everything through you."

Pausing, Will rubbed his chin thoughtfully. "I'm not really in the mood for business right now. How about some champagne?" he asked. "Jerome." He motioned to his bartender to bring over the champagne he requested to have on ice. He'd known intuitively that Lexie couldn't resist coming tonight.

Lexie narrowed her eyes. "I didn't come here for champagne."

"No?" Will smiled at the thought. He hadn't missed

the sexy little number she was wearing, which was no doubt for his benefit.

Lexie leaned in closer to whisper in his ear. "Make no mistake, this arrangement is strictly business. Nothing more."

Will stepped back and looked her up and down. The fitted halter dress was a knockout, leaving little to the imagination, and Lexie knew it. "And I suppose you always dress like this for one of your 'business meetings'?" Will asked.

The man never missed a beat! Swallowing hard, she lifted her chin and boldly met his gaze. "Oh, this?" Lexie asked, running her fingers down the satiny-smooth fabric. "Well, I *am* in the business of fashion. I always look good, darling."

"So it's going to be look but don't touch, huh?"

"That's right," Lexie answered, tossing her brunet mane over her shoulders. She'd come here tonight to bask in her womanly power and prove to Will that she was immune to his defenses; what had happened earlier was anomaly.

"If that's the way you want it, I'll agree to it *for now*. But mark my words, you will have a change of heart."

At a loss for words, Lexie fumed as a waitress came with two flutes of champagne. Not waiting for him, Lexie grabbed one and gulped the entire flute. Maybe it was best she left before she said something she would regret. And she couldn't afford to do that. She needed to stay in Will's good graces.

When Lexie remained silent, Will took that as a sign of defeat. "Well, I'm glad we've got all that straightened out. So what do you say we dance, have a good time. It is Friday night, after all." Will reached for Lexie's hand.

"I have other plans," she lied, backing away. She had no other plans for the evening, but she didn't want him to know that. She would not let William Kennedy think she was that easily had.

"Break them."

"I will do no such thing." Lexie turned to walk away, but a strong hand pulled her back.

"Are you always this stubborn? Why must you always do things the hard way?" At the defiant look in her eyes, Will continued. "Well, in case you don't remember, you're the one that needs me. I've agreed to your hands-off policy. So let's have a cocktail and get to know each other. And what better time than the present?"

Lexie started to say something, but thought better of it. "All right, you win. Are you happy now?"

"Immensely." Will smiled. Lexie sure didn't make it easy for him to get close. He guessed that was why he found her so intriguing. "Do you always make men work this hard?"

"Always."

Will's mouth curved into a smile. Lexie was all fire. After the initial challenge, Will usually grew disinterested, but Lexie was the exact opposite. He doubted he could ever grow tired of her.

Lexie joined Will at his corner booth in the VIP section of the club. The booth was Will's own private hideaway that he kept for special occasions and special guests and Lexie Thompson was definitely one of those.

"Would you like more champagne?" Will asked once they were seated.

"By all means." Lexie accepted another glass of expensive champagne. Was he trying to impress her? If so, he was off to a rocking start. Lexie took a generous sip.

"I appreciate your spending the evening with me," Will began. "Now we can get to know each other."

"Did I have a choice?"

"Yes, you did, but I think you'll discover that I'm not the ogre you believe me to be."

"No, probably not." Lexie smiled. "Though I have heard that you have a way with the ladies and your bed is never empty for long." Sebastian was familiar with Millennium and had given her the 411 on the illustrious club owner.

"So my reputation precedes me, huh? Well, rest assured, it's well deserved."

"My, my, aren't we arrogant? Do you really think you're that irresistible?"

"Baby, trust me, you'd be amazed. But enough about my playboy image—tell me what makes Lexie tick."

All Lexie needed was a willing ear to open up about her career. Anyone who knew her could see, could hear, and could feel the enthusiasm in her voice when she discussed her job as a junior buyer; Will was surprised to discover that Lexie was more talented than he thought. Ms. Thompson had designed her own clothing line.

"And you? You mentioned expanding your business. How's that going?"

Since Lexie had freely opened up about her life, Will felt compelled to follow suit and give a few thoughtful details.

Will shrugged. "It's coming. But I could use your help."

"How so?" Now Lexie was curious. Maybe she could finally get some leverage on the illustrious Mr. Kennedy.

"I am meeting with some very important investors who are interested in helping me expand the business, amongst other things."

"And how do I fit in?"

"Well . . ." Will moved closer to Lexie in the booth and grasped her hand. His fingers stroked the inside of her palm. When Lexie didn't move away, Will continued. "These men are very old-school and they would like to see that I'm settled and serious about business."

"And you need a girlfriend to prove that?" Lexie asked, trying to focus on the question at hand instead of the dizzying euphoric emotion that encompassed her when his smooth, lean fingers touched her palm. Usually she was immune to these romantic gestures, but this time was different. Will had really listened to her dreams for the future. Gone was the cocky man from the theater; in his stead was a good listener. And that was more attractive than she could have ever imagined.

"As a matter of fact, yes," Will stated.

"W—well, I suppose I could," Lexie stammered in astonishment.

"Listen, Lex, all you have to do is accompany me to dinner. It's all quite harmless."

"And tonight—is tonight harmless?"

"Tonight was just for kicks." When Lexie looked like she was ready to explode, Will placed a lean finger on her lips. "After our last dinner together, I needed to see if we could spend an evening in each other's company without strangling the other person. And lo and behold. I was right."

"Ya think?"

"Yes. More than that, I know," Will stood up and reached for Lexie's hand. "Dance with me." It wasn't a request, but a demand.

Without a word spoken between them, Lexie accepted his outstretched arm. She would let Will think he was in charge and when the moment presented itself, she would show him who was boss.

His hands were warm and strong as they grasped her, pulling her with him onto the dance floor. And just as easily, her arms found their way to his neck, while his encircled her slender waist. Together they swayed to a well-chosen song by Brian McKnight, who just so happened to be her favorite artist. Could Will have known that?

As they danced, a strange unknown force took over Lexie, forcing her to press her body against Will's. They easily found a rhythm, swaying to the sound of the music as song after song played on the stereo. They were oblivious to the world around them. Will didn't realize that most of the patrons had already left until he caught his bartender pointing to his watch.

As much as he hated to, they finally separated and Will released Lexie's warm, pliant body from his grasp. "I'll be right back," he whispered.

Within seconds, Will had cleared the club, dismissing his staff a half hour early. Alone on the dance floor, Lexie waited with eager anticipation for his return.

CHAPTER SEVEN

Once the club had cleared, Will made his move. Quickly locking the front door, he spun around to face Lexie. He found her standing boldly in the center of the room waiting for him, her slender figure silhouetted by soft candlelight.

Confidently he strode across the room, dimming the lights as he went and turning on a slow love ballad, her lust-filled eyes luring him to her web just like a black widow spider.

Lexie was riveted to her spot. Her heart pounded in an erratic rhythm as his compelling eyes raked every inch of her. She knew what was about to happen between them and felt no shame. She was merely responding to her body's needs, to an attraction she hadn't felt in a long time. Warm all over, Lexie wondered what it would feel like to have his tongue and fingers lick and caress her body. Would they know the way to guide her to profound pleasure?

When Will finally made it to her, Lexie couldn't suppress the moan that escaped from her lips when his hand lightly touched her cheek. There was no time for second thoughts as they both reached for each other at the same time. Losing all vestige of control, they kissed each other like sex-crazed maniacs. Will gathered her in his arms and crushed her to him while Lexie ground her womanly center against his full arousal. They were on fire for each other as their tongues dueled, each seeking intro into the warm inner cavern of the other's mouth.

Lexie returned his ardor and sucked on his tongue voraciously. Before she knew it, Will was picking her up and carrying her to the bar. Hoisting herself atop, Lexie took action, feverishly attacking the buttons on his shirt, and when they didn't comply, ripping them off, sending a slew of buttons flying to the floor. But Lexie didn't care. She wanted him right there, right now.

Will admired her ferocity and assertiveness, but he didn't allow her to take lead for long. Sliding her spaghetti straps down her shoulders, he pushed up her dress, bunching it at the waist. He was pleased when he found bare breasts jutting out, eager for his tongue. Bending his head, he took a taut nipple in his mouth.

"You're so beautiful," Will said, moaning as he tugged on her nipple, lightly teasing it while his other hand kneaded her other breast. Molding and shaping the soft flesh with his fingers, he squeezed the nipple until another tight bud appeared. Will fastened his mouth on the nipple and suckled generously.

A hunger built between Lexie's thighs. She needed to be closer to him and feel all his magnificence. With anxious fingers, she unbuckled his pants and felt the thick, hard, pulsating length of him between her hands. Slowly she caressed him before picking up the tempo until Will was in a frenzied, fevered pitch just like her.

So it was like that, huh? Will thought. Well, he would

show her exactly what it felt like. Seeking out the soft folds of her feminine flesh beneath her lace thong, his narrow fingers slid inside her, causing a wonderful friction that made her squirm and clutch at his shoulders. Within minutes, her eyes fluttered back and her body convulsed as he brought her to a cataclysmic orgasm.

But they were far from over. Will continued loving her body until he couldn't stand it any longer. Hearing her come had made him hot and hard for her.

Lexie heard the tear of foil seconds before he grasped her by the hips and plunged deep inside her. Her mind vaguely registered that Will was protecting them, but all she could think of was that she wanted him oh-so-desperately. "Yes, oh, yes," Lexie said, moaning as her nails raked against his back.

Reveling in abandonment, Lexie lifted her hips off the counter and rose to meet his demanding thrusts. When he almost pulled out, Lexie wrapped her legs tightly around his waist and brought him closer.

Gripping her hair, Will brought her mouth back in close contact with his. His appetite was insatiable as he sucked her tongue, her breasts, and that sensitive spot at the nape of her neck. He filled her completely, all the while making love to her with his mouth. When his hands cupped her bottom, Lexie rose to meet him for one final thrust before screaming out in ecstasy once more. Stars swirled around her as her whole body was flooded with pure pleasure.

Closing her eyes, Lexie lightly rested her head on Will's shoulder and clung to his embrace. Their union had been explosive. There wasn't a doubt in her mind that her dormant sexuality had finally been reawakened.

Taking a deep breath, Lexie tried to compose herself, because as much as she'd enjoyed their passionate encounter, feeling that kind of passion was overwhelming and a little bit scary. For the first time in her life, she felt completely exposed and vulnerable.

Mustering her gumption, Lexie pushed herself away, but not before she saw Will's passion-glazed eyes piercing hers. Flushed, she quickly jumped off the bar, pulled up her straps and adjusted her dress. Glancing around, she searched for her panties, which had somehow been cast aside during the heat of the moment. Lexie found the lacy underwear on the floor nearby and pushed them inside her purse.

"Lexie—" Will started, but Lexie put a finger to his lips.

"Don't say anything. It might spoil the moment." With a feather-light kiss on the lips, Will watched Lexie make a hasty retreat.

He was completely thrown by what had just happened. He couldn't ever remember having that kind of response with another person. What he and Lexie shared was more than just physical. It was a connection and one he wouldn't easily throw away.

Stretching out on her Egyptian cotton sheets the following morning, Lexie remembered the feel of Will's lips on hers. How soft they'd been and how oh-so-sweet they'd tasted. It had been a long time since a man had made her moist like that. The last time that happened, she'd been a natural brunette.

While a freshman at Northwestern University, Lexie had fallen deeply in love with Kevin Anderson. Tall and muscular, Kevin had fulfilled every one of her teenage fantasies. She'd fallen so hard for his smooth-talking ways, she'd been ready to toss her business career and fashion design dreams out the window to settle down and have some of this playa's babies. Lexie cringed at the memory of how willing she'd been to cast aside all her hopes and dreams on a man. Thank God someone was looking down on her from above and she'd finally gotten a clue to his womanizing ways. Soon she discovered Kevin had several women's noses wide open. The man had women paying his rent, buying his books, and his playa clothes.

But Lexie would not be played. She set out to teach him a lesson that no one messed with Lexie Thompson. With Nia's help, Lexie plastered fliers of his face all over campus, identifying him for the hustler he was. Soon every woman on campus knew to stand clear of him and before long Kevin was off to another campus to find another unsuspecting victim.

Rising from her bed, Lexie shook off her past; she had more important things to contend with this morning, such as Will. Although the sex had been good, it could never happen again. Lexie sensed that Will could be another Kevin in the making and she mustn't let herself get besotted like that again. Careerwise she was finally where she wanted to be and no man was going to get in the way of that.

"You look torn up," Damon commented. "Long night?" He was all fired up for one of their notoriously intense racquetball games at the country club, until he saw the serious look on Will's face.

"Man, if you only knew." Will looked up from tying his shoelaces and shook his head in amazement. He motioned for Damon to take a seat on the locker-room bench.

He still couldn't believe how last night had ended.

It hadn't been his intention to sleep with Lexie, but boy, was it worth it.

"Hello, is anyone home?" Damon waved his hand in front of Will. His best friend was never known to stare off into space. "All right, spill the dirt. What's got you all shook up?"

"Hmmm?" Will said distractedly. All his thoughts centered around a certain five-foot-nine beauty who had all of sudden turned his whole world upside down. "Everything's fine."

"Doesn't look that way to me," Damon replied. "I bet you haven't heard a thing I've said."

"Uh . . . you mentioned something about the wedding."

"Don't even try it. What gives?"

"Man, you would not believe what happened last night." Sighing, Will decided he needed to confide in someone. He still couldn't believe it himself.

"I'm waiting and getting older by the second."

"Lexie and I hooked up last night," Will blurted out.

"What?" Damon jumped off the bench. "Get outta here. No way. After the other evening? C'mon!"

"Have I ever lied to you about a female?"

"Well . . ." Damon could remember a time or two back in high school, but the grin on Will's face told otherwise. "Seriously, you and Lex? How did this happen?"

"Do you really want to know play-by-play?"

Damon smacked him on the forehead. "No, knucklehead. What precipitated all this?"

"Hmmm, let me see." Will rubbed his chin. "Was it my devilish good looks or my overwhelming charm?" He smiled when Damon stared him directly in the eye. "Honestly, Damon, I couldn't tell you. It was the right moment. I guess we were both on the same page."

Clearly, they weren't talking about the same woman.

"How did the two of you happen to fall into bed?" Damon knew Lexie to be the type of woman who liked to stay in control.

"Did I mention a bed?" Will smiled roguishly. He enjoyed watching the bewildered look on Damon's face. Obviously Lexie came across as more conservative in certain circles, but the woman he had been with last night was a wildcat!

"No . . ."

"Since I'm a gentleman, I will not say where, but needless to say, it was an unconventional location."

"You sly dog, you." Damon punched him the arm. "So when do you two plan on hooking up again?"

"How about her first available minute?"

"Good luck, man, I have a feeling that catching Lexie may not be so easy."

"Oh, please." Will held up his hand. "I have no doubts that Lexie and I will hook up again. Now let's go and play some ball."

Sitting in her cubicle at Bentley's two days later, Lexie stared into space, her thoughts wandering to the night atop Will's bar and what she was going to do about it. She dreaded the thought of having to interact with Will, but seeing as how the fashion show was at his club, there was no way to avoid him.

Her emotions were extremely conflicted. They teetered from despising the man one minute to daydreaming about the most incredible, mind-blowing sex she had ever experienced with a man. Atop a bar, no less!

She had to nip this in the bud once and for all. Picking up the phone, she forced her fingers to dial the number to Millennium. Lexie glanced at her watch. It was ten o'clock. She could only hope that despite his late-night hours, Will was an early riser.

"Hello?" A gruffly voiced Will answered on the fourth ring.

"Good morning."

Hearing the sound of Lexie's voice on the other end immediately caused Will to perk up. If she hadn't called, he was sure to make contact. After they'd combusted, he knew that one evening with Lexie Thompson was not nearly enough. Wiping the sleep from his eyes, he pulled the phone to his ear. "And how are you this morning, sunshine?" Will decided to take the laid-back approach.

"I'm great." Taking a deep breath, Lexie began. "Listen, Will, about the other night . . ."

"Yes, darling."

"Don't call me that," she snapped. Just because they shared a night of passion did not mean he could start calling her pet names. She had to clue him in straightaway. "Will, as wonderful as that night was, it was just one night and it can't happen again." No, she needed to be more forceful and direct. "It *won't* happen again," Lexie corrected herself.

"And why not?"

"Because you and I are not compatible."

"Were you and I in the same room?" Will smiled through the phone.

"Yes, I was and you were plain lucky, is all. The stars must have been looking down on you. Whatever the case may be, you're not my type."

"Oh, really?" Will replied. For this he needed to sit up straight and pushed several pillows against the headboard. "Well, I happen to disagree with you. In fact, I think you're a coward."

"What? How dare you speak to me like that!" Lexie

shouted with a note of annoyance. As much she enjoyed the other night, she would not give him the satisfaction of knowing how right he was.

Will heard the tone of her voice and knew he'd hit the nail on the head. "You're upset because I'm right. Why else would you choose to tell me via this medium? Over the phone—that's very cowardly of you, Lexie. You don't have the courage to tell me in person because you're afraid it might happen again."

"Uh . . ." Lexie said. "Of all the arrogant things I've ever heard . . ." Lexie rolled her eyes upward. "Listen, Will, you weren't that great. I've had better."

"Don't even try it, Lex. Just admit that you've never had it so good. And when you're ready for another dose, come back and I'll happily supply you."

"You're a pig!" Lexie yelled before slamming down the phone. The nerve of that man! And to think she'd actually slept with him. What had she been thinking? He'd just proven that he was truly as uncouth as she'd originally thought. But now she had to live with her spontaneity. The fashion show was still at the club and she'd given him her word that she would pose as his date for his dinner with his investors. They hadn't even begun to discuss the implication of the latter. What had she gotten herself into?

Will hung up the line. He had succeeded in getting under her skin, and as much as she thought she despised him, she still needed Millennium.

He smiled inwardly as he thought of the beautiful, talented Lexie Thompson. His initial inclination had been to run as fast he could. He'd been with her type before, but after spending more time with her, he'd had a change of heart. Learning more about Lexie

Thompson was preeminent. He wanted to find out what other passions lay right underneath that cool and composed demeanor. He had barely delved beneath the surface of the woman he'd thought was nothing more than a pampered bourgeoisie princess living underneath makeup and designer clothes. Maybe, just maybe, she might be a woman worthy of his time. But first he had to get a few more hours of shut-eye.

Two hours later, Lexie banged on the door of Millennium with her production staff and her assistant. Pulling off the fashion show required a myriad of different people—caterers, models, stylists, hairdressers, makeup artists, and dressers—and Lexie was in charge of pulling them all together.

After several minutes, Jerome opened the door. "What are you doing here, Ms. Thompson? Isn't it a little early?"

"I've don't have the time to wait for your master to rise from his slumber. I've got work to do." Lexie barged past Jerome and entered the club with her crew.

Scanning the main room, Lexie looked for the illustrious Will Kennedy, determined to show him that Lexie Thompson was no coward. He had absolutely no idea who he was dealing with. Her search proved futile, though; Will was nowhere in sight. It was already past noon and the only people in the place were Jerome and the chef.

Well, she was just going to have to wake up Mr. Kennedy.

A loud banging noise awoke Will from his sleep. Who in the hell would be in Millennium this early?

His staff usually didn't arrive until at least four o'clock. Will snatched his robe off the bedpost and threw it on.

Marching downstairs, he was surprised to discover Lexie and an entire crew of people roaming around Millennium while rap music blared through the speakers. Walking toward the stage, Will ignored Lexie seated at a table nearby and climbed the stairs to turn down the volume.

Yet, who could miss her? She was dressed in a cropped top that revealed her sterling-silver belly-button ring, a hip-hugging skirt, and newsboy cap, while slurping a smoothie.

"What the hell are you doing here?" he bellowed, walking down the steps. "Do you have any idea what time it is?"

Lexie, who was speaking to the sound and lighting crew, stopped her conversation.

"In case you haven't noticed, the hour happens to be past noon. Most people in the world are already amongst the living." Lexie lifted her chin to meet his icy stare. But, instead, her eyes wandered to his bare chest, which peeked out from his open robe. Her body tensed in response, remembering exactly how hard that very same chest felt against hers.

"Considering my line of work and hours of operation, I'm sure you understand that I would sleep in," Will finished peevishly, coming to take a seat beside her.

"And how is that my problem?" Lexie retorted with cold sarcasm. "As you are aware, I have to get moving on coordinating the fashion show."

Though annoyed, Will smiled despite himself. He had to admit, the woman had fire. After he'd called her a coward, she showed up two hours later to prove he was dead wrong. He wondered what else she had in store for him.

"Of course," Will replied smoothly. "But in the future, Lexie," her brow rose questioningly, "please call first to schedule use of the club."

"I'll try to remember that. Now, if you don't mind, I really need to get back to designing the stage setup." Lexie opened a folder as if to dismiss him.

"Perhaps I can be of assistance?" Will asked, closing his robe. He'd flown down the stairs with it blowing in the wind. Luckily, he had on pajama bottoms.

Lexie's ears perked up in response. She could probably use a little help. A fashion show required a runway. She and her crew had tried envisioning how to extend the stage, but just couldn't see it.

"Give me a few minutes to get dressed and I'll be right back down."

Twenty minutes later, he returned smelling of sandalwood and Lexie knew she was in trouble. She watched him complete a quick survey of the room and come up with several options, which he happily expounded to Lexie.

Lexie couldn't help but smile at Will's innovation. In a few short moments he'd already come through for her. His suggestions on how to extend the stage and where to place the podium were right on target.

"You've really given me a lot to think about. Thanks for your assistance." Lexie shook Will's hand stiffly as though they were nothing more than business partners.

"Lexie, after what we've shared, do we really need these formalities?"

"Yes, we do."

"If you insist on this stance, I'll just have to show you that you're not nearly as immune to me as you protest." His hands surrounded her bare waist and pulled her toward him.

"Easy, Will," Lexie whispered in his ear, inclining her head toward her staff waiting by the door. "I don't want the whole world privy to our previous festivities."

"Why not? I know I'm eager to feast on you all over again," Will said huskily.

Lexie stepped backward; Will's close proximity was causing her senses to go haywire. "Don't think you're going to get an invitation to my bed anytime soon. Besides which, I have a whole slew of models coming in right now."

"Oh, really?" Will took a seat next to hers and propped his feet on the table. Well, count me in. I'd love to see the view."

"You are really the most egotistical, self-centered—" Before she could continue her tirade, Portia St. James from the Elite Agency walked in. With an office in Chicago, Elite was one of the premier fashion-model agencies in the country and Lexie was lucky to have them.

"Portia, as always, it's a pleasure to see you." Lexie came forward and gave her a quick hug. Nearly six feet tall with straight blond hair that fell to her waist and what Lexie could only guess was a size-two figure, Portia looked every bit as fashionable as the models she represented. She made Lexie look curvaceous in comparison.

"You, too, darling." They kissed either cheek. "Tell me, what do you have in store for this shindig? I'm dying to know."

"Sorry, Portia, I'm keeping my theme under wraps."

"Can't you give me a few juicy tidbits for old time's sake?"

Lexie smiled. Old time's sake? They had known

each other socially for years, but they were never the best of friends. "Sorry, darling." Lexie feigned sincerity. "But come to the show on the fourteenth and you'll see all the surprises I have in store."

Knowing when to take a hint, Portia backed off. "And who is this gorgeous specimen?" she asked openly, staring at Will.

Will walked over to meet her. "Will Kennedy. I'm the owner of Millennium."

Portia batted her eyelashes at him. "Why, it's a pleasure."

Never before had Will been uninterested in a woman, but he couldn't give one flying fig about the anorexic creature standing before him. All he wanted was Lexie, who stood beside Portia with a less-than-amused expression. Was Lexie jealous at the attention he was receiving? It gave him hope. Lexie wasn't as cavalier as she portrayed. She was feeling something for him. He just knew it. He would call her on it.

"Please, make yourself at home." Will pulled out a chair.

"Can I get you something to drink, Portia?"

Glancing over her shoulder, Portia replied, "I don't see a bartender."

"Don't you worry, I'm the best bartender around." Will smiled, flashing a dazzling smile. "I'll make you something special."

"I'd like that." Portia beamed. "But it is business hours."

"I'll make it virgin." Strolling to the bar, Will busied himself preparing a virgin Incognito, one of his signature drinks. He noticed Lexie getting antsy in her seat, attempting to appear unaffected by his flirting with the agent. He didn't know why she was resisting the attraction to them when it was obvious they had chemistry in spades.

Lexie coughed to get Portia's attention; she hated it when women fawned all over men. She certainly wasn't one them, but Will was a different story. He probably had more women than Wilt Chamberlain. "Who are we seeing first?" Lexie inclined her head to the portfolios underneath Portia's arm.

"Oh, yes." Suddenly Portia remembered her purpose in coming and pulled out the portfolios. "I have several great candidates for you. I'm sure you'll be pleased."

The two were just getting down to business, looking over an array of blondes, brunettes, and redheads, when Will came over with the drink.

"For you, my dear." He placed the drink in front of Portia with a flourish. "Enjoy." He turned to Lexie. "And one for Lex."

"I didn't ask for one."

"Just enjoy."

Portia smiled up at him. "Thank you."

Will caught the look of disdain on Lexie's face and decided he'd gone far enough. "I've got business to attend to, ladies," he said, politely excusing himself.

"Really?" Lexie inquired tartly. "I rather thought club owners slept all day and partied all night."

Portia nearly choked on her drink.

"Sorry to disappoint you, Lexie, but running a club is not as frivolous as you think. Ladies." Without a further word, Will departed and Lexie could have kicked herself for letting him leave on such a sour note.

"Hmmm, I sense some chemistry there," Portia said.

"Don't start," Lexie warned. Portia was entering dangerous territory.

Portia took the not-so-subtle hint and the next three

hours proceeded with no event—except one. Lexie insisted that she see more diversity in the models.

"Everyone I've seen is great, but I need to see more diversity." Everyone was beautiful, but she wanted to see more African-American, Hispanic, and Asian women represented onstage.

"I understand, but before you write me off completely, I'd like to introduce you to our last model, Carly Matthews. She's a standout. I'm sure once you've seen her, you'll agree."

Five minutes later, Lexie was convinced. Carly Matthews was strikingly beautiful—high cheekbones, flawless skin, green eyes, and silky straight auburn hair that hung down her slender back. Carly had a perfect figure to suit Bentley's latest collection. There was no doubt in Lexie's mind that Carly was a showstopper. Ideas began to form in Lexie's mind.

"Would you like me to walk?" Carly asked after Lexie's long appraisal.

"No need," Portia replied. She'd watched Lexie's reaction and knew they'd found The One. "Carly, you'll be the lead model for the show. I assume she'll be wearing the wedding dress finale?"

"Hmmm?" Lexie heard someone speaking, but her mind was elsewhere. "Oh, yes, of course."

"Wonderful. Carly, we'll need you to show up for fittings next week, dress rehearsals on the thirteenth, and of course the day of the show."

"Excellent." Carly sashayed toward Lexie and shook her hand. "Thank you for the opportunity, Ms. Thompson. It's a pleasure to work for such a great company like Bentley's."

"It's great to have you on board, Carly. Now, if you'll head over to my assistant, he'll take your comp card." Lexie smiled; she was very pleased with herself. Everything was working out according to plan and in two months the fashion show would be a thing of the past and she'd only see Will in passing during the wedding preparations.

As if they were on the same wavelength, Will returned to the main room. A smile formed on her mouth until she saw the curious expression on his face.

He watched Carly intently for several moments before approaching her. Probably deciding upon his plan of attack, Lexie figured. The man was unscrupulous. He was hitting on her one moment and sliding up to another woman the next. Lexie's stomach tightened in response. How dare he treat her this way? She was Lexie Thompson, for God's sake! Never before had she felt jealous of another woman, and she wasn't about to start now.

She stood abruptly and walked toward the couple, already in a heated discussion. The moment she arrived, all conversation stopped. Lexie's eyes darted back and forth between the two of them. "Will; Carly." Lexie inclined her head to them. "Do you two know each other?"

"Once upon a time." Carly smiled knowingly at Will. She'd heard a troop of models were being seen in his club and had dressed fabulously for Will's benefit, hoping he'd be in attendance. "But . . ." As she looked from Lexie to Will, she sensed a brewing attraction and knew her relationship with Will was over, "we've since moved on. Lexie," Carly extended her hand, "thank you for the opportunity. I'm sure the show will be fantastic. I look forward to working with you."

Unafraid of the Carly Matthewses of the world, Lexie returned the handshake. "I look forward to working with you as well, Carly."

Will's anger at Carly dissipated. A silent showdown

had occurred and as Carly walked away, Lexie was most certainly the victor. He was sure she had picked up on a very personal vibe between him and Carly, but instead of acting jealous, she'd handled the situation with class and grace.

The mystery solved, Lexie breathed a sigh of relief. Maybe Will wasn't so bad after all. At least he'd ended a relationship first before hopping into the next. Lexie didn't know why she was buoyed by the prospect, but she was.

"I don't suppose you were just a tiny bit jealous?" Will teased.

Putting her professional hat back on, Lexie turned and flashed a smile. "Of Carly? Why should I be? I have nothing to fear from her."

"That's what I love about you, Lexie. You're all confidence and spirit rolled into one helluva package." Will stroked her cheek lovingly.

"Stop that!" Lexie pushed his hand away. Her cheek burned from the touch of his hand. "What if someone saw you?"

"They'd probably wish they were on the receiving end."

"Ugh. You're arrogant!" Lexie stormed past him and back over to Portia. Within minutes, they concluded their business, and without a backward glance, Lexie rushed out of Millennium before Will could make another move.

CHAPTER EIGHT

Strolling around Bentley's, Lexie toured the women's department to have a look at her displays and to find out from the sales staff how her selections were selling. In addition to her fashion-show duties, her day-to-day job as head buyer continued. She had to stay on the pulse of current trends and that meant meeting with the customers as well as trips to the cutting-room floor to meet with designers. Bebe was a hot line right now and Lexie was anxious to add it to Bentley's market. Although it wasn't their usual fare, Lexie was determined to convince Lauren to carry the brand.

She was stepping onto the downstairs escalator to go to moderate wear when she heard someone calling her name. Both shock and surprise registered on Lexie's face when she discovered her father waiting on the level below. What was he doing at Bentley's during the middle of the day?

"Daddy!" she exclaimed, giving him a bear hug.

"How's my pumpkin?" her father asked, kissing her on the forehead.

"Better, now that you're here." Hooking her arm

through his, the two strolled down to moderate wear. "Speaking of which, what are you doing here?"

"Can't I come by and see my best girl?"

"Of course you can, Dad. I'm just surprised, is all," Lexie replied. "Would you like some coffee? We can get some at the café downstairs."

"Love to."

Five minutes later they were seated on plastic stools at the bar of Bentley's cafeteria, giving a waitress their order. On the ground level of Bentley's, the café served coffee, pastries, and light snacks.

While they waited for their order, Lexie decided to take a detour rather than the direct approach to find out why he'd come. "So, how's the job?"

"Oh, just fine."

"And the house?"

"Hmmm?" her father asked absentmindedly. "Oh, yes, the house is fine.

After a long deadening silence, Lexie couldn't take it anymore. "Okay, Dad, how are things between you and Mom?"

"Not too good. You know your mother."

"And what about you? Are you sleeping in the guest bedroom again?" When her father didn't answer, Lexie knew the truth. "Just because she's upset with me gives her no right to be mean to you. I can't believe that woman. Of all the nerve."

"Settle down." Her father patted her knee liked a spoiled child. He'd had enough of Isabel getting riled up. He didn't need to deal with Lexie's temper, too.

"Dad, I can't believe she's penalizing you because she's upset with me."

"Your mother and I will handle our relationship. We have thirty years behind us and we'll get through this just as we have every other time before it."

"It's just not fair."

"Then it's up to you, which is why I'm here."

"Dad." Lexie turned to him pleadingly. "Why do I have to be the one to apologize?"

"Lexie," her father admonished.

Lexie remembered that tone. She'd heard it a million times before when she and Sebastian misbehaved and scribbled with crayon on his newly painted walls or when Lexie cut her own bangs.

"You know you hurt your mother's feelings very deeply. Please repair your relationship. Do this for me, okay?"

The waitress returned with steaming mugs, one a vanilla latte and the other Earl Grey tea, along with a side of milk and her father's favorite butter cookies.

"For you, Daddy, I will." Lexie took a sip of her latte and nearly scorched her tongue. "I'd do anything for you."

Lexie knew she was in for it the moment she parked her car outside Sunset Catering. Although they often disagreed, Lexie hated leaving things so unsettled with her mother. She had given her the appropriate week to cool off and Lexie could only hope that that was enough.

With all the courage she could muster, Lexie stepped inside the lion's den. A bell chimed as she walked in, but surprisingly her mother was nowhere in sight—just her world-famous pastries and delicacies in the display case. Lexie was ogling the desserts as she thought of which one to select when her mother appeared in a flour-splattered apron.

"May I help—" Isabel started, but stopped midsentence when she saw her daughter.

Lexie didn't miss the hostile glare that came her way. Instead she chose to be the bigger person. "Mom, it's good to see you." With open arms, she started toward her, but nothing could have surprised Lexie further than when her ex-boyfriend Adrian sauntered out of the kitchen eating one of her mother's napoleons.

"Adrian!" Lexie was flabbergasted. What in the hell was he doing there, and in her mother's kitchen, no less! Lexie and her father were never invited into her mother's inner sanctum. Her mother always said they never had a flair for culinary creativity. That gift went to Sebastian. How did Adrian manage an invite?

"Lexie." Adrian smiled as he surreptiously licked filling from the corners of his mouth. "How are you?" he asked nonchalantly as if she hadn't kicked him to the curb a mere few weeks earlier.

Lexie took a long assessing look at Adrian. A head taller than her, he had a square jaw with a slightly aquiline nose and overall model looks. And the man sure knew how to dress. Adrian wore nothing but the best and today was no different. Immaculate in his navy Brooks Brothers' suit and silver tie, he looked every bit the high-powered mogul—which was why she was so surprised to find him coming out of her mother's kitchen.

"What are you doing here?" Lexie asked the question that hung in the air.

"Oh, I was the neighborhood." Lexie glared at Adrian while he made himself comfortable. She watched as he walked behind the counter and grabbed bottled water from the icebox. Her blood boiled at his audacity. This was her mother's shop.

"That still doesn't explain why you're here," Lexie replied testily, waiting for the real deal.

"What's your beef, Lexie? In case you don't remember," Adrian stared back at her, "your mother and I happen to get along famously. Do you have a problem with me visiting her?"

"Of course she doesn't," her mother answered for her as she walked back into the room to add fresh pastries to the display case.

"Mother—"

"Oh, hush," her mother said, chastising her. "Adrian was nice enough to stop by and bring me several hot job prospects. He thinks about me, *unlike some people.*" Isabel ignored Lexie's blush and stalked back through the swinging doors into her haven, the kitchen.

Throwing her jacket on the counter nearby, Lexie prepared to do battle. "Well, isn't this just great!" Lexie fumed and stomped her feet. "Even though we're not dating, you still manage to out-trump me with my own mother!"

Adrian laughed. "Stop being such a drama queen. It's a quid pro quo. I send your mother deals and she allows me to come in and sponge off some pastries. What's the harm in that?"

"Because I don't like it, that's why," Lexie replied a little too harshly.

"Get over yourself. I think you'd be happy that I still bring my business to Sunset Catering and Sebastian's studio. As a matter of fact, the only person that seems to mind is you." Adrian came to stand behind her. "Seems to me you're jealous that your family is getting all my attention. You have only to say the word, Lexie, and I'd take you back."

Lexie felt his breath on her neck and tried to move away, but Adrian held her in place. His arms encircled her waist and his thin lips began to nuzzle her neck.

"Have you forgotten how good it was between us? It could be that way again. I know what you want, Lexie. I can drape you in the best clothes, furs, and diamonds. You can have it all with me. You only have to reach out and grab it."

Lexie may have been tempted before, but not anymore. As much as she hated to admit it, she'd finally found a man that excited and challenged her. She couldn't put a name on whatever it was they had yet, but she wasn't prepared to toss it out like yesterday's trash.

And the more Adrian tried to entice her with her former shallow ways, the less Lexie wanted to hear it. She was revolted that she'd stayed so long with a man she didn't love and wasn't at all attracted to. All of a sudden, Adrian's hand felt hot and clammy and Lexie pushed him aside.

"Stop, Adrian." Lexie strode several meters away. "What you're saying would have worked before, but I'm not the same person I was before. I'm sorry to say this and hurt you again, but I don't want to be in a relationship with you."

"You have no idea what you're missing," Adrian replied, disappointed.

Lexie hated to hurt him again, but the truth had to be said. If he was helping her mother and Sebastian on the off chance that he could win her back, then he had gambled and lost.

With his head hung low, Adrian walked to the door. "Don't you want to say good-bye to my mother?" Lexie asked.

At the door, Adrian turned around. "Why? What would be the point?"

Lexie felt horrible. She didn't know what this would mean for her mother, but she couldn't let Adrian go on believing they had a second chance. That ship had sailed. She'd known even before she and Will hooked up that Adrian wasn't the right man for her. He didn't have enough courage, enough strength, or enough sex appeal to get her fires burning. She wasn't sure if she and Will would crash and burn. But she would *never* know if she fell back into her old ways.

A few minutes later, her mother walked back in the room. Looking around, Isabel shook her head in disgust. Once again her daughter's impulsive behavior had lost her a good man.

"I guess I don't need to ask where Adrian went," Isabel said with a huff, wiping off the counters. "I swear, Lexie, you're going to be the death of me."

Whatever her mother needed to say, Lexie would let her have her say. She'd promised her father she would resolve the tension between them, no matter the cost to her own pride.

"All right, Mom, let's hear it," Lexie began. "Let's get this over with."

Her mother furiously turned on her heel. "You just let Adrian walk out the door and for what? For some fashion career?"

Her mother was dead wrong—she wasn't letting him go because she wanted to focus on her career, she was letting him go because she'd found someone else.

"Don't you dare criticize my fashion career, Mom." Lexie ran her fingers through her hair, trying to calm herself. Obviously this was not going to be easy.

"That man"—her mother pointed to the door—"could give you all the riches and prestige you claim to desire, but what do you do? You throw it all away."

"Is that what you think of me, that I'm that superficial?"

"If the shoe fits."

Grabbing her coat, Lexie headed for the door. Father or no, there was no reasoning with the woman.

"Go ahead, run away, that's what you do best."

"Oh, yeah?" Lexie turned to look her mother dead in the eye. "Well, if that's the case, then why don't you admit why you're really upset?" Trying to ease the tension, Lexie tried another approach. "Listen, Mom. I know you were upset that I didn't give you the catering job for the show." Lexie followed her to the kitchen and stared while her mother beat several egg whites within an inch of their lives. "And I'm sorry I hurt your feelings." Her mother huffed aloud at the statement. "But you know the two of us are like oil and water. We don't mix. And this show is too important for to me to leave anything up to chance."

"Are you quite done yet?" her mother inquired. "I have work to do." Isabel was not to be swayed. She wasn't a woman who easily forgave or forgot. And Lexie knew this. So she was prepared for a little more groveling.

"Please don't be this way." Lexie shook her head. How was she going to get through to the woman? She'd promised her father she would make amends and keep peace in the family. The poor man had had a horrendous week with her mother on the warpath. "I'm sorry I hurt you. But what's done is done. Plans have been made and deposits sent. I can't go back and change it." Lexie wasn't going to apologize for doing her job. A promotion depended on this fashion show succeeding.

"As if you would," her mother whispered under her breath.

"Mother," Lexie warned. She wasn't going to continue to stand here and be berated, not even for her old man.

"Fine." Her mother looked up. "You're forgiven. Are you satisfied?"

"No, I'm not." With the biggest pout a grown woman could muster, Lexie looked beseechingly at her mother. "But if that's the best I can get, then I'll take it."

"Good, now let me get back to work. I have a catering job to finish. So when is this shindig anyway?" her mother asked.

"In two months."

"That's cutting in close with Nia's wedding isn't it? Are you sure you can manage your maid-of-honor duties and plan a fashion show?"

Lexie smiled. "Of course I can. I'm superwoman."

"Hmmm," her mother said. "Don't bite off more than you can chew."

"Don't worry. I've got it all under control."

Or so she thought, but as Lexie later rifled through a rack of fall inventory that had arrived in the day's shipment, she still had no idea of what pieces would make their final destination on the runway.

With her pencil behind her ear, Lexie paced the conference-room floor.

Tap. Tap. Tap. Lexie glanced up to find Sydney at the door. Stylishly sophisticated in a two-piece DKNY suit with her gleaming blond hair slicked back in a ponytail, Sydney walked inside. Lexie wanted to strangle the witch who was patiently awaiting her downfall.

"Sydney." Lexie inclined her head.

"Lexie, how's it going?" Sydney took the liberty of stepping forward and circling the rack, just like a fox circling a henhouse.

"All is well," Lexie replied, continuing to sort through the racks of clothes.

Sydney sniffed with an air of disdain. "These are

nice, but you're still missing something. You know what I'm talking about."

"A silver bullet."

Sydney smiled knowingly and turned to face Lexie. "Quite frankly, yes. You need something that will capture the audience's attention." Sydney fingered the clothes. "You've got the usual Christian Dior, Gucci, and Dolce, but if I were you, I would come up with something dazzling or you'll be the laughingstock of the town."

"Thank you so much for that candid observation." Lexie snatched a scarf out of Sydney's hand.

"Don't bite my head off. I'm merely offering some advice. You would do well to take heed."

"Sydney, you didn't come here as a concerned colleague offering some good advice." Lexie grabbed her by the wrist and turned her around to face her. "You came in hear to get in my face and make me doubt myself. And why?" Lexie's voice rose. "Because you want what I have? Well, let me tell you something, missy, you're *not* going to get it."

"Oh, really? It only takes one mistake, Lexie." Sydney held up her index finger. "Only one." She snatched her other arm out of Lexie's grasp.

"Well, it won't be mine. Don't get in my way, Sydney." Lexie eyed the blonde. "I haven't made it this far in the business without eating little tarts like you for breakfast."

Sydney sniffed before turning on her heel and stalking out of the room.

Taking a deep breath, Lexie's turned around to face the rack. As much as Lexie hated to admit it, Sydney was right. *But what am I missing?*

* * *

Lexie opened her apartment door with a grand flour-ish the following Saturday night and was awestruck by the sight that greeted her: Will in a formal black suit and tie. He'd come by to pick her up for dinner with his potential investors, but all Lexie could think about was how handsome he was. *It ought to be illegal to be that good-looking.* "Good evening," she finally managed.

"Good evening to you, too," Will replied. He was ex-cited to see Lexie in pleasant spirits. It was a good sign of the evening to come. Always up for a challenge, Will stepped inside Lexie's world. His eyes darted around the room, taking in the decor. Her home was every bit as complex as the lady herself. The floors were filled with sketches, rolls of fabric, and design easels, while her walls were covered with photography and African masks. Her apartment was a mass of or-ganized chaos.

Lexie felt secure as she watched Will peruse her liv-ing quarters, from her large hanging plants to her contemporary art and retro violet furniture.

"Wow, this is impressive, Lexie." He stopped when he spotted a huge eat-in kitchen. He loved the cherry-wood cabinets, funky table painted in a myriad of col-ors, and Calphalon pots hanging from ceiling racks.

"You have an eye for design, Lex. Your apartment is very homey. Most women's apartments I've been to are very minimal with no personality whatsoever."

"I'm not the average bimbo you usually date, Will. I'm a strong black woman who is completely self-reliant."

"I can see that." Will smiled in return. Lexie was spoiling for a fight, but he needed the evening to run smoothly and he needed Lexie's help to do it. "And I respect it," he added.

Lexie didn't expect to hear that. She didn't know

why she was purposely sparring with him. Could it be because for the first time in her life she felt alive? Will had awakened a passion that had been lying dormant for so long, she had almost forgotten it existed. None of the men she'd ever encountered had made her feel like this. Sure, they threw diamonds, clothes, and furs at her, but none of it ever equaled the fire that was steadily growing in her belly as he walked toward her.

"Sweet Lexie," Will whispered as he neared and his big strong hand reached out to caress her soft mocha-colored face. "Hmmm, you feel so good. I just wanna have more of you." Will pulled her into his arms and Lexie didn't resist. Instead she allowed him to run his fingers through her hair until their faces were mere inches apart. Seconds ticked by with barely a breath between them. Their eyes connected and Lexie was caught in the allure of his deeply set black eyes and long curling lashes. His eyes told her to come to bed and she surely wanted to obey. She waited for Will's lips to descend over hers, but instead of putting that deliciously succulent mouth on hers, he brought her hand to his lips and placed a quick peck on it.

Lexie snatched it away from him. "You're a tease."

"And you, my dear, were just waiting for me to kiss you."

"And what if I were?" Lexie asked, taking a step backward to regain her composure.

"I would be more than happy to oblige," Will answered in return.

Lexie's heart did a somersault and butterflies fluttered in her stomach.

"But not right now."

Her heart took a nosedive.

"We've got more important business to attend to." Will glanced at his watch. "To which we will be late if you don't get a move on." He slapped Lexie's bottom. "Now, go. Are you always this late?"

"Usually," Lexie retorted over her shoulder before hurrying to her bedroom. Looking in the mirror, she reminded herself that she only needed William Kennedy's club, not his body. *Get it together, Lexie!*

A few moments later, Lexie emerged, adorned with diamond teardrop earrings and a matching necklace that was carefully nestled in the cleavage of her V-neck lace dress. After their previous encounter, she had decided upon a more subdued, but classic black dress. The dress was more demure than her usual, but it was a business dinner after all.

Will whistled as she entered the living room. "You look absolutely marvelous!"

"Why, thank you, Mr. Kennedy."

"Shall we do dinner?"

"Yes, I suppose so." Lexie couldn't resist returning his smile with one of her own. She wondered what the evening held in store for her; knowing Will, it was sure to be memorable.

CHAPTER NINE

They arrived at Houston's Restaurant that evening thankfully ahead of their guests and Will took the liberty of ordering a bottle of champagne. As he poured her a flute, Lexie watched him over the candlelight.

"To a wonderful evening," Will said, raising his glass in a toast.

Lexie clicked her flute with his and sipped the delicious rare vintage champagne. It was light and crisp and tasted divine. She wondered where he'd learned about wines. It was then that Lexie realized there was a lot she didn't know about Will. Curiously, she wanted to find out more about this intriguing man.

Will smiled from across the table as he watched her sum him up. He was sure she was usually the one in control in her previous relationships, which was why they'd all failed. Lexie needed someone strong with a backbone, not someone she could walk all over if the mood suited her. Was he thinking he was the man for the job? He didn't have time to answer that question because the DuBois brothers arrived at their table along with another couple.

Rising from his chair, Will shook hands with Evan

DuBois and greeted his twin brother, David. The DuBoises owned a local black investment firm and had expressed an interest in helping Will expand after a recent fund-raiser held at Millennium. They'd told Will they had a client who might be interested in the venture as well and brought him along to meet Will.

"Evan. David." Will shook the latter twin's hand. "It's good to see you again."

"You, too, Will," Evan replied. "You're looking well."

"Thank you."

"Allow me to introduce Matthew Russo and his wife, Cynthia."

"Mr. Russo, it's a pleasure to finally meet. I've heard a lot about you." Will accepted Mr. Russo's generously firm handshake. "And Mrs. Russo. Dare I say, you look quite stunning this evening." Will smiled at the older Italian woman.

Cynthia was attired in a dress way too tight and way too short; Will could only smile at the older woman's attempts to stay young. He was sure she didn't go out too often.

"Thank you, Mr. Kennedy," Cynthia replied. "My husband did warn me that you are quite the flirt. You better be careful, Matthew, he might steal me away."

"I highly doubt that with this lovely creature beside his side," Matthew Russo replied.

Lexie looked up from her flute and found Mr. Russo leering at her.

"Young man, aren't you going to introduce us?" Matthew inquired, openly staring at Lexie's cleavage across the table.

"Of course." Will assisted Lexie from her seat. "Allow me to introduce Ms. Lexie Thompson, my fiancée."

Lexie eyes widened in amazement and her mouth fell open seconds before Will swept her in his arms and planted a deliciously long, fervent kiss on her warm lips. As he did, Lexie felt a cool piece of metal close around the third finger on her left hand. When she pulled away and looked down, Lexie was surprised to find a beautiful diamond ring on her finger. She stared back at Will in bewilderment as he steadfastly held on to her hand while she unsuccessfully tried to escape his clutches.

"Where did you get this?" she whispered in his ear as he helped her back into her chair.

"It's my mother's. Now go with me on this," he said.

Lexie nodded in agreement and gazed down at the diamond solitaire on her finger. It was truly the most exquisite piece of jewelry she'd ever received. He'd thought of everything. The man continued to surprise her.

"Wow, fiancée, huh?" David inquired. "I didn't even know you were seeing anyone, Will."

"Yeah, man," Evan agreed. "I thought you were a confirmed bachelor."

"In another time I would have agreed with you." Will laughed. "But when you meet the right person like my Lex, here," Will grabbed Lexie's hand and placed a tender kiss on it, "you know you've struck gold."

Detecting the laughter in his eyes, Lexie went along with the ploy. "Thanks, baby."

The evening progressed smoothly with talk of locations and investment terms. Lexie jumped in when needed and provided a lively diversion. Will appreciated her efforts as she kept the conversation rolling from entertainment to politics. The Russos and DuBois twins were hooked on her every word. Will watched how effortlessly Lexie adapted herself to any given situation and was impressed. Here was a woman who was comfortable in her own skin. It was a helluva turn-on.

"Isn't that right, Will?" Lexie added, bumping his shoulder and giving him a sexy wink.

"Hmmm, what was that?" Will asked, forgetting all rational thought when he was around her. How could he think straight when she was giving him those sexy little looks under those incredibly long lashes?

"I was telling the Russos how we met." Lexie smiled mischievously at him.

Will sat up straight. What the devil was she up to? "And how was that, sweetheart?" he inquired.

"Don't tell me you forgot how we first met!" Lexie's mouth turned downward in a little pout.

"C'mon, tell us, Lexie," David inquired, his eyes wide with rapture. "We want to hear all about it."

Will didn't like the hint of excitement in David's tone. He wasn't oblivious to the appreciative male glances the DuBoises and Mr. Russo had sent Lexie's way throughout the evening. And they were surely enjoying Lexie's figure; when she'd excused herself to go to the ladies' room, he'd watched as all three men watched her tight backside sashay off with the plump Mrs. Russo close behind her. When Lexie tossed her hair, she had the ability to make all the men at the table salivate.

Could he be a little jealous? No, he couldn't be. Will dismissed the notion. He just didn't appreciate men panting after his date.

"Well, it's a simple story, really." Lexie smiled at David flirtatiously. She knew she really shouldn't. She wasn't blind to the fact that Will tensed at her side every minute she played up to David. To combat it, she reached underneath the table to squeeze the hard expanse of Will's thigh. "Our best friends hooked us up, isn't that right, Will?" Lexie sipped her champagne and waited for a reaction from Will.

Will couldn't believe the little minx. She was trying to get him all excited. Well, he wouldn't have it. He would show her he was immune to her charms.

Turning to face her, Will laughed in response. "Of course it is."

So he was trying to ignore her touching him, eh? Lexie was no slouch in the lovemaking department. She'd had her share of lovers and knew it didn't take long to get a man's blood pumping. Sensuously, she stroked his thigh until she finally made contact with his manhood. His muscles tensed beneath her wandering fingertips and Lexie knew Will was ready to jump out of his skin, but instead he maintained an air of coolness.

As much as Will would have loved for Lexie to continue to seduce him underneath the table, he had to wrap up dinner. "I want to thank you gentlemen and you, Mr. and Mrs. Russo, for coming out this evening."

"It was great, really, Will," Evan agreed. "We are looking forward to working with you on this project. Aren't we, David?"

"Absolutely," David finished. "You've prepared a thorough proposal that would be an excellent investment for us."

"I couldn't agree more," Matthew said. "And with a fine woman like Lexie behind you, you surely won't go wrong."

Will leaned over and placed a kiss on Lexie's unsuspecting cheek. "Thank you."

"That's me." Lexie replied, joining in. "The woman *beside* her man." Men like Matthew probably only trotted out their wives for special occasions. Lexie refused to ever have a relationship like that.

"After-dinner aperitif?" David inquired.

Before anyone could get a word out, Will declined. "Um, none for us. Lexie and I have plans for the rest of the evening."

If it was possible to blush with her mocha coloring, Lexie did. She couldn't believe Will. Given the hour, which was somewhere in the vicinity of eleven o'clock, it was a clear that she and Will couldn't possibly have any plans other than those in the bedroom.

"Don't be embarrassed, old girl." Cynthia rose from the table and shook Will's hand. "Be happy that you have a young stallion such as our William here that can keep you satisfied in the boudoir."

Lexie couldn't help but laugh at the middle-aged Italian. She surely didn't mince words. Raising her head, she stood up for the final farewells.

After they were gone, Lexie turned her claws on Will. "Plans for the evening?" Lexie inquired, pushing her chair back. "And what might those be?"

"Let's discuss it on our way to the car."

Grabbing her purse, Lexie stalked out of the restaurant to Will's car. She waited for him to open the car door, but instead of opening it, he pressed her against the cold metal. There was no denying that Will's arousal had not dissipated.

Pulling her firmly to him, Will did what he had wanted to do all night. He ground his lips into hers and Lexie accepted all his pent-up frustration, returning it with some of her own. She responded to his feverish kiss and opened up her mouth to receive his demanding tongue.

While his tongue ravished her mouth, his hands had a mind all their own and were slowly raking every inch of her.

"Will, stop this." Lexie tried pushing at his hard, firm chest. "We can't do this," she insisted.

"And why not?" Will asked, his breathing ragged and uneven as he pulled away. "Why can't we do what comes naturally?" Will cupped her chin and searched her upturned face for an answer. "Why can't we do what we both want to do?"

"Because we have a purely business arrangement."

"Lexie, you and I have been dancing around each other for days. Why not just enjoy each other until we both decide otherwise?"

"What happened the other night was a mistake, a moment of weakness, a lapse in judgment. Now open my door."

"Okay, okay." Will clutched his heart. "You're really killing my ego, you know?"

"Don't worry." Lexie touched his chin. "I'm sure you'll recover."

"Ouch, are you always this brutal?" Will asked, opening the car door. He knew when to call it quits. He wouldn't beat Lexie over the head with the idea of a love affair. He would bide his time, allow her to get used to the idea. Slowly but surely he would ease her into the transition of the inevitable that the two of them would become lovers.

"Hmmm, not always." Lexie bent down and slid into the passenger seat.

"I guess I bring out the worst in you," Will commented once beside her.

"As I told you before, Will, you and I are not a good match."

"The other night would say otherwise, but perhaps you ought to remember this conversation the next time you attempt to seduce me underneath a restaurant table. I am only a man, you realize."

"Point taken. Now are you going to take me home or not?"

"All right, all right. I'll take you home. But don't think you and I are over." Will kicked the ignition into gear and pulled out of the parking lot. Taking a direct route to Lexie's apartment, Will had her there in twenty minutes.

Lexie smiled self-confidently. It was clear that Will didn't appreciate her turning him down, but Lexie had to keep him at the bay. Her feelings were all over the place and she had to get in control of them again. She did want Will as much as he wanted her, but there was no way she would give any man that kind of control or the power to hurt her ever again. When she was ready she'd allow William Kennedy into her bedroom, but not a moment before.

When they pulled into the parking lot of her building, Lexie breathed a sigh of relief. The sexual tension had crackled inside the car and Lexie was afraid of what she might do if Will made a move. Would her defenses crumble if he tried to touch her again? Kiss her again?

Not giving him the chance, Lexie jumped out of the Lexus and trotted toward her building.

"Lexie, wait!" Will yelled after her, hopping out of the car. He grabbed her arm in an iron grip.

"What is it, Will?" Lexie twisted around angrily to face him. She hated that her body reacted to him even when her head told her to run in the opposite direction. "You know I'm not inviting you in."

"In time you will," Will replied as he slipped the diamond ring off her finger and bounded down the stairs back to his car.

What would it be like to be Will's girlfriend? Lexie wondered as she and her staff took a second measurement of the clothes already selected for the show.

She was just finishing up when Lauren walked in the room.

"How's it coming?" Lauren asked over her shoulder.

Swinging around, Lexie answered, "Everything is going along perfectly. The venue and caterer are booked, the collection is in order, and the models are on their second fitting."

"If those models in the lobby are any indication, it looks like you have everything under control."

"You bet." Lexie gave her a thumbs-up signal. "Thank you for your faith in me, Lauren."

"It's well deserved. Continue on, then, I didn't mean to interrupt." With a pat on the back, she was out the door.

Lexie wrung her hands. Even with the well wishes, she still had a nagging feeling in her gut.

She was still fretting when Will called that afternoon.

"Put down those fabric swatches and purchase orders and meet me at the corner of Rush and Division."

"What's going on?"

"Don't argue with me, woman, just meet me."

Glancing at her watch, she decided she had time to play a little hooky. "Okay, I'll meet you in thirty."

Lexie pulled beside Will's car in the parking lot of a vacant one-story brick building in the commercial district of Chicago's Northwest Side.

"Hello!" Lexie yelled as she knocked on the door and stepped inside a wide-open space that had been completely demoed. All that remained of the structure were the steel frame and bare concrete floor. Lexie hoped her Manolo Blahniks wouldn't scuff.

"Hey, gorgeous." Will smiled, coming forward to grace her with an unapologetic kiss in the lips.

Lexie didn't scoff because she really didn't mind it all that much.

"What do you think of my new place?"

"This is yours?" Lexie asked, waving her arms around.

"Yup." Will had finalized the details with his real estate agent and was set to close at the end of the month.

"It's incredible!" Lexie exclaimed. "And what about this?" she rushed forward to caress a baby grand piano with mahogany finish in the corner of the room. "Do you get to keep it, too?"

Eyes twinkling, Will answered, "Yeah, it comes with the place. Now c'mon, I'll give you a tour." Will held out his hand. Accepting it, Lexie allowed Will to lead her from the soon-to-be remodeled bar adjacent to the piano to the upgraded stainless-steel kitchen with ceramic tile flooring.

"Hmmm, what's this room going to be?" Lexie inquired when they stopped in a front of a closed door.

"That's for me to know and for you to find out. Put this over your eyes." Will handed Lexie a silk scarf.

"What for?"

"Just do it, Lexie," Will ordered. Smiling, Lexie acquiesced and slid the scarf around her head and over her eyes.

Opening the door, Will led her by the hand inside the room. Will left her side for a few moments to open the drapes before returning to her side to remove the blindfold.

Lexie blinked several times, allowing her eyes to adjust to the light. She was surprised to discover a picnic lunch spread out on a blanket in the center of the room.

"Well, what do you think?" Will asked, coming forward to kneel on the blanket.

Lexie shook her head. "Just when I think I have you all figured out, you surprise me, Will Kennedy. You wouldn't be trying to romance me, would you?"

"Is it working?"

Lexie nodded.

Will held out his hand. "Good. Come join me."

Lexie took it and joined him on the blanket. Opening up the basket, she found a gourmet lunch of Brie, cold meats, potato salad, and fresh fruit. Lexie prepared plates for herself and Will while he opened a bottle of white wine.

After they'd stuffed their bellies, Will and Lexie laid out on the blanket and stared at the ceiling. Lexie was impressed when Will revealed the rest of his plans for Risqué, his new club.

Lexie visualized the crowds beating down the door to get in. "Oh, I like the name. It's very sexy." Lexie rolled over to face him. "When do you plan to open?"

"If all goes well with the renovation, six months, tops."

"Wow, that's fast."

"Not really. I've already selected a contractor and I have all the licenses and permits."

"That's fantastic, Will. Sounds to me like you've thought of everything."

"I hope so. This is a big venture to me and will take me away from Millennium. That's why I have to make sure all my *i*'s are dotted and all my *t*'s are crossed."

"It will all work out." Lexie stared at Will. Now more than ever, she was even more assured that if she wasn't careful, Will could be come a habit she couldn't quit.

"More wine?" Will asked.

"Are you trying to get me drunk?"

"Could be. Now come here," he said. "You're pretty far away over there." Will had observed that Lexie had settled herself on the opposite side of the blanket. Just the sight of her flesh imprisoned in those sexy lace-up pants and wraparound shirt flustered him to no end.

Unable to resist, he stretched out across the distance to pull Lexie closer to him. "Is it so bad being near me?" he asked, his hand stroking her hip haphazardly.

Holding her breath, Lexie allowed him to hold her against his solid frame and nuzzle at her neck. His warm breath caressed her skin and Lexie knew that soon she would be a goner. Abruptly, she stood up.

"I have to go." Lexie looked around for her purse.

"Why? We're having such a good time. Why do you keep running away, Lex?" Will asked, rubbing his head. He couldn't understand why every time they got close, she ran.

"We were, but I have to get back to work." Lexie answered the first question and avoided the last. "Thanks for lunch."

Hardly hazarding a glance at Will, Lexie stooped to pick up her purse and rush out the room.

Will fell back onto the blanket. He'd almost gotten to her this time. She hadn't wanted to go. He'd seen it in her eyes, but she was still fighting the attraction between them.

CHAPTER TEN

"All right, sista girl, give up the goods!" Christian glided into Lexie's cubicle several days later. Finding no place to perch his Esprit-covered bottom, Christian tossed several designer clothes onto a chair and fell on the small couch.

"Watch those, Christian, do you know how much those cost?" Lexie sighed in frustration.

"Yes, I do, dearie. You're not the only one who scours the pages of *Vogue* and *Cosmo*," Christian replied.

Lexie chuckled. Even on his worst day, Lexie could never get angry at him.

"Now what gives? You've been far too quiet for me to let this go. You know I've been dying from curiosity. So please, try me on for size. What happened with Mr. Dream Boat the other night?"

"Christian, you're too much." Lexie shook her head and swiveled her chair around to face the wall, but Christian already read the guilty expression on her face and rightly deduced the truth.

"Girlfriend, don't tell me. You gave up something, didn't you?" Lexie turned back and lowered her eyes, unable to look Christian in the eye. He doubled over in laughter on the couch. "I warned you. Turns out you were one of the lucky many to wind up in his bed."

"Christian, don't make fun. I can't believe what I did. I hardly know the man. I—I've never been so carefree . . . or so reckless . . . in my entire life."

Christian giggled with excitement. "I can't wait to meet the fella that brought the great Ms. Lexie Thompson to her knees. He did bring you to your knees, didn't he, Lex?" Christian inquired with a look of pure devilment in eyes.

"Why, Christian Blair!" Lexie threw a magazine at him that landed square on his head. "You watch your tongue."

"All right, all right, Lex." Christian joined Lexie at her desk. "You look tense, let me come and give you one of my massages." Christian walked behind her desk and stood behind her, slowly rubbing her shoulders.

Lexie felt a little bit of tension ebb away. How had she let one man get her all worked up?

"May I make one frank observation and then we can lay this subject to rest?" Christian asked as he squeezed her shoulders.

"By all means."

"It seems to me that you are not as immune to Will as you thought," Christian whispered in Lexie's left ear.

"Well, I have to be." Turning slightly, Lexie answered with what she hoped was a ring of finality.

"If you say so."

"Don't worry, Christian. It's just been a while since I've felt that kind of animal lust and Will happened to be there to fulfill a primitive need. But make no mistake, it was one night and it shan't happen again. From this point forward, I'm going to focus on the job at hand. The show is in five weeks and I haven't got a moment to spare for all that yucky relationship stuff."

Lexie noticed the look of disbelief on Christian's face.

"What do you mean you aren't coming?" Lexie asked her mother over the phone. "Nia is expecting you. You know how she likes reinforcements at those Bradley gatherings. Plus, you RSVPed."

"I know that, Lexie." Isabel sighed into the phone. "But this can't be helped. This job came unexpectedly and with the loss of Adrian's three jobs, I have to take it." Lexie understood, but she wasn't sure Nia would. Unfortunately her mother was a sole proprietor and had to follow where her business took her, which apparently wasn't near Adrian's companions. True to form, Adrian had been using her mother to get back into her good graces, because when Lexie had dismissed him again, he'd cut her mother off at the knees.

Goes to show you about some people, Lexie thought. Her mother was a fighter, though; Lexie had no doubt that she would bounce back.

"Please do me a favor and give her my regards," requested Isabel. "Let her know that I would give anything to be at her big party. Reassure her that I'll see her at the bridal shower."

The way Isabel carried on, you'd think her mother liked Nia more than her own daughter. "Okay, okay," Lexie promised. "By the way, Mother, I'm bringing a guest for Sunday dinner." Lexie dropped the bombshell.

"A guest? And who might that be? I know it's not Christian. That boy's already like one of the family."

Trust her mother to think that the only person Lexie could convince to join a family dinner would be her gay best friend. Lexie had other ideas. She was tired of her mother's constant whining about Adrian, so she'd decided to spring Will on her and end all nagging that Lexie needed a man in her life.

"Is it someone I know?" Isabel asked curiously.

Lexie knew her mother was bursting at the seams, but she wasn't going to give her any details. It would be better to leave Will's existence clouded under a shroud of mystery until his appearance. She couldn't resist making her mother squirm in anticipation.

"Nope. You've never met him. He's someone new I've recently started seeing."

"You sure don't let the dust settle under you, do you, Lex?"

"No, Mother, I do not. Life is way too short."

"You want me to do what?" Will asked a short while later when Lexie stopped by the club on her way in from work. Even on a weeknight the career set was already lounging about the club, having a cocktail or enjoying dinner. Later a salsa band was lined up to entertain the crowd. And there was Will, front and center, mingling with his patrons making sure they were satisfied with the service.

Lexie watched from the bar as she waited for the bartender to fix her an Appletini. When he was done, he set the tart, green drink in front of her. "I have a family dinner on Sunday and I'd like you to come as my guest," Lexie repeated.

"Did I hear this correctly? You actually want me to come?" Will asked, arching his eyebrows. He was in disbelief that Lexie actually cared enough to allow him to meet her family. Things were going even better than he expected.

"Yes," Lexie whispered softly in his ear. "I need you to run interference with my mother. Provide me with an alibi of sorts."

Will was intrigued. "Why would you need an alibi?"

"Well," Lexie paused for a moment. "I'm coming off a breakup with my ex-boyfriend, who was near and dear to the family, and it's like he's breaking up with my family, too. So right now I need a diversion."

"And I'm to provide this 'diversion,' as you call it." Will's heart sank. Lexie didn't really want him there. She was just using him. Will was disappointed; he still wanted Lexie to want him for him. The other night he'd ached with wanting to be with her. To make love to her tight little body all night long. Instead he had dreamed of her and woken up disgruntled with a major hard-on that even a cold shower hadn't been able to cure.

"Yes, so as you can see, you weren't the only one with an agenda." Lexie smiled.

"Touché." Will raised his Scotch and soda next to her martini glass and clinked. He hadn't seen that coming, but he couldn't let her have the upper hand. "Though it does appear to me that you're getting awfully comfortable with our arrangement."

"In your dreams, buddy. Do as you're told and pick me up at seven."

"I'll be there with bells on."

"Hmmm, and nothing else," Lexie teased.

Will laughed. "That could be arranged, but it would have to be a private showing."

"Mmmm." Lexie licked her lips in anticipation. "I might have to take you up on that."

"Anytime, Miss Lexie." Will squeezed her thigh gently. He wanted to do more but they were in public and a modicum of decorum was in order, especially in front of his staff.

Even after she'd left, her legs still tingled where Will touched her. It amazed her that every moment with him was truly unforgettable.

Leave it to her mother to cool any sparks, Lexie thought the following Sunday. Like a pit bull ready to attack, her mother raked Will over the coals. From the moment they set foot in the door, her mother wasted no time in finding out who Will's parents were, what they did for a living, and if he had ever done drugs or gone to jail.

Meanwhile, her father and brother hovered in the background, content to talk photography and watch the festivities.

Lexie couldn't remember her mother being quite so rude when she'd brought Adrian over. Her mother had taken to him right away. Of course, Adrian had come dressed like a yuppie straight out of prep school.

"So, you're college educated?" her mother asked Will inquisitively as she handed him a cup of English tea. "Milk?"

Will shook his head. He preferred his tea all natural. "Yes, ma'am. I'm a Harvard alum and proud of it."

"Harvard educated? I'm impressed." Her mother smiled approvingly and Lexie breathed a sigh of relief. Her mother firmly advocated education after she attended NYU in the late sixties. Will had indeed won her mother over and Lexie, too.

Tonight she'd learned more about Will than in any of their previous encounters.

As if reading her mind, Will patted her knee and responded to Isabel.

"I obtained a full academic scholarship to Harvard and, after finishing school, I toiled for a few years in the Chicago stock market, but eventually decided to branch out into entreprenurialship," Will replied, ignoring Lexie's shocked expression.

Now that her mother could appreciate! "Indeed. I can testify that there's nothing like being one's own boss."

Finally speaking, her father joined in. "So, Will, what kind of business are you in?"

"I own my own supper/nightclub."

"I've been to it, Mom," Sebastian chimed in. "It's a great place, Will. It's got a lot of class."

"Thanks, Sebastian." Will turned. "I've hired one of the best chefs in the Chicago area, not including yourself, Mrs. Thompson, and I maintain a loyal staff by rewarding them accordingly."

"That's the secret to being a great boss that not many people accomplish," Wesley replied. As the senior property manager for Trammell Crow, her father was responsible for all the financial aspects as well as maintenance, security, groundskeepers, landscapers, and custodial staff that it took to a run a large business park like Landmark Center. All his staff looked up to him and considered Wesley a smart and fair man.

"I agree, sir. If more people showed honesty and fairness, the world would be a better place."

"Well said. Why don't we all go into dinner?" Isabel offered before leading Will to the dining room.

Lexie hung back and whispered to Sebastian, "I thought she was going to eat him for breakfast, but somehow Will has managed to charm that old woman."

"And that ain't easy to do." Sebastian laughed. "He's endured the firing squad, so let's chow."

After a delicious gourmet meal of beef tenderloins, rosemary potatoes, and a fresh green bean and portobello sauté, they enjoyed one of her mother's famous delicate pastries of fruit tarts, napoleons, and chocolate éclairs. Gracious as ever, Will exceeded Lexie's expectations and, she hoped, cured her mother's speculations on her love life.

What was all the more surprising was the fact that he'd gone to Harvard. Turns out he was her kind of man after all. He'd just decided to follow his own path like Sebastian.

"Why didn't you ever let on about your education?" asked Lexie on the ride home from Highland Park. "You had to know that I was thinking the worst."

"Why should I have told you? Maybe you shouldn't be so quick to judge a book by its cover," Will commented harshly as he kept his eyes firmly affixed to the road.

Much to Lexie's dismay, Will dropped her untouched again at her doorstep.

"Be ready at six-thirty on Friday night."

"For what?"

"You're accompanying me to the Bradleys' thirty-fifth anniversary party."

"I don't need an invite. I'm already going," Lexie replied smugly, upset that Will hadn't even tried to make a move. Maybe it was best that he was killing her libido because the more time she spent in Will's company, the more trouble it would mean for her.

"Good. Be ready at eight P.M."

Eschewing all that "what do you want to do" stuff, Will was a man who took charge, and although she would never admit it, Lexie loved it. Will Kennedy was no wimp.

"And who am I going as this time?" Lexie inquired from the sidewalk.

"My date, what else?"

Later while driving home in his Lexus, Will thought about the entire evening. It had surprised him to discover exactly how much Lexie needed her mother's approval. Oh, sure, Lexie acted as if she didn't jump when her mother said how high, but Lexie was constantly trying to win her mother's acceptance. Gone was the confident, self-assured woman he'd met that first night at the theater, and in her place was an insecure daughter in need of her mother's love and affection.

Will recognized the feeling because he'd seen it in himself. Eve Kennedy was not an easy woman to love. She constantly saw Will as his father, always blaming Will's father for what went wrong in her own life. At times he'd wanted to walk away and leave her, but he'd endured for his little brother. And he'd do it all over again because family meant everything.

CHAPTER ELEVEN

"I thought we were going to the Bradleys'?" Lexie asked when they drove in the opposite direction of the Bradley family home in Country Club Hills the following weekend.

"We are."

"What's the big mystery?" Lexie wondered aloud.

"We have to make a pit stop first," Will replied and slowed down the car as the traffic signal turned red. Will hazarded another glance over at Lexie. When she'd opened the door earlier, he'd nearly fallen over. The woman was stunning.

Her tumbleweed of hair had been all swept up to reveal a beautifully slender neck, while a few wisps of hair graced either side of a perfectly divine face. Was she wearing any makeup? With her clear complexion, Will couldn't tell. Surely a heavenly creature like her didn't need any. And the dress—if you could call it a dress—was two pieces of satin fabric that clung to her slender body like a second skin. Will didn't see any panty lines so he could only imagine she wasn't wearing any underneath the ensemble. Was she trying to drive him crazy with desire? It appeared she had no idea of the effect she had on him.

He'd fantasized about her all day, unable to focus on any one thing. He'd stared endlessly at the computer screen, attempting to complete his monthly reports, but to no avail. He didn't know how, but somehow Lexie Thompson had gotten to him and there was no cure in sight.

He'd nearly gone out of his mind thinking about the smell of her fragrant her hair and her pert breasts. He was ready to continue their relationship on a physical level so why was Lexie keeping him at arm's length, yet still wearing enticing outfits?

Gripping the steering wheel, Will turned the corner to his mother's house. He'd promised his mother that he would pick her up. Pulling into a parking space, Will jumped out to open Lexie's car door.

"Where are we?"

"My mother's."

"What!" Lexie eyes widened in fear. "Will, what are you pulling here? I can't meet your mother now, not dressed like this. Is this punishment for Sunday dinner with my mother?" She had selected tonight's dress with the thought of pleasing Will. Putting the dashing club owner out of her mind hadn't worked and now she was standing in front of his mother's door looking like a harlot.

"Don't worry." Will grasped Lexie's hand. He was surprised to discover how cold and clammy they were. Was Lexie, Miss Ice Princess, actually afraid of meeting his mother? Surely she could charm Eve.

"Will, I can't." Lexie snatched her hand away.

"Don't worry; my mother is very excited to meet you." Lexie pulled her hands from her side and placed it in the crook of his arms. "You told her about me?" Lexie asked as she cautiously walked toward Mrs. Kennedy's front door.

"Of course I did." Will pulled out his keys and opened the door, allowing Lexie to precede him. "I think she'd be curious to meet my new girlfriend."

Lexie smiled to herself. First he was romancing her at the club and now this. If he kept it up, she'd be in the position permanently.

Meeting Lexie would settle his mother's worries about his future. The idea had come to him last night while he watched a bevy of beauties parade around him at the club. None of them held a candle to a certain woman who was naturally blessed with a wealth of silky jet-black hair and a pair of killer legs.

"Mom!" Will called up the stairs. "Are you ready?"

"There is no need to holler," his mother answered testily, rising from her seat in the adjacent living room. "I'm right here. And ready to go. You do realize you're a half hour late. We're going to miss their arrival."

"I'm sorry, ma'am, that was my fault," Lexie interjected, coming forward to shake Eve's hand. "I wasn't ready when Will came to pick me up. It's really a pleasure to meet you, Mrs. Kennedy."

"My, my, well, aren't you all fine and proper?" Eve Kennedy chuckled, returning the handshake. "There's no need for such formalities around here. Please call me Eve."

"It's a pleasure, Eve."

"We really should be going, ladies, if we're going to make this party," Will interrupted. He didn't miss the astonished look on his mother's face that he'd actually brought a woman home to meet her. Had he ever done it before? Not that he could remember, but then again he had never met a woman that fascinated him as much as Lexie. She had spirit, fire, and beauty, and all in one dynamite package. Had he finally found that diamond in the rough?

"All right," Eve conceded. "Will, grab my present on the cocktail table." Eve nodded to the large box decorated with wedding bells.

"Where's Ryan?" Will asked, searching downstairs. "I thought he was coming with us."

"He had other plans with the boys."

"What boys?"

"I don't know, Will. Don't twenty-question me to death," his mother fired at him.

"Well, you should know who he's hanging with."

"Boy," his mother began, "don't tell me how to raise my son."

Will held up his hands in defense. "Mom, I don't like the idea of him associating with the hoodlums in this neighborhood."

"I know, but leave the boy be. So he didn't want to spend the evening with a bunch of stuffy adults. What's the big deal?"

"I agree with your mom." Even though it wasn't her place, Lexie stepped in. "I doubt the Bradleys are a place for teenagers this evening."

She detected the concern etched on Will's face and was glad to see that he cared about his family as much as she did hers. The more she learned about him, the harder it was to ignore her growing feelings.

"Okay, okay." Will knew when he was outvoted. "But I'm still going to have a talk with him later."

"C'mon, Lexie." Eve took Lexie's hand and together they walked outside to the car. "I'm eager to hear all about you and Will. I know most of the women he usually dates aren't too bright."

Will laughed heartily and locked the door before

following them outside. Starting the car, he noticed that the crew he'd seen the other day was nowhere in sight. Will could only hope Ryan wasn't with them wherever they were.

On the opposite side of town, Ryan welcomed J.T. and his crew into Millennium. When the hostess disappeared on a fake errand he'd dispatched, Ryan let his delinquent friends into the side entrance. If he hadn't agreed, J.T. would beat him to a pulp or, worse yet, make his life completely miserable. Ryan did not want to get on J.T.'s bad side.

Wanting to keep his head atop his shoulders, Ryan agreed to let in a *few* people as long as J.T. appeared inconspicuous. He was shocked when J.T. entered with not one or two of his boys, but a dozen.

Looking them over as they crossed the threshold, Ryan shook his head in amazement. Most were dressed in baseball hats, T-shirts, and baggy jeans that hung off their hips. Who wouldn't notice the bling-bling in their mouth and tattoos displayed all over their arms? And J.T. was no better. Although he was wearing the latest in Sean John fashion, he looked every bit as menacing as usual with his glistening bald head, gold chains, and abundance of tattoos. How was this crew supposed to be invisible?

"Thanks, dawg, for getting us in." J.T. shook Ryan's hand at the door. "So, where's the best spot?"

Ryan searched the club for any place where he wouldn't get caught and noticed that Will's private booth was open. It would be tight, but surely he could fit them all in. Luckily the place was crowded. Maybe no one would notice.

"Over there." Ryan inclined his head and led them

over to the booth with an oversize leather couch—but not without incident. One of J.T.'s friends pinched a girl on the behind on the way over.

"Could you please tell your crew not to handle the merchandise? This is my brother's club," Ryan whispered in J.T.'s ear.

"Aw, man, don't worry about it." J.T. blew off his concerns. "Did you see how that hoochie was dressed? These girls come to the club wanting to get laid and I'd be more than happy to oblige them. Ain't that right, boys?"

All of J.T.'s boys high-fived him.

Why had Ryan ever agreed to this? Now there was no backing out; he had already opened Pandora's box.

Lexie was impressed when a uniformed butler greeted them at the door and ushered the threesome into the Bradleys' foyer. She had heard about their fabulous Country Club Hills home from Nia. Her initial description, Lexie recalled, had been intimidating, but Lexie loved the grand staircase, Oriental rugs, and elegant tapestry.

Eager to show off the most phenomenal woman in the room, Will captured Lexie's hand in his. "C'mon." Apparently he wasn't alone in his opinion because Lexie and Eve hadn't stopped chatting the entire ride there. Eve approved of the new woman in his life—Lexie had wowed her as usual and he would forever be grateful.

Guests and friends of the Bradleys were already milling about the formal living and dining room, drinking champagne and eating caviar, prawn cocktails, and lobster bisque.

Will looked around and saw his longtime friend

and rival Paige Armstrong with her often overbearing husband, Maxwell. Will and Paige had butted heads since preschool. Fortunately Maxwell kept a strong hold on the four-foot-eleven spitfire.

His buddy Julian was there with his girlfriend Whitney, who'd obviously returned from her business trip, and as looks would have it was giving him quite an earful that very second.

Will was about to leave his mother to fend for herself when Marcus Bradley, Will's surrogate father, stepped forward to greet them.

"Eve, you look wonderful as always." Marcus kissed both cheeks.

"Thank you, Marcus." Eve Kennedy blushed wildly, smoothing down the simple black evening dress Will had purchased for her cruise last year.

"Did you ever think you'd see the day that Simone and I would be married for thirty-one years?"

"Actually, yes. Unlike some, you were a good man," Eve remarked. "By the way, where's Simone?" Looking over Marcus's shoulder, Eve missed the scorn etched across Will's face. But Lexie didn't miss it. Was Will's relationship with his mother on shaky ground, too?

"Off being the hostess with the mostest," Marcus said.

"Well, I'm going to find her and give her my heartfelt congratulations." Eve left the group in search of best friend.

Will hated that his mother used every opportunity to put down his father. Why couldn't she let him rest in peace? But he refused to let Eve ruin his evening. Shaking his head, he turned to his mentor. "Marcus, have you had a chance to meet Lexie Thompson?" Will asked, eager to introduce Lexie to the one man he respected most in his life.

"Ah, yes, Nia's friend. I've heard a lot about you."

Marcus brought Lexie's hand to his lips and placed a light kiss on her wrist. "It's a pleasure to finally meet you."

"Likewise," Lexie returned with a dazzling smile.

"You've got quite a catch in Will." Marcus beamed with pride at his second son. He'd known Will from the moment he was a babe in his mother's womb. He and Will's father, Joseph Kennedy, went way back. High school buddies, he and Joe dreamed they could conquer the world. If only Joe hadn't tried accomplishing it a little too quickly, then maybe he wouldn't have ended up with a bullet in the chest. On his deathbed, Marcus promised Joseph that he would keep his boy safe, and after all these years, he'd never broken that promise.

Lexie winked at Will. "Don't I know it."

"So, when did you guys arrive?" Nia asked, discovering Lexie on Will's arm shortly after they arrived.

"Nia, you're looking fabulous as always." Will was the first to speak as Lexie's mouth suddenly dried up like the Arizona desert. The look of obvious delight on Nia's face made Lexie feel like her hand had just been caught in the cookie jar.

Swallowing, Lexie found her voice. "Hey, girl." Lexie attempted nonchalance and detached herself from Will's clutches to give her best friend a quick squeeze.

"When did the two of you become an item?" Nia asked. "If I remember correctly, the first time you met it wasn't love at first sight."

"Are you wondering about your best girl and me?" Will pulled Lexie back to his side. "Yes, Lexie and I did get off to a rocky start, but now we're enjoying each other's company. Isn't that right, darling?" Will peered down at Lexie lovingly. When she appeared frozen and incapable of speech, Will continued. "We'd like to thank you, Nia, for hooking us up."

"What's going on over here?" Damon asked, strolling over to join the trio.

"Honey, you've missed all the excitement." Nia laughed as Damon handed her a glass of champagne. "Will was explaining that he and Lexie are an item now."

"Hmmm, so it's true. I had heard rumors."

"What?" Nia looked up at her fiancé questioningly. "And you didn't tell me?" Nia gave him a nudge for holding out before turning her gaze on Lexie.

Once again, Lexie tried unsuccessfully to remove Will's arm, which he'd kept permanently attached to her waist. Clearly she wanted to keep their little tête-à-tête a secret, but the cat was out of the bag.

"And how long have you been seeing each other?" Nia wondered aloud.

"Not long." Lexie answered.

"So, where is Simone?" Will asked, changing the subject. "I saw your father earlier and he was on cloud nine." He was glad to be a part of the Bradleys' special day. Thirty-one years of marriage was an accomplishment and Will was impressed. Marcus Bradley was a man he trusted and respected. He'd single-handedly been a profound male presence in Will's life since the death of his father when he was seven years old.

There was never anything Will lacked that Marcus hadn't tried to provide for. If Damon was in private school or having tennis or piano lessons, Marcus was sure Will had the same advantage. He never forgot his second son and for that Will would be forever thankful.

"Oh, my parents?" Damon looked over his shoulder, but they had disappeared. "They're probably off somewhere necking like a couple of teenagers."

"Even now, after all these years, that's surprising," Lexie commented.

"Really, how so?" Will asked curiously. It was a revealing statement coming from Lexie, who so far had been rather closemouthed about Isabel and Wesley. "Your parents are still together."

"Yes, they are. But trust me, not all marriages are like the Bradleys'. If you'll excuse me."

Will wanted to chase after her, but sensing her hesitancy to discuss the topic, he allowed her some space.

"Excuse me." Nia followed after Lexie.

"Was it something I said?" Will asked, turning to Damon.

"Maybe you hit a sore spot."

"I guess so." Will glanced down the hallway after her, but she'd already disappeared. "Let's find your folks."

"I can't do it," Ryan said stubbornly. He was already in so much trouble, but this he couldn't do.

"I said I want a couple of beers for me and the boys." J.T. stood in front of Ryan.

"No way, my brother could lose his license for selling liquor to minors. I'm not going to do it."

"So you're telling me you can't hook us up with a couple of brews?" J.T. glared at him.

Ryan knew J.T. was trying to bully him, but he couldn't have it. The club meant everything to Will and if anything ever happened to it, Ryan would never forgive himself.

"Come with me for a minute." J.T. grabbed Ryan by the arm. Ryan knew what was coming as J.T. escorted him to the men's restroom. He was probably taking him off for a beat-down out of plain sight.

Once inside, J.T. threw Ryan up against the restroom wall. "So you won't do this little favor for me, huh, punk?" J.T. hissed.

"I'm sorry, man, but I can't," Ryan replied nervously. He was scared to death, but if Will found out, the situation would be much worse. He would just have to take the hit. Ryan bowed his head and waited for the blow.

J.T. laughed in response and released him by the shoulders. "I'm not going to hit you, man. At least, not yet."

Ryan breathed a sigh of relief. He was in no mood to get beat up today, and how would he explain the bruises to his mother and brother?

"Thanks, man, I'm glad you understand." Ryan turned to walk away, but J.T. blocked his path.

"I'm not done yet."

"Sorry, sorry." Ryan backed away and stopped uneasily when he saw the sinister look in J.T.'s eyes.

"You can do me another favor instead." J.T. smiled, showing off a pair of gold teeth in the front.

Ryan wanted to wipe the smug look off his face. Although he had height and J.T. was a full five inches shorter, J.T. was used to street fighting and Ryan wasn't at all sure he could take him, especially with J.T's entourage here.

When he didn't respond, J.T. told him instead, "I want to be sure you understand that me and my boys have a standing invitation to roll up into Millennium anytime the feeling moves us, got it?"

"J.T., I can't get you in. We barely got in tonight. Technically I'm not even allowed at the club. You know the whole minors-can't-work-at-a-place-that-sells-liquor. As I told you before, this is a one-time thing."

J.T. slammed Ryan against the concrete wall again and, for added benefit, smacked him hard across the face. "What did I just say?"

"I heard you, but I can't help you," Ryan replied. That's when J.T. punched him in the jaw a second time.

"Do I care? You gon' jump whenever I say how high, aren't ya?" J.T. pointed his index finger at Ryan's temple and pulled the trigger. "Because otherwise you may not like what happens to your mom or that pretty-boy brother of yours." Seeing stars, Ryan nodded his head in agreement. "Good, me and the boys are going to be leaving now, but I'll be seeing you again real soon."

Rolling down the wall, Ryan fell on the tile floor and let the tears he'd held inside run down his cheeks. He'd thought that if he got J.T. into the club once, he would stop pestering him in the neighborhood, but it wasn't enough. How had he gotten himself into such a mess?

"So where are you hiding her?" Jordan Bradley questioned Will, her pseudo-brother, upon his approach. Since she was a kid barely reaching her father's knee, Jordan had adored Damon's best friend Will. She'd always envisioned that one day they would fall madly in love. It was too bad that someone else beat her to the punch.

"What are you yapping about?" Will asked, playfully ruffling her hair. Jordan was supposed to be Damon's little sister, but what a woman she had become. The geeky teen with the braces and flat chest had filled out to become one fine-looking woman. Almost as tall as he, her usually curly ringlets had been straightened and her mane hung perfectly down her square shoulders. While other women had arrived in designer gowns, Jordan went against the grain and wore slinky black pants and an off-the-shoulder top.

Jordan caught Will's hand. "Don't muss the hair."

"J, why don't you go harass someone else? Like Julian. The two of you would probably make a good couple, being lawyers and all," Will teased. A career woman and a junior lawyer at Hamilton Morgan and Gilbert, Jordan Bradley was well on her way to becoming partner.

"Don't change the subject," Jordan retorted with a pout.

"I'm talking about the beauty you walked in with and whose side you've never left all evening." Jordan looked around the room but couldn't find the model figure in the couture gown.

"I guess you're right," Will commented, looking around the room. Lexie was no place in sight. "She seems to have disappeared."

"What did you do, run her off?"

Will whispered in her ear, "I don't have to run women off. Women flock to me."

"Not this one," Jordan commented. He moved away, but Jordan persisted. "Is it possible there's a woman that exists who could actually tame you?"

"Who says I'm tamed?"

"C'mon, Will," Jordan teased, "everyone can see it. I'm sorry to tell ya, my friend, but you're sprung."

Was he really? Had that love jones snuck up on him when he wasn't looking? If so, he'd been a goner the moment he first laid eyes on Lexie.

When Nia approached, Lexie was sitting in a lawn chair with a plate of uneaten appetizers in her lap and a full glass of champagne at her feet.

"I've been looking everywhere for you. Where you'd go?" Nia asked, taking a seat beside her.

Lexie shrugged her shoulders. She'd been angrily berating herself for the last ten minutes for not taking advantage of the wealthy patrons in the room. She should be out there promoting the joys of shopping at Bentley's and showing off queen-bee Simone Bradley's Vera Wang original or the mayor's wife in Carolina Herrera. Instead she'd walked off. She'd needed a breath of fresh air, away from Will. When she was standing next to him, he took up all the available air in the room and she couldn't think straight.

And then there was her mother. The topic of conversation had had hit a little too close to home for Lexie. Her mother had still not warmed up to her, despite her attempts to repair the damage. Sure, she'd accepted Will, but Lexie could tell Isabel was still upset that Lexie had chosen another caterer over hers. How did she know? Because her mother's daily telephone calls had gone to zero.

"I noticed you looked rather strange when we discussed your parents. Is anything wrong?"

"My parents are having a bit of trouble."

"You're kidding." Nia was shocked. She'd always thought the Thompsons had the perfect marriage. "I've always looked at your parents' marriage as the one to aspire to."

"Well, don't," Lexie stated bitterly. "Nia, things aren't always what they seem. No one is perfect. And my mother certainly is not. She's being totally unreasonable and giving my father the cold shoulder because she's mad at me."

"Why? What happened?"

"She's upset that I didn't hire her to cater the fashion show." Lexie noticed the shocked expression on

Nia's face and didn't care. Nia had no idea what Lexie had endured over the years having a domineering mother like Isabel Thompson. The cloud of perfection she'd had to live under. It was Isabel's way or the highway. "I know what you're thinking, Nia, but I had a different idea in mind. And yes, I do usually throw business my mother's way, but I won't be held hostage any longer. I had a decision to make and I made it."

"Okay, I'm not here to beat you up—I think you're doing a good job of that all on your own—but you did make your own bed. I guess now you have to live with the consequences."

"My father shouldn't have to pay for my mistakes."

"I'm sure he won't—at least, not for long." Nia rubbed Lexie's back to soothe her frazzled nerves. "Your parents have weathered many a storm. They'll weather this one, too. Now, c'mon, let's go inside." Nia stood up.

"Wait." Lexie grabbed her arm. "Are we still on for Saturday? We need to finish your dress."

"Absolutely." Nia's face creased into a smile. "Wild horses couldn't keep me away."

When they returned, Lexie found Will's arms laced up with another woman's. Whoever this incredibly beautiful and poised young woman was, they clearly knew each other because Will was hanging on her every word. Immediately Lexie tensed back up. Times were a-changing. Since when did she become the jealous type?

"Who's that with Will?" she asked Nia pointedly. Nia turned at Lexie's harsh tone and laughed at Lexie's vehement glare at the other woman. "Oh, that's Jordan, Damon's sister."

"She's gorgeous."

"And available." Nia couldn't resist a little tease. She

was surprised to see Lexie sweat over some competition. "But don't worry, she's like his little sister. You have nothing to worry about."

"Of course I don't," Lexie reiterated, attempting lightheartedness. Venturing another look, she found Will staring back at her. If she hadn't known any better she'd think he'd actually sensed her presence.

Will noticed Lexie the moment she returned. He hoped to find out what he'd said to make her walk off in the middle of a conversation. "Listen, sweetheart," Will squeezed Jordan's shoulder, "I'd love to talk more, but . . ."

"Your woman has returned. It's okay, Will. Go after her," Jordan ordered.

Will complied and swiftly strode across the room. "I missed you," he said before sweeping Lexie in his arms for a long, slow, and torturous kiss.

Lexie was indeed surprised at such a public display of affection, but the second his lips claimed hers, she succumbed to the sensations his lips and tongue evoked. When he finally pulled away, her knees felt like jelly and Lexie grabbed hold of his shoulders for support.

Nia watched them both with amazement before slowly moving away to give them their privacy and go back to her fiancé.

Seconds ticked by before either of them spoke. "Wow, what was all that about?" Lexie asked, wiping at her smudged lipstick.

"I don't want you to leave me tonight," Will replied all of sudden.

"A little possessive, aren't we?" Lexie tried moving away, but Will's massive hand remained at her side. "Will, I doubt more is possible. We do have your mother with us tonight."

"We'll drop her off and afterward I'm going to ravish you all night long," he said huskily.

"How do you know I won't resist?" Lexie's almond-shaped brown eyes connected with Will's heavy-lidded passion-filled orbs.

"You won't."

Cling. Cling. Cling. The sound of champagne flutes awoke Lexie and Will from their haze.

"I have a toast to make." Will searched the crowd and found Damon and Jordan standing center stage with their parents. "First off, I want to thank all of you for coming to my parent's thirty-first anniversary party."

Overjoyed at the way Marcus held Simone firmly at his side, and seeing love in their eyes, Will wondered if that kind of happiness was staring him right in the face.

"Indeed, tonight is an auspicious occasion for these two lovebirds," Damon began. "They've endured the ups and the downs of marriage and have still come out on top. We salute you two for your loyalty and commitment to each other. I only hope that Nia and I can live up to the gold standard that the two of you have set. To our mom and dad, Marcus and Simone."

The room exploded with applause and everyone clinked their flutes in toast to the anniversary couple.

Lexie smiled. She had never known that kind of enduring love. All her relationships had been fleeting. A quick roll in the hay here, a trip to Rome there. She had always been looking for the quickest way out of a relationship and had never stuck around to see if any of them would ever last. Take what you could get and get out before your heart got trampled on was her MO.

"You okay?" Will inquired.

Snapping out of her reverie, Lexie realized that Will was speaking to her. "Yes, I'm fine."

"What were you thinking about just then?"

Should she tell him that she was thinking of making the pseudo-relationship permanent? Mind you, she wasn't ready for any diamond rings, but maybe she could commit to being a one-man woman. When she tried to open her mouth, no words escaped. Instead, out of habit, she did what she always did: relied on her sex appeal.

"I'm about ready to explode. Let's get out of here," she whispered in his ear.

"That was a wonderful party," Eve commented on the drive home. "It was so great seeing Simone so happy. It's funny, but I can still remember the day we all first met. Your father, Joseph, and Marcus were handsome as the devil and equally as arrogant, though the latter hasn't changed much." Eve chuckled at the memory and continued on. "Stars of the football team, they approached Simone and I. They thought that as cheerleaders we'd be fawning all over them. Instead, Simone and I ignored them, but that didn't stop your father. He piled on the charm by sending us two chocolate milkshakes."

Will laughed heartily. "That must have really done it."

"Don't mock me, boy. Your father was quite a man." Eve Kennedy's eyes misted up.

Although outwardly she appeared wistful, Will knew how much it hurt Eve to talk about his father. Usually she condemned his father's choices because they'd led him to live in the fast lane . . . and had eventually cost him his life. But tonight she was different; she had remembered happier times and Will was grateful. Will wondered if perhaps it wasn't Lexie's presence that caused her to speak such kind words.

"So he and Mr. Bradley won your hearts," Lexie finished.

"They sure did, and all it took was a milkshake." Eve smiled as she reminisced about her past.

"That's a wonderful story. I'm sorry I won't have the opportunity to meet the man that helped create this handsome devil." Lexie caressed Will's cheek.

"It's a shame, too. If only he could have stayed as innocent as he was that day in the ice-cream shop."

As he pulled into a parking space outside her home, Will turned to give his mother a venomous glare. She couldn't resist at least one dig.

Eve responded by patting his shoulder to settle him down. She knew her son didn't appreciate any obtuse comments about his late father. It was always a forbidden topic of conversation because they never saw eye to eye on the subject.

"It's been a long evening." His mother yawned, showing her exhaustion. "I'm going to retire to bed. You two enjoy the rest of your evening."

Stepping out of the car, Lexie and Will accompanied her inside. Once inside, Lexie gave Will's mother a hug. "Good night, Mrs. Kennedy. It was lovely to meet you."

"The pleasure was mine," Eve replied, going to her bedroom upstairs and leaving Lexie and Will alone in the foyer.

As soon as he heard the click of his mother's door close shut, Will lifted Lexie in his arms and buried his nose in her sweetly scented hair. Will knew what he wanted and nothing was going to stop him tonight from having his heart's desire. He nuzzled her neck, slowly traveling a path up to her ear, then her cheek, until finally covering her lips hungrily.

Lexie leaned into his massive chest and his urgent kiss sent shivers up her spine. She returned the favor by teasing the sides of his mouth until his lips parted, allowing her entry. Her tongue met his and stroked his while her body achingly rubbed against his until her nipples tightened against his lapel and his groin grew.

With all the strength he could muster, Will pulled away. "Not here," he rasped. "Let's take this to your place."

CHAPTER TWELVE

Usually calm and in control, Lexie fumbled as she attacked the lock on her door. When she finally managed to open the door, Will was right behind her, showering her with hot, moist kisses.

Closing the door, Lexie trembled in anticipation of what she knew was sure to come: some of the best sex she had ever had in her entire life. But first she had to set some ground rules.

Turning around, she faced him. "Will, you know I want you. . . ." Her voice trailed off.

"But what's stopping you?" Will quizzed as he quickly removed his coat and moved forward to wrap his arms around her waist. "Lexie, you remember how good it was between us before. Imagine how much better it could be."

"I'm not looking for a relationship, Will." Lexie finally said the words she'd wrestled with her entire life. Her career was on the fast track and she couldn't afford to let anything stand in her way.

"Neither am I," Will replied in a velvety smooth voice. "I just want to breathe you in all night long. Can you handle that?"

"Are you willing to accept my terms?" Lexie returned.

Will's response was a lingering kiss on the lips. She leaned into his embrace and allowed his smoky masculine scent to waft over her. Should she step into a minefield?

Will didn't give her any time to think about it; naked hunger was lying in his deeply set dark eyes. "You are so beautiful, Lexie," Will whispered.

Before she had time for second thoughts, he pinned her against the wall. His hands roamed and caressed her shapely bottom, and from the sound of her soft moans, Will could tell she enjoyed everything he was doing to her. Lexie liked spontaneity, enjoyed the unexpected, and Will was going to give it to her.

Will kicked his shoes off. They landed with a loud thud on the other side of the room. At first he wanted to take her right there standing up, but he'd reminded himself that the next time he was privileged enough to be invited to have her body, he would enjoy it. Savor it. Inhaling, Will slowed the pace.

"What's wrong?" Lexie asked as her breathing slowly became ragged.

"Not a damn thing," Will said, walking toward her.

"Good," Lexie replied as a sense of urgency took over her. She attacked his clothes with fervor and tugged at his tie and cummerbund until they fell to the floor.

"Wait." Will stopped her hands. "Let's take this slow and enjoy the moment. We've got all night."

Lexie understood. Their first coupling had been wild and frantic. Because they had wanted each other so bad, they hadn't cared about where they were, but now they had all the time in the world.

Each time he was near, Lexie was as powerless as

that first night when she'd been unable to resist his virility, and she was even more so now. His pull and attraction had become stronger than any lover she ever had. So, willingly, she offered her hand up to Will. He took it and followed her into the bedroom. Inside the dark room, Lexie slowly pushed him toward her bed and left him waiting there while she headed to the bathroom. She returned several moments later with candles and a lighting stick. Soon the glow of scented lavender and vanilla candles filled the air and Will began to relax. He intended to take his time making sweet love to Lexie Thompson. She was his tonight—mind, body, and soul.

For the first time in her life Lexie was a little hesitant. It surprised her, but it didn't stop the moment. Reaching out to touch his face, Lexie allowed herself the chance to study him. By candlelight, she traced the outline of his face from the top of his curved brow to his high cheekbones and down to his firm, square jaw. When she fingered his lips, Will trembled. And Lexie was surprised to discover Will equally as nervous and tense as she. Cupping his strong chin, she leaned down and placed a gentle kiss on his warm and inviting lips. His lips parted easily beneath hers as desire rushed through her.

Lexie thought she was in charge, but Will couldn't resist taking over. He kissed her mouth fervently, nipping, sucking, and stroking her tongue until she was weak with need.

He tasted so good. It was a taste she had tried hard to forget, but had lived inside her memory since that very first kiss at his club.

Reaching down, she unbuckled Will's pants. Will lifted his hips and allowed Lexie to slide them down his legs. Anticipation was building inside his loins as his manhood strained against his briefs, eager for what lay ahead.

Lexie continued her ministrations and slowly unbuttoned his shirt, easing it off his shoulders. Again she was awed by his powerfully built chest. Hard and firm, Lexie ran her fingers down his chest and encircled his nipples. Flicking her tongue across one, she brought it to a turgid peak before turning her sights to the other. Will groaned. He couldn't take it any longer. He needed to mate with her. It was a primal urge; the feminine scent surrounding her was driving him mad.

Within seconds he was grabbing Lexie by the waist and in one quick fluid movement he rid her of her damning dress and thong. Will smiled; he knew she hadn't been wearing much underneath.

"I want you so much, Lexie," Will rasped, easing his briefs down his legs. "Do you want me as much as I want you?"

"Yes, I want you," Lexie replied, glimpsing a view of his swollen shaft. It was just as big and emboldened as she remembered and she was more than ready to receive him.

But first, Will's hands were exploring the soft shapely lines of her legs to her slender hips and waist before finally settling on her small but ample breasts. When his hands found their way to those mounds, he took one nipple and rubbed it between his fingers until it turned into a rocky pebble. Then he took one taut nipple into his mouth and suckled on it like a newborn babe.

"Hmmm, that feels good." Lexie moaned as he laved the other nipple with his hot, wet tongue while his long, deft fingers explored her flat stomach. When they came to the juncture between her thighs, Will found her moist, tight, and ready for him. Reaching over the bed, he pulled a condom out of his pants on the floor. Snatching it from him, Lexie slid it onto his engorged shaft.

"Now, Will. I need you," Lexie said.

Easing her legs apart with his knee, Will braced himself on his elbows and slid into Lexie's moist center. When her wet feminine fold clutched him like it was made for him, a guttural sound escaped from Will's lips.

There was no time to savor the moment as Lexie wrapped her legs around his waist and matched his urgency with that of her own. Before he knew it, he was pushed over the edge. His body erupted seconds before he heard Lexie's screams of passion as she too met him in oblivion.

Lexie awoke the next morning to find herself wrapped in Will's arms, her body perfectly curved with his. It stunned her that she had lost self-control last night. No man had ever made her feel this way, not even her college boyfriend Kevin. Lexie wasn't at all sure what she would do next. Her emotions were running rampant.

As she looked over at Will, Lexie found him sleeping with a satisfied smile on his face. He was probably dreaming of all the wicked things he had done to her.

Despite her protestations, Lexie enjoyed Will's company in and out of bed. Not that the former wasn't the best she'd ever had. Will was an amazing, inventive lover. He knew how to touch and caress her body to bring her to a heightened awareness. Last night with Will felt like the first time she'd ever made love with a man.

Sure, she'd been with other men, but none like Will. He actually took the time to get to know her. Lexie truly felt that he understood her, respected her.

Will's eyes fluttered open and he found Lexie awake and staring at him curiously.

"Is something wrong?" Will asked, running his hand through her mass of tangled curls.

"No, of course not," Lexie answered. She couldn't exactly tell him the truth that she was starting to fall for him.

"Good, because I intend to acquaint myself with every inch of your amazing body this morning," Will murmured and, within two seconds flat, had Lexie flat on her back.

Lexie looked up into his sexy onyx eyes and smiled. "And do I have any say in the matter?"

"Hmmm" Will pondered for a moment. "Nope." He smiled, shaking his head before kissing her, long and deep, just like she liked it.

Two hours later, they were *both* flat on their backs, bathed in sweat, yet completely satiated from their morning activities.

When Lexie finally tried to move, Will cast a possessive arm around her middle. "And where do you think you're going?"

"I have to get to the office." Lexie pulled away. Sliding from his embrace, Lexie pulled on her robe from a nearby chair.

At Will's sardonic smile, Lexie continued. "I have work to do. As much as I would love to, we can't stay in bed all day." Lexie started toward the bathroom.

"And it couldn't be that you're running away?" Will asked, sitting up in bed, uncaring that the sheet revealed all of him, every inch of the rock-hard body Lexie had reveled in all night and all morning long.

Lexie heard the catch in Will's voice, but when she turned around Will was already gathering his clothes strewn across the floor. Had she imagined the tender tone of love in his voice? Or was she imagining what she needed to hear?

It suddenly dawned on her that she was thinking the word *love.* Did that word come into play with someone like Will? Hell, with someone like her? They were both made from the same cloth. Maybe they weren't meant for love.

"Why would I run away?" Lexie asked, turning around suddenly. "You know I thoroughly enjoyed last night."

"Then why are you leaving?" Will asked. "I thought we could spend the day together." The moment the words were uttered, Will was surprised. He had never spent the day with a woman the night after being in her bed. He usually hit it and quit it. But for some reason, this time was different. He enjoyed spending time with Lexie and didn't want the day to end. But Lexie obviously didn't feel the same and Will wanted to know why. He wouldn't let her escape so easily.

Pulling on his trousers, Will followed her, bare-chested, into the bathroom.

"Why are you following me?" Lexie asked, placing her toothbrush on the counter and facing Will.

"Because our discussion is far from over. You can't dismiss me, Lexie, like you do your other beaus."

"That wasn't what I was trying to do." Lexie smiled and batted her eyelashes, attempting to make light of the situation. "I had a fantastic evening." Lexie came toward him and ran her fingernails across his hairless chest. "But I have to go to work." Turning away, she started brushing her teeth, successful ignoring him.

"On a Saturday?"

"Yes, sometimes I work on Saturdays. Plus I have Nia's dress to finish," Lexie answered and continued with her morning ritual of cleansing and moisturizing her face. Unaffected, Will sat on the toilet seat and waited until she was done. He would not be dismissed.

"What, Will?" Lexie asked, annoyed. "So we've spent a couple of nights together. You think that entitles you to know my comings and goings? What more do you want from me?"

"Are you going to stand there and deny that you felt nothing in my arms? Because trust me, I could make you eat those words." Will stood and like a tiger ready to pounce on his prey, took a dangerous step toward her.

At the dark and primitive look in his eyes, a lump formed in Lexie's throat and she found it hard to speak. Will took her silence as acquiescence.

"I want you to admit that we're good together."

Swallowing, Lexie found her voice. "And?"

"And that we should continue seeing each other."

"Why? Because you're allowing me to use your club?" Lexie asked mistrustfully.

"No, of course not. The club is yours, Lexie. You're free to use it for as long as you need it." Of course Will knew it was just a decoy to spend more time with her. After that first night on top of the bar, he'd known there was no going back. He hadn't been able to get her out of his mind. There was no way he was going to let Lexie Thompson slip through his fingers.

"You really mean that?" asked Lexie. She wanted to believe that Will was sincere. Was it possible that she could trust what her heart was telling her?

"Yes, I do," Will brought her hands to his lips. Lexie felt her insides warm at the touch of his tongue on her skin as he placed moist kisses along the center of her palm.

Will's eyes spoke the truth that she could believe him, but Lexie wasn't so easily fooled. She had been down this road before. And although she loved taking risks, this time she would show a little more caution.

"All right, all right." Lexie succumbed, giving in a little. "Based on our last two encounters, I would agree that perhaps there's something here."

"Hmmm, ya think?" Will asked, encircling her in his arms. Once they were eye to eye, Will gripped Lexie's hair and pressed her mouth against his. Her lips parted in response to his invading tongue. And when he slowly stroked his tongue sensuously across hers, Lexie welcomed the invasion.

"Oh, yes," Lexie said, moaning in agreement. "I most definitely think we should be *lovers*." Will opened her robe and it fell to the floor.

The following afternoon Lexie met Nia for a final fitting of her wedding dress at Bentley's bridal boutique. Having worked nonstop for months, Lexie was now focusing her attention on the design, a delicate array of intricate patterns and fabric. There was still plenty of work to be done on the dress before its debut. The lace and pearls still needed to be installed along the bodice and at the hem. Not to mention the veil, which she hadn't even started on. Luckily they had two months left before the wedding. The dress would be Lexie's most prized accomplishment and was sure to give her maximum exposure at one of the premier events of the season! Somehow she would

An Important Message From The ARABESQUE Publisher

Dear Arabesque Reader,

I invite you to join the club! The Arabesque book club delivers four novels each month right to your front door! It's easy, and you will never miss a romance by one of our award-winning authors!

With upcoming novels featuring strong, sexy women, and African-American heroes that are charming, loving and true… you won't want to miss a single release. Our authors fill each page with exceptional dialogue, exciting plot twists, and enough sizzling romance to keep you riveted until the satisfying end! To receive novels by bestselling authors such as Gwynne Forster, Janice Sims, Angela Winters and others, I encourage you to join now!

Read about the men we love… in the pages of Arabesque!

Linda Gill
PUBLISHER, ARABESQUE ROMANCE NOVELS

P.S. Watch out for the next Summer Series "Ports Of Call" that will take you to the exotic locales of Venice, Fiji, the Caribbean and Ghana! You won't need a passport to travel, just collect all four novels to enjoy romance around the world! For more details, visit us at www.BET.com.

SPECIAL OFFER!
4 BOOKS FREE!

BET★ BOOKS

www.BET.com

A SPECIAL "THANK YOU"
FROM ARABESQUE JUST FOR YOU!

Send this card back and you'll receive 4 FREE Arabesque Novels—
a $25.96 value—absolutely FREE!

The introductory 4 Arabesque Romance books are yours FREE
(plus $1.99 shipping & handling). If you wish to continue to
receive 4 books every month, do nothing. Each month, we will send
you 4 New Arabesque Romance Novels for your free examination.
If you wish to keep them, pay just $18* (plus, $1.99 shipping &
handling). If you decide not to continue, you owe nothing!

- Send no money now.
- Never an obligation.
- Books delivered to your door!

We hope that after receiving your FREE books you'll want to remain
an Arabesque subscriber, but the choice is yours! So why not take
advantage of this Arabesque offer, with no risk of any kind. You'll be
glad you did!

In fact, we're so sure you will love your Arabesque novels, that we
will send you an Arabesque Tote Bag FREE with your first paid
shipment.

* PRICES SUBJECT TO CHANGE.

YOU'LL GET
4 SELECT
ROMANCES PLUS
THIS FABULOUS
TOTE BAG!

ARABESQUE

**Visit us at:
www.BET.com**

THE "THANK YOU" GIFT INCLUDES:

- 4 books absolutely FREE (plus $1.99 for shipping and handling).
- A FREE newsletter, *Arabesque Romance News*, filled with author interviews, book previews, special offers, and more!
- No risks or obligations. You're free to cancel whenever you wish with no questions asked.

FREE TOTE BAG CERTIFICATE

Yes! Please send me 4 FREE Arabesque novels (plus $1.99 for shipping & handling). I am under no obligation to purchase any books, as explained on the back of this card. Send my free tote bag after my first regular paid shipment.

NAME _____

ADDRESS _____ APT. _____

CITY _____ STATE _____ ZIP _____

TELEPHONE ( ) _____

E-MAIL _____

SIGNATURE _____

Offer limited to one per household and not valid to current subscribers. All orders subject to approval. Terms, offer, & price subject to change. Tote bags available while supplies last.

Thank You!

AN075A

ARABESQUE

Accepting the four introductory books for FREE (plus $1.99 to offset the cost of shipping & handling) places you under no obligation to buy anything. You may keep the books and return the shipping statement marked "cancelled". If you do not cancel, about a month later we will send 4 additional Arabesque novels, and you will be billed the preferred subscriber's price of just $4.50 per title. That's $18.00* for all 4 books for a savings of almost 30% off the cover price (Plus $1.99 for shipping and handling). You may cancel at any time, but if you choose to continue, every month we'll send you 4 more books, which you may either purchase at the preferred discount price. . . or return to us and cancel your subscription.

* PRICES SUBJECT TO CHANGE

THE ARABESQUE ROMANCE BOOK CLUB
P.O. BOX 5214
CLIFTON NJ 07015-5214

THE ARABESQUE ROMANCE CLUB: HERE'S HOW IT WORKS

PLACE
STAMP
HERE

find enough hours in the day for the dress and the fashion show.

Nia turned to get a closer look at Lexie when she noticed the additional details on the dress bodice.

"Lex!" Nia cried out. "You've done such a fabulous job. The dress . . . it's everything I've ever wanted."

"I'm so happy, girlfriend." Lexie grinned. It meant the world to her that Nia allowed her to design the most important dress of her entire life; Lexie did not take it lightly.

They were admiring the dress in front of the three-way mirror when a livery driver delivered a large bouquet of red roses to Lexie.

"And who are those from?" Nia inquired even though she had some idea. Nia leaned over Lexie's shoulder and tried reading the inscription, but Lexie pulled away.

"Aren't you nosy?" Lexie smiled, sliding the card back into the envelope.

"Hmmm, and are you going to tell me who they're from?"

"Don't be coy, Nia. You already know."

"So you and Will are an item, huh?" Nia asked when Lexie sat back on the floor to pin the hem of her wedding gown. "I would never have believed it if I hadn't seen it with my own eyes. At the Bradleys' anniversary party, the two of you side by side making polite chitchat, dancing, feeding each other. . . ."

"There's more to the story than you know."

"Really? Well, dish, girl. Last night you were upset about your mother, but now I want the whole story out of you, 'cause a certain person has been MIA over the last couple of weeks."

Lexie hung her head in shame. She really did feel

bad about avoiding her friend, but if they had spent any time together, Nia would easily have recognized her growing feelings for Will.

"Will and I have decided to become lovers until one of us decides otherwise." Lexie revealed a little bit of the truth.

Nia nearly fell off the stool. "Well, I knew you were dating him, but . . ." Nia stopped when Lexie began focusing on another task. "But why do I have a feeling you're holding out on me? Are you starting to fall for Will?"

Her best friend knew her so well, Lexie thought, hiding her face in her sewing basket. Nia wasn't going to take Lexie's simple explanation at face value. Did she sense that there was more under the surface? It had definitely been a surprise to Lexie. The other evening, when Will held her in his arms, it had felt good and so right.

Closing her eyes, Lexie envisioned the touch of Will's hand on the small of her back as he pulled her to him and pushed their bodies in close, or the feel of his smooth hands as they caressed her sensitive skin. Even now her lips were still swollen from his kisses while her breasts ached for his touch.

Will Kennedy had captivated her every waking thought. But she mustn't let herself get carried away in the cold light of day after all the hugs and kisses. She had to be careful not just with her heart, but with the fashion show, too. She couldn't afford any screwup, not with Sydney waiting in the wings. Even if the man did glide across the floor like Fred Astaire.

"I enjoy Will," Lexie answered, standing up. "He's fabulous in bed, but beyond that . . ." Lexie's voice drifted off. She wasn't ready to admit her true feelings to Nia or anyone. Maybe if she kept them bottled inside, they would just disappear.

"Are you sure that's all it is?"

Lexie paused for a moment. She hated lying to her best friend, but if Nia knew her underlying attraction, she would encourage a relationship with Will and Lexie didn't need the added headache.

"Nia, really." Lexie laughed her off. "Will Kennedy is a smooth playboy. After he's done with me, I'm sure he'll have no problem finding a replacement to capture his attention."

"I doubt he wants any other woman," Nia barked, moving unceremoniously off her perch to confront Lexie. But each time Nia dared look in Lexie's eyes to gauge her true feelings, Lexie moved in the opposite direction.

"What are you doing?" Lexie finally asked.

"Appears to me the lady doth protest too much," Nia replied and lifted her arm so Lexie could unzip the side zipper. "Here, help me out of this dress." When Nia was finally undressed, she commented on Lexie's sex life. "As hot to trot as you are, I doubt even you can resist a man as sexy as Will."

Lexie blushed. She couldn't deny the attraction and fessed up immediately. "I haven't."

"You mean you and Will slept together? Lord, have mercy!" Nia fanned herself. "When did this happen? I want to know all the details."

"A couple of weeks ago," Lexie murmured demurely.

"And you didn't tell me this!" Nia hit Lexie on the shoulder. "How dare you keep something like this from your best girl? See, I knew something was up. Remember when I first met Damon and I proclaimed I wanted to have nothing to do with him?"

"And?"

"And you called me on it," Nia replied. "So I'm going to return the favor. I think you're falling for Will and you're afraid to admit it. I'll let you off the hook for now, but you mark my words, you two will be hooking up again before long."

Lexie sighed. She hated predictions. Once they were out, somehow they always seemed destined to come true.

Now that she'd had a taste of Will, Lexie wanted him more than ever. After putting the finishing touches on Nia's gown at the bridal boutique, Lexie drove over to Will's loft to surprise him. She'd made a pit stop at home first and donned her sexiest strapless mini that barely covered her backside. Adding a few dollops of her favorite fragrance by her ears and a little makeup, she was good to go.

When she arrived at Millennium, Will was looking as scrumptious as ever in black slacks and a black silk shirt, casually opened at the neck. He was talking to several customers when he noticed Lexie walk by. His eyes nearly fell out of their sockets when he caught the hot little number she was wearing. He watched as she turned the corner that led to the restrooms. "Gentlemen, if you'll excuse me." Will followed her into the hallway. "Lexie, what are you wearing?" he asked, less than amused.

Lexie glanced down. "Oh, this little number?" Lexie slid her fingers down the side of her slender frame. "Well, this is strictly for you, baby."

"And everyone else." He nodded to the men who were staring as they came out of the men's room. Why did the woman love to push his buttons?

"Now don't tell me you like to share," Lexie teased.

"Not with my women," Will murmured before hauling Lexie into a nearby linen closet. Kicking the door shut, Will reached for Lexie and forced her against the door. His hands sought out her face, neck, and buttocks, while his mouth went to work nibbling on the sensitive spots on her neck. When he heard her moan, Will's tongue darted out and trailed a hot path to Lexie's ear, where he stayed and suckled generously. "Yes, oh, yes," Lexie cried.

"You like that?" Will murmured against her hair. "Well, I've got more for you." Starting at her lobe, he continued a leisurely journey to the valley between her breasts. When he reached his destination, Will wasted no time in pulling down Lexie's dress and feasting on the rock-hard pebbles.

He laved one nipple with his hot, moist tongue before bestowing the other with the same attention. Will knew from the way she was writhing against his increasing rising manhood that she wanted him and, boy, did he want her. Throwing her hands in the air, he divested her of the scrap of material she called a dress. Within seconds, Lexie was standing before him naked, save the tiny lace thong she wore covering that tiny patch of triangle.

Will's manhood grew hard as he gazed into her passion-filled eyes. He couldn't think straight when she looked at him like that. All he could think of was being sheathed in her wet heat.

Lexie, on the other hand, couldn't wait. She was already down on her knees unbuckling his pants. One hand reached inside and clasped around his manhood, stroking him into a frenzy while the other squeezed the firm cheeks of his buttocks. Soon she had him calling out her name. "Lexie, oh, Lexie."

When she was complete with her ministrations, Will hauled Lexie to her feet and turned her to face the door. Bending her bottom toward him, he pushed the tiny scrap aside. He couldn't wait any longer. He had to have her. Reaching into his wallet, he found a foil packet and quickly sheathed himself before plunging inside.

Lifting her slightly off the ground, Will rode her from behind while his hands splayed across her chest, molding and shaping her breasts. His fingers brought the soft mounds back to rock pebbles as he squeezed them tighter and tighter.

Lexie was right there with him, complementing his every thrust with a gentle sway of her hips. When Will gave one final thrust, they both fell against the door as each reached an apex quickly. Lexie was the first to recover, moving away from Will to search for her dress in the dark while Will slid to the floor. Finding it, she put it back on. She could only hope it was on the right way.

"You okay?" Lexie asked Will, bending down in front of Will, who was holding his head in his hands.

"I'm fine. And you?"

"Never better." Lexie winked. "We'd better go." Lexie held out her hand and helped Will off the floor. "Or your staff might send a posse out looking for you."

"Wow, what happened downstairs?" Lexie asked a short while later while they shared a steamy hot shower together in his loft.

"Hmmm." Will let the water trickle down his face before answering. "Quite frankly, I don't know what came over me, Lexie. I was a man obsessed. I hope I didn't scare you."

He knew he'd been a little intense. Lexie brought out the animal in him.

Lexie turned around to face him. "I kind of liked

it." She grinned. "You're so put together, Will. Who knew you had such a wild streak in you. Anyone could have come in there." Lexie smiled again, reaching for the shampoo on the dolly.

"Here, let me." Will took the bottle from her and poured a generous amount his hands. Bending her head back, Lexie allowed Will to wash her hair. She enjoyed the feel of his hands as they gently massaged and kneaded her scalp.

She sighed.

"Feels good?"

"Yes, oh, yes," Lexie said, moaning.

It didn't take long for them to end up right back where they had started earlier that evening. Except this time, they found their way to a bed.

A stream of sunlight forced an exhausted Lexie awake the next morning. Wiping her eyes, she was surprised to discover where she was.

Glancing down, Lexie took in the blue satin sheets and remembered. A smile crossed her face as she thought of her and Will making love until dawn. He was fast becoming very addictive to her system.

And Lexie couldn't have that. Things were moving too quickly. She had to slow things down. Sure, the sex was good, but they were headed for commitment and it had been a while since she'd tried that one!

Lexie was sliding out of bed when a hand reached over to halt her. Having been caught in the act again, Lexie backpedaled. "How about some coffee?" she suggested chipperly. "There's a Starbucks around the corner."

Will smiled. Had she been about to run out on him again? He hoped not. The more time they spent together, the more he knew Lexie was some kind of special lady.

"I'm game," Will responded, rubbing his eyes. "Give me a second to get dressed, okay?"

Fifteen minutes later, they were both at the Starbucks counter, Lexie ordering a low-fat vanilla latte, and Will a strong Colombian coffee and low-fat blueberry muffin. Once they'd completed their order, they took a seat outside underneath an umbrella and breathed in the clean morning air.

As she sat on the wrought-iron chair, Lexie eyed Will's muffin dangerously. "Hmmm, that looks delicious," she said, craving a little sugar.

"Want some?" Will asked, placing the warm muffin directly under her nose to tempt her.

"Mmmm, I'd love to, but I can't eat that stuff. No carbs." Lexie patted her flat stomach. "You want me to maintain my figure, dontcha?

"Oh, yes," Will replied and leaned over to plant a tender kiss on her lips.

Lexie quivered as she drank in his sweet, drugging kisses. "God, you have no idea what you do to me." The words came out of Lexie's mouth before she had time to give them pause. Will appeared dumbfounded at her unrehearsed statement. Never let them see your hand, Isabel always said. Lexie sighed.

Could she be falling for him, too? Will wondered. He stared at her for several long moments before taking a leap of faith. "The feeling is mutual," he said. A little nervous, he tore off a piece of muffin and plopped it in his mouth.

"So," Lexie was almost afraid to ask, "what are we doing here? Where is all this leading to?" she sipped on her latte.

Will shook his head. "I don't know. Can't we just enjoy it and see what happens?" Will wiped the foam off her upper lip and licked it with his fingers.

"Sounds good to me." Lexie smiled, hoping she'd made the right choice.

CHAPTER THIRTEEN

"What happened to your eye?" Will asked Ryan the next afternoon when he stopped by the house.

Ryan was lying on the sofa with an ice pack over his eye.

"Oh, this?" Ryan laughed nervously, pointing to his black-and-blue eye. "Some guy got a little rough on the basketball court."

"Let me take a look," said Will. Turning Ryan's jaw from side to side, he assessed the damage. It looked minimal, but he'd still better keep the ice pack on it.

"It's okay," Ryan replied when Will continued to stare at him. Avoiding Will's eyes, Ryan reached for the remote on the coffee table, but Will grabbed him by the arm.

"How'd it happen?"

Ryan felt awful lying to Will, but he was scared. J.T. had warned him that he'd be in a world of hurt if he told anyone about their little arrangement. But on the other hand, he was equally terrified of Will finding out. He would have a fit if he knew, but sometimes you had to do what you had to do.

"And you're sure that's all it was? A friendly game of

basketball?" Will asked. Ryan was acting awfully strange and it made him uneasy. He hadn't liked it when Ryan wasn't home the other night and Eve had no idea of his whereabouts.

Chewing on his bottom lip, Ryan tried to answer more confidently. "Sure, bro. It just got a little rowdy. One of the guys elbowed me in the eye when I tried to block his shot."

Will regarded him quizzically for a moment, trying to assess if he was telling the truth. But why should he worry? Ryan had never really given him one moment's trouble.

"You believe me, don't you?" Ryan asked.

"Of course I believe you. Listen, I gotta get going," Will replied. "I have plans with Lexie later on."

"Well, you'd better get a move on it then," Ryan said and clicked on the television.

Scratching her head, Lexie contemplated her next approach. She had to get this design right—she'd been working on it for more than an hour and it still perplexed her. She noticed Will staring at her from the opposite end of the couch and asked, "And what are you looking at?"

"You, my dear." Will smiled. "And your designs." Will leaned down and picked up several that were strewn across the floor. "These are wonderful. You're really very talented, Lex."

"Thanks, but you're a little bit biased," Lexie retorted. Though neither had said it aloud, somehow when they weren't looking they'd slipped into a relationship.

"'Cause we're sleeping together?" Will shook his

head fervently. "I know a gift when I see it and you've got it."

"You really think so?" Lexie inquired, holding one of her sketches to the light. It was great to have someone believe in her. Sure, her father and Sebastian loved her sketches, but the one person she longed to have faith in her always fell short. Isabel Thompson was not one to give compliments. The only comment she could muster about Lexie's designs were "They're pretty pictures." Isabel didn't see how anyone could ever make a living in fashion.

"Someday you're going to have your own line, Lexie. Just you wait and see." Will squeezed her thigh.

"From your lips to God's ear."

"One day it'll happen," Will said wholeheartedly. "Why? Because I have absolute faith in you, baby." He leaned in to plant a warm kiss on her lips.

"And what else do you have for me?" Lexie asked, sliding her hands into his shorts.

"Oh, that, too. . . ." Will's voice trailed off as Lexie's fingers began to work their magic.

Will was working on figures for Risqué when Lexie yelled at him from his closet. He wanted to make some adjustments to his presentation for the DuBoises before they went to North Avenue Beach for a little fun in the springtime. When he didn't respond right away, Lexie stormed into the living area with her hands on her hips.

"Will, I'm talking to you!" Lexie shouted from the doorway.

"Lexie," Will smiled as he glanced up from his laptop, "what's wrong?"

"I can't find my new bikini anywhere." Lexie pouted. "Have you seen it by chance?"

"I'm sorry, Lex. I haven't seen it," Will said before returning to his work.

Lexie stomped her foot. "That's just great. I live like a gypsy carrying my underwear in my purse traveling back and forth between our apartments and you couldn't care two hoots. Thanks a lot, Will."

Irked by his cool, aloof manner, Lexie stalked over to the kitchen and grabbed an apple juice out of the refrigerator. She hated being dismissed. Opening up a cabinet, Lexie found some chips and slammed it behind her. She munched loudly, waiting for a reaction from Will.

So she wants attention, Will thought. What was she, two years old? Taking a deep breath, Will finished his last calculation and shut down his laptop. He had an idea what the bigger issue was and knew instantly how to solve it. Reaching inside the drawer of his desk, Will removed a key off a keychain.

"Come here, gorgeous," Will ordered from his chair.

"No." Lexie refused. "I like it right here." She happily munched away on potato chips at the breakfast nook.

"Don't be mad," Will teased. "I have something for you."

Lexie instantly turned around to face him. "A gift?" Will watched as her eyes gleamed. "You know how much I love gifts." Lexie raced over into his lap. "Well, what is it?" she asked, looking behind his back. When she didn't see anything, a frown creased her mouth.

"It's this." Will dangled a key from his index finger. "In case you're wondering, it's a key to my apartment. Now you can keep some things here and not have to live pillar to post."

Nothing could have surprised her further. Will was

giving up his freedom by giving her a key. The key represented a commitment. Without his saying so, he'd revealed that he wasn't seeing anyone else. The tiny act truly touched her heart.

Will breathed a sigh of relief when after several long moments, Lexie finally snatched the key. He was starting to think he'd made a mistake when she said, "You do realize what you're giving up?"

Reaching for her hand, Will brought the small, delicate fingers to his lips and kissed them one by one. "I have everything I need right here."

Lexie's eyes welled with tears as a torrent of emotions washed over her. Was he for real? Had she really found her Prince Charming?

Later that afternoon, Lexie donned one of Bentley's new bikinis, a deep-plunge halter bra top with matching string bikini bottom. Knowing she looked hot, Lexie openly stared at herself in the mirror. Sure, there were some slight signs of cellulite creeping in— she would just have to work harder at the gym—but all in all she was holding up pretty good. Tying a sarong cover-up around her torso, she finished the look. Will caught sight of her when she ventured out into the hallway; the piercing look in his eyes caused her to shiver excitedly.

Growling, Will swept her up in his arms and pushed her back into the bedroom for a passionate kiss. Lexie smiled. They were definitely taking a detour before heading to the beach.

Hours later, exhausted from their day at the lake, Lexie flung herself onto her towel. After picking up a picnic basket from Will's local delicatessen that included fresh fruit, seafood salad, pâté, crackers, and meats and cheeses, along with wine, Perrier, and an assortment of sodas and juices, she and Will had headed to North Avenue Beach.

They'd taken full advantage of the good weather by sunbathing, playing volleyball, and swimming in the lake. After exhausting themselves, they'd waded in the cool water, allowing it to slick their skin deliciously. And when Will's mouth came down to claim hers in the coolness, Lexie relished every delicious moment. Will wasted no time nudging her thighs apart with his knees. She'd nearly lost it when he pressed his rising desire against her hot feminine flesh. She'd wanted to have him take her right there in the water, but they were not alone.

After reminiscing in her head about their wonderful day, Lexie rolled over onto her stomach and laid her head face-down against the bright orange terrycloth towel. She allowed the wind to dry her damp tresses and the sun's rays to caress her skin. Soon she felt the warmth of Will's hands as he firmly massaged her shoulders. Lexie didn't realize how stressed she'd been until the tension slowly ebbed from her body.

"Did I happen to tell you how great you look in your bikini, babe?" Will whispered, giving a cursory glance to her skimpy bathing suit.

Twisting around, Lexie squinted up at him. "No, I don't believe you did. Why don't you show me?" Lexie replied, reaching up to bring Will down onto the towel with her.

"I think that can be arranged," Will responded and nuzzled at her neck while his fingers lightly brushed the length of her arm.

A short while later, Lexie murmured, "Thank you for encouraging me to take a break. I really needed it. All the stress for the show was really getting to me."

"I know," Will replied. The day had all been to please his favorite girl.

"You do, don't you?" Lexie searched his face. "You think you know me that well, huh?"

"I do," Will answered matter-of-factly. Trailing a finger down the side of her face, Will stopped and pinched her nose. "I know because you and I are very similar creatures."

"Oh, really?" Lexie raised an eyebrow.

"Yes, really. We're both very determined, passionate individuals with an all-consuming desire to succeed, whatever the cost. Maybe because we both had very domineering mothers who we've been at odds with all our lives and who have never believed in us, we're both still searching for something more. Something that always seems to be a little out of our reach."

"I wonder if we'll ever get it?" asked Lexie.

Will brought her hand to his lips and kissed it. "We will, baby. I've no doubt in my mind."

The next few weeks sped by in a frenzy of activity as Lexie finalized the last-minute details from clothes fittings for the models to sending out the invitations. The production and art staff had designed an amazing stage and fabulous backdrops.

While reviewing the fashion-show script at her desk, Lexie realized there was still more to be done. The runway was in the final stages of being built and the models were due to arrive later at Millennium for a full runthrough to coordinate the choreography and staging.

Tickets had been sold to the public through Ticket-Master, with the proceeds from the show being donated to the Children's Memorial Hospital AIDS wing. Of course, Bentley's wasn't interested in the proceeds, but rather all the free publicity their donation would provide. The show would no doubt be in the paper and *Chicago Magazine.*

Invitations were sent to every major media outlet in Chicago, from the *Tribune* to fashion mags in Chicago. WLS television station was even a running a segment on Bentley's in their ten o'clock broadcast the day before the show. *Women's Wear Daily* was set to cover the show, even though it wasn't taking place at Bentley's flagship store in New York. Lexie had asked one of her old contacts to twist their editor's arm and send a reporter. The editor had agreed, provided Lexie comp said reporter with an outfit for the show. Lexie hadn't minded one bit. What better way to market their season? Several influential society matrons in the Chicago area were also due to attend.

Lexie was beside herself with excitement. The evening was sure to be a success, and part of that reason was Will. He had been instrumental.

Will had a fabulous idea to simulcast the fashion show on Bentley's Web site. Lauren had been thrilled with the idea, and a media blitz was well underway. Sure, she'd thought of including the usual Paris couture themes—luaus, country rodeos, Las Vegas nights—but Will had finished it off and brought Bentley's show into the twenty-first century.

Bentley's had never done anything like this before and was a little bit cautious, preferring to stick with its usual couture fashion show, but it was time for a change and Lexie was just the diva to provide it.

Feeling a presence behind her at her desk, Lexie turned around to find Sydney's blue eyes piercing her from the door.

"It's down to the wire now." Sydney smiled. "I've heard the rumors. You've caused quite a buzz. I sure hope you don't fall flat on your ass."

"You would love it if I did, wouldn't you?"

"Your failure is another person's gain," Sydney replied, walking away.

Lexie stared at her retreating figure and vowed to knock the little bird off her high and mighty perch.

CHAPTER FOURTEEN

When Lexie arrived at Millennium the following day, the stage was already transformed into a pharaoh's palace. The models would enter through the palace doors, decked out in varying Cleopatra looks, and walk along a runway paved in gold.

Pharaoh's guards were set to greet the distinguished guests, benefactors, members of the press, and unsuspecting public to their seats. The caterers were already on hand setting up a lavish display complete with an ice sculpture of a pharaoh, a champagne pyramid, and a decadent feast of Mediterranean cuisine.

The models, stylists, hairdressers, and makeup artists were already preparing backstage in the dressing room while dressers remained on hand to help models during outfit changes.

The production crew had arrived several hours earlier to set up the chairs and props and correct any lighting or music issues. Now, as Lexie looked around, she was a nervous wreck. What if something went wrong?

Lexie was checking her notepad for last-minute details when a flurry of feminine *oohs* and *aahs* prompted her attention elsewhere.

Will sauntered into the club clad in a black tux and fitted white tuxedo shirt that in no way hid the muscular physique and six-pack lying underneath. Lexie understood their disquiet. Will had an undeniable presence, an aura that was difficult to resist, and she didn't have to. He was all hers.

Lexie longed for one of his prolonged kisses, but she needed to go backstage before the guests arrived and allow the hairdresser and makeup artist to work on her hair and face. Tonight was a big night and she had to look as sensational as her models.

When Will noticed her, he turned and gave her one of those grins of his that she'd come to love. His eyes took her in from head to toe, but his brown nose scrunched at her straight tresses and clean face.

"Soon," she mouthed.

Even without makeup, Will was awed by Lexie's beauty all the way from across the room. The woman looked beautiful even when she wasn't trying to. Will smiled to himself. He was truly smitten. Somehow Lexie had eased herself into the very core of his soul and now he had to have her and not just the tiny piece she was offering. He wanted all of her. It surprised him to realize it; Lexie had indeed stolen a piece of his heart.

Lexie was giving her assistant instructions when she felt a pair of strong arms around her middle and a smooth, sexy voice whispered, "Hey, babe."

"Hey, you." Lexie spun around to give him a delicious kiss. It was short and sweet. Still, the waitresses and models hanging out in the dining room gave her withering looks.

"Hmmm, I like that greeting," Will whispered against her ear. His mustache tickled her neck, sending tiny shivers up and down Lexie's spine. "But why aren't you ready?" Will touched her unmade face.

"Because I have to make sure everything's perfect."

"Nervous?"

"Are you kidding?" Lexie swatted him on the shoulder. "This event could single-handedly either make or break my career. Of course I'm nervous." She had waited a lifetime for this moment. To prove what she was made of.

"Don't worry, Lex. Everything will be fine. I have absolute faith in your leadership abilities. You've worked hard to make this night a success."

In Will's eyes she found peace and serenity. It was moments like this when Will showed the kinder, sensitive side that surprised Lexie the most. Lexie was sure not many women had the opportunity to see it, but for some reason he had chosen to share that side with her. It meant the world to her that he believed in her.

Standing on her tiptoes, Lexie leaned forward to place a kiss on his cheek. "Thank you, Will. I needed to hear that."

"You can't come," Ryan whispered into his cell phone. He'd left all the brouhaha over that hot chick's fashion show to call J.T. and beg him not to come to the club tonight. Millennium would be crawling with reporters looking for a story or an angle and Ryan didn't want any trouble.

"Forget about it," J.T. answered him. "Friday night's been one of our best nights at the club."

"J.T., there is a big show going on here tonight."

"Yeah, I heard your brother agreed to host some girlie fashion show. What's up with that?"

"Never mind, you just can't come tonight. The

place is going to be crowded with folks. You're sure to get caught."

"Hey, the more the merrier."

Ryan shook his head. How was he going to convince J.T. not to come to the party? It could ruin everything.

While Lexie manned the slew of models backstage, Will set about making sure everything else was perfect on his end. He'd checked with the caterers and everything was right on schedule. His staff that he'd volunteered for the event was already bedecked in pharaoh attire. He would never hear the end of that one!

Leaving the kitchen, Will went in search of Ryan. Will noticed that Ryan seemed quiet and sullen lately, and whenever he went over to the house, his brother was never there. Their mother always said he was at the library studying or at basketball practice, but Will didn't buy that for a second. Something was definitely up and he was going to find out what it was.

Climbing the stairs to his loft, Will entered and found Ryan whispering on his phone.

"Ryan, what's going on?"

Startled, Ryan dropped his cell and it crashed onto the tile floor. "Crap!" Ryan bent down to pick it up, but Will snatched it out of his hands.

"Give it to me." Will looked the phone over, pressing the arrow keys, but the front display would not turn on.

"Is it broken?" Ryan asked.

Will couldn't tell, but then he saw a hairline crack in the front display.

"I'm sorry, Will." Ryan moved back and forth on his heels. "I don't know what happened."

"It's okay, Ryan. I'll just get you a new one, but that's the least of my worries. I want to know what's going on with you."

Will had graciously agreed to allow Ryan to watch the show from his window in the loft. What could it hurt to allow his kid brother to see some women dressed in skimpy clothes? Hell, he saw more than that on television these days. Will searched Ryan's eyes for a sign of what was bothering his baby brother, but found none. Ryan's eyes were clouded.

"What do you mean?"

"C'mon, Ryan, I've noticed your odd behavior lately. I mean, look at you." Will pointed at Ryan. "Your eyes are red, your hands are clammy, and you're a wreck. What's going on?"

"I've got a lot going on, is all. You know, chores, school, b-ball, and now this job. Sometimes it's all too much." Ryan avoided Will's eyes.

"Is there anything I can do?" Will asked. Maybe he was putting too much pressure on the boy, expecting too much.

Before Ryan could answer, Jerome rang him from downstairs. "Will, you're needed down here."

"All right, we'll finish this discussion later, okay?" Will patted Ryan's tense shoulders and left the room. Ryan, on the other hand, breathed a sigh of relief.

The dressing room was a mass of activity. Models clad in lace and satin Bentley's lingerie were seated in director's chairs while their hair was blow-dried, curled, waved, updoed, twisted, or made into any other outrageous style the hairdressers could come up with. Makeup stylists finished their effects.

Surveying the room, Lexie looked around for her

beleaguered assistant Mina. She had sent her to rever-
ify that all the items and accessories had made it from
Bentley's and were all accounted for. Four premier designers would showcase their spring collection, one of
which was D&G. Lexie was thrilled to add Dolce & Gabbana to their store. Bentley's had tried for years to convince them to add Bentley's to their repertoire, with no
success. And now Lexie had succeeded where others
had failed. It was quite a coup for her.

As she walked past a model, Lexie stopped and
touched the hairstylist's arm. "Lydia, I don't like the
hair. Try something else."

"Sure thing, Ms. Thompson."

"I don't want demure. I want diva." Lexie gestured
with her hands. "I want goddesslike. Like that model."

Lexie pointed to Carly, whose hair and makeup
were almost complete. Her usually gorgeous mass of
red hair was piled high on her head. "See her? That's
what I want," Lexie ordered.

Finally Lexie saw Mina coming toward her, looking
frazzled. "Where have you been? I've been looking—"
Her assistant's usually sunny smile was replaced with
one of sheer terror. Something was wrong. "What is it?"
Lexie said. "Just say it." Lexie noticed that Mina's bottom lip trembled.

"The Vera Wang collection is missing."

"What do you mean missing?" Lexie's voice cracked.

"I mean it's not here. It's not at Bentley's. It's not
anywhere. It's MIA." Mina's eyes brimmed with tears.

All the air in the room suddenly seemed to dissipate
and Lexie's legs nearly collapsed under her. Mina
helped her to a seat nearby as Lexie struggled to
catch her breath.

"Are you okay?" Mina asked, her voice full of
concern.

"Oh, my God, oh, my God," Lexie said starting to hyperventilate.

"Someone get me a bag!" Mina yelled at anybody that was listening. Within minutes Lexie was breathing through a brown paper bag and trying to get in control of her faculties.

She couldn't afford to let the models and crew see her crack any farther under pressure or they would lose confidence in her and the whole show would fall apart.

"Are you sure?" Lexie asked finally.

Reluctantly, Mina answered. "Lexie, I've searched everywhere. Millennium, storage, the warehouse, even your office. And they're just not there."

"Where could they be?" Lexie racked her brain. The blood in her veins ran cold. "What am I going to do? There are . . ." Lexie looked down at her watch, ". . . less than two hours to go and I don't have my premier collection!"

"Lexie, I'm sorry." Mina's voice faltered. Lexie saw tears fall down her poor assistant's cheeks. "I should have taken better care."

"Please don't cry on me, Mina. I can't deal with that right now. Just find Christian," Lexie barked. "Get him in here."

"Lexie, there's women in here."

"Trust me, Mina. Christian has no interest in any woman standing here. Now, go! And find Will!" Lexie yelled at her retreating figure. Lexie needed to regroup, and who better than Will and her best friend to help her figure all this out.

Minutes later, Christian rushed through the curtains and flew into Lexie's arms. "Darling, what is it? You look as white as a ghost."

"Chris, please." Lexie stood up and pulled Christian

into a nearby corner. "The Vera Wang collection is gone. What am I going to do?" Her voice broke slightly.

"The first thing you're going to do is rip your production assistant a new one for letting this happen," Christian said with a huff. This was the happiest day in Lexie's life; he couldn't believe this was happening.

"Christian, it's not her fault," Lexie said, defending her assistant. "I'm in charge. I should have ensured the collection was here."

"Don't beat yourself up. There's no sense in crying about spilled milk now. We've gotta be creative instead. Let's put our thinking caps on and come up with a solution." Christian grabbed a program from the makeup artist's table. "What about premiering a current collection that's a little less fabulous than Vera, and save the Dolce & Gabbana for last?"

"Chris, that would require reworking the whole program and I can't afford to do that. Not at this hour." Lexie tried to think of another idea. But at the moment, fear was taking over. Lexie saw her career going down in flames.

"What about your designs?" Will offered. He'd seen the commotion when Mina came out and immediately knew something was wrong. This show meant everything to Lexie and if there was anything he could do, he would be there. He'd quickly walked backstage past the curious stares of the half-clad models in the room. Will had no eyes for them. His mind was on singular focus: Lexie. "Lexie, it's going to be okay," Will said, wrapping her in his arms and giving her a firm hug.

"Will, I can't put my designs out there. They're not finished yet. There's still so much to do."

"Hogwash," Christian joined in. "They're ready."

"Listen to me." Will's hands grabbed either side of

her face. "I've seen your designs, Lexie, and they're as good as any I've seen on a fashion runway."

"I don't know. . . ."

"Yes, you do. Your work will speak for itself." Will was a true believer in destiny. Sometimes fate had a funny way of forcing you along and tonight was no different. Fate was handing her the chance of a lifetime and he'd be damned if she didn't take it. "The only one who's not ready is you, Lexie."

"But the program . . ."

"Forget the program—a new line will throw the press and guests completely off-kilter and only add to the appeal. But first things first, you've got to tell Vera's publicist. She's in the audience right now."

Lexie laughed bitterly. "What about my boss?"

"She'll have to see it unfold like everyone else."

"I don't know, guys, this is a huge risk. If my designs fall flat with the audience, it could destroy my fashion career before it has even started."

"Or it could be the start of something new that leads you in the direction of your dreams," Will said.

"Aren't you the optimist?"

Will laughed. "In life, you have to be."

"All right, we'll have to hustle," Lexie conceded. She was going to put her career and reputation on the line tonight, come what may. "Christian, I need you to go back to my apartment. You know where everything is. I need you to bring back the entire collection. We'll work with the shoes and accessories when you get here."

"I'm on it." Christian rushed through the curtains.

"Mina, Will, could you help me look around and double-check that the collection isn't here?"

"It's the least I can do," Mina responded.

Twenty minutes later they all came up empty; after

rummaging through all the wardrobe, the collection was still missing.

"Oh, Will." Lexie crumbled onto the tile floor in a heap.

"I'm a failure! How could I have let this happen?"

"Don't give up yet, Lexie. There's still time to spare. Listen, baby." Will picked her off the floor and grabbed her by the shoulders. "You've got to pull yourself together. You've got to prepare a new program for your collection and finish your hair and makeup. Now get a move on it." Will patted her on the bottom and pushed her forward.

"Give me some time, okay?"

"I'll give you five minutes while I go check on some of the production staff."

Stepping through the curtain, Will looked for Sebastian. If anyone could put a smile on her face and get her back on track, it was him. He knew Sebastian wasn't a cheerleader of his; Sebastian had been to Millennium a few times and had noticed that Will was quite the ladies' man, so he was sure it had come as a surprise when Lexie showed up to Sunday dinner with a smooth club owner like him on her arm. But Will had endured. He survived a Sunday grilling session by Lexie's mother and that was no small feat, and despite initial misgivings, Sebastian had treated him fairly and now Lexie would need her brother's support more than ever.

The moment Will walked through the curtain onto the stage, he noticed that more than a few guests had arrived. Searching the crowd, Will found Sebastian schmoozing with wealthy widow Camille Bartlett. Due to her late husband's unfortunate demise in a car accident, Camille was now a multimillionaire. She would be a great benefactor for tonight's event. Apparently, Sebastian had the same idea.

"Excuse me, Mrs. Bartlett," Will said. "Would you mind terribly if stole this guy away for some backstage issues?"

"No, of course not, young man," Camille replied. "And you are?"

Ever the diplomat, Sebastian introduced him. "Camille, allow me to introduce William Kennedy, owner of Millennium."

"Oh." Camille batted her eyelashes. "You're the man all the ladies are talking about."

"My reputation is a little overblown."

"Hmmm, I'm sure it's well worth it," Camille replied, open staring at Will. "It was quite gracious of you to agree to host tonight's charity event at your club."

"Yes, well, Lexie is quite convincing," Will replied, annoyed that Mrs. Bartlett was holding him up.

"And where is our lovely hostess?"

"Backstage putting the finishing touches on her hair and makeup. If you'll excuse us." Will pulled Sebastian away from Camille's curious gaze.

"What's going on, Will?" Sebastian whispered as Will pushed him through the crowd. "That woman could help my sister. And give a great big fat donation at the end of tonight's event."

"Well, there won't be any event if you don't get back there and pull Lexie together."

Not waiting for an answer, Sebastian ran backstage.

"I'm ruined," Lexie wailed when he appeared. She spilled all the ghastly details to Sebastian including the missing collection and Will's solution to use her own designs.

"I think it's a fabulous idea, Lex." Sebastian smiled. He had an easy, laid-back vibe that could always soothe Lexie even in the most tense of times. He knew she needed reassurance. She was undertaking a very risky move, albeit a brilliant one, that he hoped would work in her favor.

"Why in the world would someone steal dresses for a charity event?"

"I wondered the very same thing myself." Will returned with a decanter of sherry and encouraged Lexie take a sip. "Quite frankly, it sounds like sabotage to me."

Lexie face shot up. A suspect instantly came to mind. One with a motive for seeing the fashion show turn out disastrously. Sydney. That she-devil! thought Lexie.

"If it's anyone in my club, Lexie," Will continued, "I'll have their hides, you can believe that."

Wiping the tears from her face, Lexie rose from the floor. "You won't have to do that. I think I know who did this. And she'd better watch out. Thank you so much, Will. I'm much better now."

"You're most welcome. Is there anything else I can do?"

Looking in a nearby mirror, Lexie replied, "No. But I can sure use some work." With purpose, Lexie walked over to her favorite hairstylist and said, "Finish me up."

Will watched the hairstylist furiously work her magic. He was glad to see the old Lexie coming back to the forefront, to see the fighter he'd come to love so well. Wait, did he just think *love*? Could he have fallen in love with Lexie without his knowing it?

He didn't have much chance to think about it because he was pushed aside by the makeup artist who'd come to work on Lexie. Dazed, Will walked toward the front stage.

"Will, Christian is due to arrive with my collection.

Can you see that he's able to come through the back entrance?" Lexie called out.

Taking his head out of the clouds, Will sprung into action. Love he knew nothing about, but fixing problems was his forte.

Dropping the trash into the receptacle, Ryan turned around, as he walked to go back inside the loft, he saw several shadowy figures ambling toward him.

His heart raced. He'd told those dumb fools he couldn't let them in tonight. Why were they here? Will was here tonight!

J.T. slithered up beside him. "What's up, RK?"

"Hey, man." Ryan tried to sound cool even though he was scared as hell. "What are you guys doing here?"

"Listen up, we heard a lotta hype about this event your brother is having tonight. He must have a sunk a lotta money into this thing. Figured we could get in on some of the action."

"Naw, man, no can do." Ryan backed away and started walking toward the door. "You see, Will's girl, her company is paying for the whole thing. I can't have you guys here tonight. My brother could get into a lot of trouble."

"Listen, Ryan." J.T. grabbed Ryan by the collar. "You musta misunderstood me. I'm not asking, I'm *telling* you, that me and the fellas are coming. We're good enough to hang out with all those high-society folks. So we'll see you tonight, my brotha." J.T. put his arm around Ryan's shoulder. "You gon' let us in tonight."

Ryan didn't want another busted lip. Reluctantly he let them in, provided they stayed in the men's restroom and left as soon as the event was over.

J.T. agreed to the proviso. Trembling, Ryan closed the door behind him to the men's restroom and prayed J.T. kept his word.

Lexie was ready. Her mass of black hair had been stylishly layered and now hung in big curls down her back. Her makeup consisted of dark eyes and sensuously red lipstick; now she was ready for display. While the hairdresser and makeup artist had worked their magic, Lexie had managed to finalize the sequence of her collection in her head and scribbled a few notes for her commentary. She was sure all the models and stylists wondered what the fuss was all about, but she wasn't giving out details. The less people who knew about the switch, the better.

"Help! help!" Christian yelled as he came through the back entrance carrying an armful of wardrobe bags.

Lexie grinned from to ear to ear when she caught sight of her collection. Having slaved over each handmade piece for the last six months, Lexie never dreamed that they'd ever see the light of day, but tonight the runway was their final destination. Jumping off her director's chair, Lexie rushed forward to help Christian with the bags. "I was starting to worry," she whispered.

"Have I ever let you down?" he asked. At Lexie's silence, Christian added, "Well, then, I ain't about to start now. So come on, we got to look these over and figure out what comes first." Christian blew a kiss skyward and thanked his lucky stars that Lexie lived only twenty minutes from Millennium or it would have been all over.

"Mina!" Lexie yelled over to her assistant. "Bring that steamer over here and steam all these outfits."

With barely a half hour to go, Lexie and Christian forced the models to try on her designs for a quick fitting. Bentley's seamstress was on hand for a few quick adjustments, but there wasn't much time left before the show.

"I also brought this." Christian held up Nia's wedding gown.

"Christian, no!" Lexie cried.

"Every fashion show has a signature showstopper, one wedding gown to finish off the night," Christian continued. "I know that no bride wants her wedding dress debuted before the big day, but I'm sure Nia would understand."

"Understand what?" Nia asked, coming forward to join their small huddle. Then she noticed the translucent bag Christian was holding up. "Lex, what's my wedding dress doing here?" Nia grabbed the bag out of Christian's arms.

Christian understood her haughtiness and stood back.

"Nia, under normal circumstances I would never ask you this, but I need to borrow your dress for the show."

A look of sheer horror crossed Nia's face and Lexie was overcome with guilt. She hated doing this to her at the last minute, but there was no other way. Lexie slowly recounted the happenings of the last two hours.

"I can't believe it," Nia said. She shook her head and clutched Lexie's hands in hers. "I'm so sorry, Lex. This was supposed to be your big night."

"And it still will be. With your help." Lexie patted Nia's hand. "I'm going to use my collection in place of Vera Wang's."

"Lexie, are you sure? It's a huge risk."

"Don't give me that look." Lexie stood up, dropping her hands. She had to have Nia's blessing to use the dress. Taking a deep breath, Lexie sat back down. "Nia, I need a showstopper and your wedding dress is it. Your dress will spotlight my whole collection. It'll show what I'm capable of. I know this is a lot to ask—" Lexie's voice broke. "But please, Nia, I need your blessing."

Nia's eyes widened and a lone tear fell down her cheeks. It was her wedding dress and no one was supposed to see it until the big day, but at the moment her best friend needed it more than she did. "Okay." Her voice was barely audible, but Lexie heard it.

"Christian, take this dress." Lexie grabbed the wardrobe bag. "Have it lightly steamed."

Christian began to walk away, when Lexie called out: "Guard it with your life." Smiling, Christian crossed his heart and headed to find Mina.

Wiping her face, Nia grabbed Lexie's Badgley Mischka dress from a chair and stepped forward. "Okay, it's time to finish you up. You only have fifteen minutes left."

"Thank you," Lexie mouthed the words to Nia before going behind the screen to dress herself. Lexie had no idea what awaited her tonight, but she would go down fighting.

CHAPTER FIFTEEN

Lexie walked through the palace doors on the stage fifteen minutes later looking like Cleopatra herself. Dressed in a long, flowing toga dress with a golden roped belt and diamond-studded mules, Lexie looked the part of the beautiful, flirty seductress ready to woo the crème de la crème of Chicago society.

Searching the crowd, Lexie smiled when she found Will beside the bar cheering her on, Sebastian at the end of the runway photographing models, Nia and Damon clapping at a front table, and her boss, Lauren, sitting with the possible saboteur of tonight's event, Sydney. Her parents were nowhere in sight, but alas, the show must go on.

Lexie tapped the microphone to get the crowd's attention. The noise level soon died down and Lexie began her monologue.

"I would like to thank everyone for coming out to Bentley's Tenth Annual Spring Fashion Show. It is my pleasure to be your hostess this evening." Lexie paused while the audience clapped customarily. "And as all of you know, the staff at Children's Memorial Hospital work every day to saves the lives of our most precious possession, our children. Because of their dedication, we are here. The money raised tonight will go to the Children's Memorial Hospital's AIDS wing. And Bentley's will donate all proceeds from tonight's events to their campaign. I hope everyone will reach deep in their pockets to help make this event a great success. I thank you all for coming and let's get on with the show.

"We will be premiering three of Bentley's spring collections this evening, Dolce & Gabbana, Gucci, and Donna Karan's DKNY."

A stunned silence ensued when Lexie didn't include Vera Wang, as per the program. Heads wagged, including Lauren's, as everyone wondered if Lexie had noticed the faux paus.

Lexie continued on. "All of tonight's fashions were generously donated from these designers and are available for bidding this evening. A silent auction is available in the Nefertiti room for you to bid on the clothes seen this evening. Now sit back and relax. We've got an amazing show for you."

Soon the models hit the stage. Sashaying through the palace doors and gliding down the runaway, they were decked in Cleopatra wigs and makeup to show off the best of the Bentley's spring collection. Lexie had chosen every piece showcased this evening and had prepared a small blurb on each outfit.

"From casual sports wear to fine, elegant dresses, the Dolce & Gabbana, Gucci, and Donna Karan's DKNY collections offer a wide range of styles to suit your needs," Lexie informed the eager crowd.

The audience and press appeared to be loving every minute and the models played up to it, but the pièce de résistance was yet to come.

Lexie broke for a brief intermission to give the audience a chance to mingle, bid on clothes previously seen on the runway, and to listen to the sights and sounds of local jazz singer Ethel Andrews.

Lexie's skirt rustled as she made her way down the stage steps. She was on a mission. Several patrons stopped her along the way, offering their support and thank yous for a wonderful evening. She found the source of her anxiety waiting next to Will at the bar.

Holding her head high with pride, Lexie walked to her parents. "Mom, Dad." Lexie breathed a sigh of relief. Coming toward them, she offered her father a hug first.

"What about me? Don't I get one?"

Looking back and forth between the two men, Lexie weighed her thoughts before leaning in to quickly squeeze her mother's shoulders. "Thanks for coming."

"We wouldn't miss it, baby girl. You've done a fine job." Lexie saw the pride in her father's eyes and it filled her with joy.

"Yes, it must have taken quite a lot to put this together," her mother replied, glancing at the tables filled with Mediterranean delicacies. "I'm sure the caterers were a great help."

"Isabel, don't start," Wesley warned.

Lexie smiled. She wasn't surprised. She was waiting for her mother's first dig, but her father jumping to her defense so vocally—now, that surprised her.

"Would you care for a glass of wine, sherry, or cognac, perhaps?" Will suggested from her side.

"I don't drink," Isabel commented. "I like to keep my head and my mind clear, thank you very much."

Taking a deep breath, Will replied smoothly, "Of course. And you, Mr. Thompson?"

"I would love a glass of cognac, if you have it."

"I have a great vintage in the cellar. Jerome?" Will motioned to his bartender to take care of the order.

"This is some place you have here," Lexie's father said. Lexie appreciated her father's attempts at polite conversation while her mother stood ramrod straight, seemingly unimpressed by her surroundings.

"If you'll excuse me, I have to make my rounds. Will, would you mind escorting my parents to their table?" Lexie winked at him and blew him a kiss before turning on her heel and disappearing into the crowd.

Will caught the wink. So she was leaving her adorable mother to him? She knew he'd prefer to check on the club, but he acquiesced for the woman he adored.

After all the collections premiered, Lexie began what she hoped was her finest hour.

"And finally, what you've all been waiting for." Lexie waved her arm from the podium toward the palace door. "I introduce to you, the Lexie Thompson collection."

The crowd was stunned. Expecting to hear Vera Wang, a rush of speculation ensued, but all gossip died when the first model burst through the palace doors wearing the best in her designs.

Immediately Lexie introduced her first moderate-wear design. "Check out this first piece. It's a salmon crocheted tunic with sequined trim and spaghetti straps accompanied by white corded crop-top pants. It's a perfect outfit for the evening out on the town. Finish the look with a pair of stylish drop earrings and open-toed, rhinestone buckled shoes."

The model strutted down the runway before stopping at the end for effect. Photographers were up and out of their seats, eager for the first shot of the mysterious Lexie Thompson collection.

"Get ready for spring in our second ensemble, a rose front halter and pinstriped flat-front pants. Open-toed, crisscrossed, ankle wrap sandals and shell earrings complete the outfit."

The model sashayed to the end of catwalk and paused for effect before continuing. "Our third model is wearing a cascading chiffon, ruffled miniskirt and fitted key-hole, knitted black and white top.

"In the mood for sassy? Try out this, a strapless button-down shirt with a bow above the chest, available in raspberry or azure with a knee-length satin skirt. Don't forget your bejeweled thong sandals made of Italian leather with pyramid heels."

Carly appeared next in one of Lexie's sassiest outfits, wearing black leather pants and a sheer black lace top with a side slit at the shoulders. "Don't forget, the look isn't complete without those studded black mules," Lexie added as Carly walked down the catwalk, leaving the crowd dazzled.

Lexie waited with bated breath as the first round of models neared completion. Critics and patrons alike were quiet, stunned into submission. Did they hate the collection? If this was her only show, then she would finish it with a bang.

Out of her peripheral vision, she noticed Lauren standing up. *Boy, am I in trouble,* Lexie thought. But there was no turning back now.

Suddenly one critic popped out of his chair and applauded her designs. Before long the entire audience followed in succession. Buoyed, Lexie continued to the next round: evening wear.

"Our first piece of evening wear is an elegant vanilla strapless dress with bone lace overlay and a fitted bodice. It's perfect for that informal occasion. Next up, we have a paisley print, silk chiffon gown teamed with a matching stole. Halter-style twisted bodice, back zip. Try this ensemble for an evening at the opera."

Pausing, Lexie allowed the model to pose for one final photograph before continuing. "Discover the amazing feel of silk in this crinkle ombré dress with beaded single shoulder strap, side seam, and asymmetrical hem. Or this sequined black flapper dress with a vintage velvet swing coat matched with a pair of Manolo Blahnik satin mules. Now doesn't that look fabulous!"

As the final evening-wear model cleared the stage, Lexie gave them a warm round of applause. She was so proud to see all her hard work displayed on their lithe bodies.

Finally the lights went dark and the spotlight shown on a lone figure on the stage.

"And now, ladies and gentleman, I give you the showstopper." Shock and surprise, registered on Will's face when he saw Nia glide down the runway wearing none other than her own wedding dress.

He applauded wildly over Lexie's brilliant thinking.

As the crowd moved forward to look at the biggest surprise of the season, Will caught a glimpse of the gang of thugs from around his mother's neighborhood. Surely his eyes were deceiving him? Will blinked several times, but what he saw before him did not disappear. Will was furious. How the hell did some underage kids get inside his club?

Ryan pulled J.T. into the restroom. "What are you doing out there? I told you my brother is out there. He probably already saw you. You've got to get out of here."

"I don't think so." J.T. got up in Ryan's face. "I'm

doing good business tonight." J.T. inclined his head to the corner where a white man dressed in a tuxedo was whispering to one of J.T.'s crew. "And I'm not going to let a snide little preppy-school b-ball player get in my way."

Ryan saw the young white professional man, who appeared to be in his twenties, hand one of J.T.'s crew a hundred-dollar bill and hide a small bag of white powder in his breast pocket before rushing out of the restroom.

"I can't let you do this anymore. This is over."

"It's over right now," said a strong masculine voice.

At the sound of his brother's voice behind him, all the color drained out of Ryan's face and he turned beet red. Ryan slowly whirled around and came to face the brother he loved so much. Ryan hadn't even heard him enter. He wasn't surprised when he saw disillusionment in those dark depths.

"What has gotten into you, young man?" Will roared from the doorway.

Even now, Will could hardly believe what he saw with his very own eyes. His own brother was behind letting these criminals into his place of business? Ryan knew how much Millennium meant to him. Millennium was his heart and soul. He'd put everything into the place. His sweat, his blood, and his tears. And his brother had systematically set out to destroy that dream. Anger burned in the back of Will's throat, but he found the words to spit out. "How could you do this, Ryan . . . bring this . . . this trash into my club? And let them sell drugs, no less?" Will, too, caught a glimmer of white powder before the thug hid it in a nearby bag.

"Will, I . . ." No words came to Ryan's mind. What could he say? That he was tired of being picked on?

That he feared for his life? It all seemed empty when faced with the sort of betrayal he'd committed.

"What? Nothing to say?" Will yelled as disgust filled his stomach. "I'm calling the authorities right now."

Will reached for his cell phone, but never made it. At the mention of the police, J.T.'s crew ran for the door. When asked to recall what happened later, Will couldn't say. Everything happened in slow motion. One moment he was yelling at Ryan and the next he was rushing toward the three guys in J.T.'s crew, trying to catch them before they made it out of the club. He caught one of them by the collar. The rest went scurrying out of the room like the rats they were, but not before top dog, J.T., launched a knife into Ryan's middle. Will saw the wide-eyed look of fear on his brother's face moments before he crumpled to the floor. Will raced toward him, but not before he caught J.T.'s grin as he ran out the club's side door, leaving it swinging in the wind.

"Ryan!" Will cried and gripped Ryan's unconscious body in his arms. Ripping off his tuxedo jacket, Will tried to stop the bleeding, but blood gushed from the open wound. "Help! help!" Will cried out to anyone who was listening.

Ignoring the sirens blaring in the distance, Lexie basked in the limelight of the press. Even after Nia had left the stage, the crowd was still on its feet, giving Lexie a standing ovation. But instead of dissipating, the sirens came closer and closer, until eventually a herd of firefighters and ambulance workers burst the doors of Millennium.

A sinking filling formed in Lexie's gut and she rushed offstage, oblivious to her surroundings. The press smelled a story and chaos ensued as they followed her to the men's restroom. When she arrived, Lexie was shocked by what she found there. Will was holding Ryan in his arms while pressing his jacket into Ryan's middle. That's when Lexie saw it, the blood staining Will's white tuxedo shirt.

Fear knotted in her stomach. "Oh, my . . ." She covered her mouth. *Oh, please God, please don't let Will be hurt, too.*

As if sensing her thoughts, a medic turned to see if Will was injured, but Will pushed him away. "It's not me, you idiot. My brother's the one who's hurt, just work on him."

Perturbed, the medic turned his focus back on Ryan and, for once in her life, Lexie wished she was not in the spotlight, because now she was finding it very difficult to escape the eager press. Several reporters were firing questions and several cameras were aimed right at her. Unfortunately, this press was not in Will's favor. They wanted to know if she had any idea that Millennium was a cover for a drug-dealing business.

Will ran his hands over his head as he watched the medics try to stop the bleeding. He just didn't know how they'd gotten to this point. How had his little brother mixed up with that punk's crew? How could he have let those drug dealers into his club? All these were questions he desperately needed answers to and only his brother could answer them.

Soon the medics were picking Ryan up and placing him on a stretcher. The crew transported Ryan into the ambulance at the side of the curb outside. Dazed, Will followed close behind them, looking completely disheveled.

"I'm right behind you, Will!" Lexie cried out to him,

but she doubted he heard her as the sirens blared all around. The policemen prevented Lexie from telling him everything was going to be okay. It didn't take long for reporters to push her aside as each scrambled to get a shot of Will.

When Lexie returned to the main room, she found the place in utter chaos, but she didn't care. Searching the crowd of policeman, guests, and onlookers, Lexie looked for Sebastian and Christian. Pushing through, she found them fielding questions from the press.

When the reporters discovered she was back in the room, several descended on her like vultures. "Ms. Thompson, were you aware of the drug ring going on at Millennium? Are you and Mr. Kennedy an item?"

Lexie's answer was a quick, "No comment." She threw a pleading look for help at Sebastian, who immediately came flying over to save her. Although slender and not much of a shield, Sebastian wrapped his arms around Lexie and pushed her through to backstage. "That's enough, guys, back off and give the lady some room."

Christian followed behind them.

"Thanks for the save, Sebastian." Lexie said. "Those people are animals. They smell a new story and they are out for blood."

"How's Ryan?" Sebastian asked. "Is it serious?"

"I don't know." Lexie's eyes welled up with tears. "Which is why I need your help." Her voice faltered as she tried to catch her breath. "I . . . I need you to finish up for me. I've got to get to the hospital."

"You've got it, sis." Sebastian gave her an enormous hug and tightly squeezed her hands. They were as cold as ice. Sebastian had never seen Lexie this way. It dawned on him that Will had come to mean more to her than any man ever had. "Whatever you need,

Christian and I have got you covered. Isn't that right, Chris?" Sebastian asked, handing Lexie a tissue.

"Of course, sweetie. You go check on your man. We'll get this mess sorted out for you."

"Don't worry, you've got us, and I see Nia and Damon helping out too." Lexie glanced over her shoulder and found Damon, in his usual fashion, was all authoritative and galvanizing the staff into action to the put the club back together again. He was already delivering instructions to Millennium's staff while Nia escorted people out the door.

"Thanks." Lexie sniffed, blowing her nose. She was about to rush out the door when the last person she wanted to see stepped in her path. Lauren.

If looks could kill, she would be dead in an instant. But none of that mattered to Lexie right now. Will needed her.

"Not now, Lauren," Lexie replied, putting a hand up. "I know we need to talk, but right now I've got to get to the hospital. I promise you, we'll speak when I get back. But first, I have to make sure his brother is okay."

"Go," Lauren barked sternly. "We'll talk later." Her tone was ominous, but Lexie didn't have time to care. She merely nodded and hurried out the door.

CHAPTER SIXTEEN

The call Will dreaded to make never came. His mother heard word of her youngest son's stabbing on the news before Will could telephone. He'd been so busy making sure his brother received the best care at St. Luke's Medical Center that he hadn't had time to call. Now they both sat on opposite sides of the waiting room while they waited for word on Ryan's condition. Apparently the stab wound had punctured his kidney and they'd taken him immediately to surgery.

Eve Kennedy was devastated. She blamed Will for the accident, telling him that if Ryan hadn't been at the club, none of this would have happened. Was she right all along? Was he in the wrong business? What if Ryan didn't make it?

Will didn't have a chance to think about it further because a few moments later, Lexie rushed into intensive care. Will saw her the moment she arrived at the nurse's station and flagged her down.

Concern was etched across Will's face and he was still wearing blood-stained clothes. Lexie rushed into his arms. "Oh, baby."

When they finally broke apart, Lexie touched his

cheek. "Are you okay?" she asked, glancing at Eve, who sat on the other side of the room, wringing a Kleenex.

"How's Ryan? Have you heard anything?"

Will shook his head. "Not yet. He's still in surgery."

"I know you're worried, Will, but he'll make it. He's young and strong."

"I pray he does." Will's voice broke.

"Well, I'm staying here with you for as long as you need or want me to."

"What about the show?"

Lexie patted his knee. "Stop worrying about me. I can take care of myself. Plus, the situation is handled. I left Sebastian in charge of the show and Damon was handling the club for you."

Will rubbed his temples. "I completely forgot about the club."

"As well you should," Eve replied from the across the room. "It's that very place that has us here to begin with."

"Please, Mrs. Kennedy," Lexie spoke up. "Now is not the time or place."

"Well, when is?" Eve retorted sarcastically. "When my son is dead and buried?"

Lexie didn't dare answer any further. The woman was obviously distraught and Lexie was only adding fuel to the fire. Just then the surgeon came flying through the double doors. Will and Lexie both stood up and searched the surgeon's eyes. As they waited with bated breath, Lexie tucked her hand inside Will's. Glancing down, he attempted a halfhearted smile.

Eve rose from her seat and clutched her purse beside her. "How's my son?"

"Don't worry, Mrs. Kennedy." The surgeon smiled as he pulled off his cap and wiped his brow. "Your son sustained only minor damage to his kidney and we were able to repair it. He came through surgery with flying colors and is in recovery right now."

Will shook his hand. "Thank you, doctor."

"When can I see him?" Eve asked.

"You can go in now, but only one at time."

Eve looked up at her older son with beseeching eyes.

"You go, Mom. I'll wait here and speak with the doctor."

Eve rushed down the hall toward intensive care.

Once Eve was out of earshot, Will asked the doctor about Ryan's basketball career. The doctor assured Will that the injury would not affect his career in any way, but would only put him on the bench until he healed.

"See? I told you." Lexie squeezed his arm.

Once the doctor left, Will was overcome with emotion. Tears of joy sprung into his eyes and he reached out and pulled Lexie forward and held on to her tightly.

"Shhh." Lexie stroked his back. "He's okay now, Will."

Pulling away, Will clutched her face in his hands. "If anything had ever happened him to, Lex . . ."

"But it didn't. He will recover from his wounds."

Will leaned down and pressed his lips against hers. "Thank God," he said. After several long moments, he released her.

"Now that he's in ICU, you should probably go and check on things at the club," Will suggested.

Lexie frowned. Why was he pushing her away when he needed her by his side? "No, I want to stay here with you," Lexie replied adamantly.

"Wouldn't it give you peace of mind to know everything was handled?"

"I suppose, but . . ."

"No buts. You go. Make sure the club is still standing."

"Will . . ." At his pleading look, Lexie consented. "Okay, but I'll call you later." Snatching her purse from a nearby chair, Lexie raised on tiptoe and gave Will a quick kiss before leaving the room. On her way out, she ran into Damon and Nia. The couple walked anxiously toward her.

"How's Ryan?" they asked almost simultaneously.

"He's fine, but Will could sure use a hand." Lexie gave Nia's hand a gentle squeeze before leaving the hospital.

Walking into the waiting room, Damon came and gave his best friend a gigantic hug. He'd never seen Will look like such a wreck.

Exhausted, Will fell onto the couch. Nia followed suit and sat beside him, holding his hand while Damon sat opposite them in a nearby chair.

"He's doing fine. He made it out of surgery and he's in recovery right now."

"Thank God," Nia exclaimed, squeezing his hand. "We were so worried, Will."

"I know, I know. But thank the Lord; he's going to be okay." Will closed his eyes and looked upward. "So how's everything at the club?" Will was thankful he had a friend like Damon. Seeing how crazy the situation was quickly becoming, Damon and Nia had graciously stayed at the club, cleaning up after the event, fielding reporter questions, and dismissing the mass of staff it took to pull off an event of that magnitude. Will couldn't be more grateful.

"It's fine. I've handled everything, but, Will, the press is after this story," Damon warned.

Furious, Will stood up and walked over to the window. What he saw only infuriated him further. A

crowd of reporters was waiting for him on the sidewalk, ready for blood.

"I'm in trouble, aren't I?" Will asked.

Damon looked at Nia. He hated to be the bearer of
bad news. "Looks like it." Standing up, Nia walked
over to Will and put a hand on his shoulder. "After
the milieu, you'll get everything straightened out and
your name cleaned up."

Will shook his head in amazement at Nia's faith.
"I hope you're right. I hope you're right. Because
if not . . ." his voice trailed off.

Damon hated to see Will in so much anguish and
vowed to do everything within his power to see him
through it.

"Can I get you anything?" Nia asked. "Coffee? Sandwich? I bet you haven't eaten anything all night."

"No, thanks."

Dejected, Nia walked over and sat on Damon's lap
and together they stayed with Will until his mother
came back from intensive care. When Will stood up to
go see his brother, his mother touched his arm to stop
him. "Why don't you wait until tomorrow?"

"But, Mom, I just want to make sure he's okay."

"Just take my word for it, okay?" his mother replied
testily. "He's fine. Let the boy rest until tomorrow.
There'll be time enough for all your questions in the
morning."

Will wanted to say a few choice words to his mother,
but they were not alone. Of course, Damon knew all
too well about the kind of hell Will endured from
Eve's tongue lashings. Many times he'd offered a
shoulder when Will came to vent about one of his
mother's tirades. That was one of Damon's great qualities; he was a great listener.

Taking a deep breath, Will consented. He was in no

mood for a fight—all the fight had gone clear out of him. "You're right, Mom. I'll let Ryan sleep and I'll see him in the morning." Will stalked to the window and stayed there until daybreak.

Lexie returned to Millennium and discovered a myriad of reporters still perched outside the front door. Damon must have banished them out of the club. Walking past them, Lexie headed to the front door. She was in no mood for their antics at that hour.

"You're not getting a comment from me," Lexie said to whoever was listening. "So don't ask."

"How do you feel about this?" One insistent reporter jammed an early edition of the *Chicago Tribune* in her face. Lexie read the headline and felt sick to her stomach. Pushing past him, she unlocked the front door and shut it firmly behind her.

Had Will seen this? Lexie wondered. If so, it would kill him. Lexie tossed the newspaper in a wastebasket in the foyer. Walking to the main room, she was surprised to discover the club in order, with nothing much to do.

The stage had been dismantled, the decorations removed, and the tables and chairs all returned to their proper places. Damon and Sebastian had taken care of everything. All that remained was the stage with its big fake pharaoh's palace doors and tall golden pillars— and a whole lot of leftover food. But she didn't see Sebastian or Christian anywhere. All that remained were a few various Millennium staff members. Walking backstage, Lexie prepared to assess the damage, and found Sebastian, Mina, and Christian packing up the designer clothes.

"Sis." Sebastian ran toward her. "How's Ryan?"

"He's doing fine. The stab wound only injured a kidney, but they sewed him up in surgery and now he's resting comfortably in ICU."

Sebastian gave her a hug. "That's great news."

"Indeed it is," Christian replied as he and Mina put the design wear into wardrobe bags.

"What a night!" Lexie looked around for an empty chair and plunked down in it. Could it have gotten any worse? "You guys have been great. Why don't you go on home? I'll finish this."

"Lexie, I'm not leaving you here," Sebastian stated.

"Please, it's been an exhausting night. I just need some time to myself to figure out what to do, okay? There's nothing left but to take these to the vault, and I would prefer to do it myself."

"Are you sure, Lex? I can stay." Sebastian didn't like the idea of leaving his sister alone with the vultures outside.

Mia nodded in agreement.

"It's nearly midnight, Mina. You go ahead and get some sleep. You deserve it," Lexie ordered her steadfast assistant.

"All right." Mina kissed her cheek. "Call me if you need anything."

After several minutes, Lexie finally convinced her brother and Christian that it was best to give her some breathing room. But first Lexie had to find out if her parents had made it home safely.

"How are Mom and Dad?" Lexie asked.

"They're fine," Sebastian responded, squeezing her hand. "I was able to usher them out the side door right when all the hoopla broke out."

"Thank God!" Lexie breathed a sigh of relief. "They must be so embarrassed and disappointed in me." Lexie's eyes welled with tears.

"They would never be disappointed in their favorite girl." Sebastian stroked her cheek. "And once you explain the whole story, they'll know the truth. You'll see." Sebastian wrapped her in his arms for a bear hug. "Now, are you truly going to be okay?"

"I will, I promise," Lexie vowed, walking them to the front door.

Sebastian raised an eyebrow. "All right, but give me a call when you make it home." Lexie crossed her heart. "Oh, by the way, your boss was here a little bit ago," Sebastian mentioned haphazardly.

"Is she still here?" Lexie asked, looking over her shoulder.

"Haven't seen her. We've been backstage for a while. I'm sure she's already left by now," Christian answered. "Get some rest, sweetie." He gave her a kiss on either cheek.

Lexie breathed a sigh of relief when they both finally left. Now she could feel sorry for herself and Will in private. What were they going to do?

His club was going to be on the verge of financial disaster. And her? Well, her night was ruined even after she debuted her first and probably last collection. She'd thought they had saved the night when her designs were a hit with the press, but instead the night turned out worse than even she could have ever imagined. And let's not forget her girl Nia. She'd premiered her own wedding dress before the blessed event. And for what? Look at how the evening ended!

How could everything have gone so terribly wrong?

Boom. A loud noise came from backstage. Lexie's heart stopped. The designs. Running backstage, Lexie found Sydney fingering her collection. "What the hell do you think you're doing?" Lexie snatched her dress out of Sydney's hands.

Shaking her head, Sydney laughed. "How did you do it?" she asked, circling around Lexie. "I don't get it."

"Do what? Manage to pull a rabbit out of a hat in the midst of the jaws of defeat?"

"How did you manage to still come out on top at the fashion show? For that I have to applaud you." Sydney clapped her hands. "But just when I was ready to hand in my resignation, your boyfriend's club goes up in flames. I have to hand it to you, Lexie, you don't do anything small, do you?"

"Don't mess me with me, blondie." Lexie swung her right finger in Sydney's face. "You thought I was something before—you ain't seen nothing yet. You see, I'm on to you now."

Sydney smiled. "Oh, please, Lexie, stop being so melodramatic. You have nothing on me." Sydney turned on her heel to walk away and tossed one final comment over her shoulder. "Happy hunting."

"You wanna bet?" Lexie grabbed her by the arm. "I know you were behind tonight's sabotage and you can bet your last dollar I'm going to prove it. Pretty soon your butt will be thrown out of Bentley's so fast your head will be spinning. As a matter of fact, why are you back here?" Lexie glanced at her watch. "It's nearly two A.M."

Looking away, Sydney feigned ignorance. "I have no idea what you're talking about."

Lexie rubbed her jaw thoughtfully and returned the favor by circling Sydney. "Hmmm, this is all very interesting. Why come back to the scene of the crime? You had it made. Lauren's sure to fire me after tonight's debacle. So why come back?" Lexie glimpsed the wardrobe bag over Sydney's shoulder. "If for no other reason"—she saw another wardrobe bag hanging from a nearby rack—"than to return the evidence." Lexie walked over and unzipped the bag. Opening it, she discovered none other than the Vera Wang garments hanging inside.

Fury rushed through her veins; Lexie wanted to rip the little skinny witch's eyes out, but she would wait. All dogs had their day. With a forefinger to her lips, she decided to play along. "Now, these weren't here before . . ." Lexie fingered the dresses inside.

"No?" Sydney smiled a devilish grin. "Well, you can't prove I put them there."

Over Sydney's shoulder, Lexie caught Lauren walking backstage. Obviously, her boss hadn't gone home. All she had to do now to nail Sydney's coffin was to have her admit the truth from her very own mouth.

"Why don't you just admit it, Sydney?" Lexie taunted her. "It's just the two of us here. Admit that you took the dresses. I know you want to."

Sydney sighed and paused for a moment while she thought about the consequences. It was only the two of them backstage. And if Lexie ever revealed what was said, it was hearsay. Lexie's word against Sydney's. Sydney would say she fabricated the whole story. And after Lexie's incompetence, Bentley's would never believe her. "What could it hurt, right?" She shrugged coldly. Boldly staring Lexie in the eye, Sydney revealed the truth. "Yes, it was me."

Lexie smiled as she saw the frown on Lauren's mouth and the color rush to her face.

"You and I both know I've wanted your job for months now. I saw an opportunity with all the chaos surrounding your grand event and I took it." Sydney grinned mischievously. "Now pack your stuff and leave Bentley's for good."

"Correction," Lauren said from behind her, walking forward. Lexie watched as a look of horror crossed

Sydney's pale face. "Make that your stuff, Sydney. Effective immediately, you're fired. As of this moment, you are no longer allowed entrance to the building. I will have your personal effects delivered to your home."

Ding-dong, the witch is dead. Lexie stood back and watched with relief as Lauren finished her off.

"You can't believe all this, Lauren." Sydney tried the practical approach. "Be reasonable. Lexie set me up. She knew she was in hot water after tonight. She set this all in motion."

"No!" Lauren yelled. "You are the reason my butt is on the chopping block. So you had better get out of here, and make it quick, before I have you arrested."

Sydney threw Lexie a killer look before storming out the back door.

Lauren shook her head. "Lexie, I apologize for this nightmare. Who knew what the woman was capable of."

"Who knew?" Lexie replied, shrugging her shoulders.

"I promise you. I'll make this right."

"Thanks, Lauren."

"But you know that Sydney's actions don't excuse you from putting your collection out on that runway, and we will have to deal with that. But tonight," Lauren glanced at her watch, "let's just go home and get some rest."

"I couldn't agree with you more." Lexie smiled. "I'll see you in the morning."

CHAPTER SEVENTEEN

After the hellish evening he'd endured, Will realized life was too short. He was going to enjoy it to the fullest. Instinct led him to Lexie's doorstep.

Tap. Tap. Tap.

Lexie heard the tapping from in her bedroom. The clock read three A.M. She'd tried to get some sleep—not that she'd gotten any. Her dreams were filled with images of Will's blood-stained shirt and the sight of his brother lying on the floor.

Slipping on her silk robe and tying it at the waist, Lexie padded to the door in her comfy bunny slippers. She didn't need to wonder who was on the other side; she knew it was him. Lexie quickly unchained the link and unbolted the door.

Will stood before her, and if his appearance was anything to go by, he was completely exhausted. Bloodshot eyes, clothes rumpled, and his usually stellar hair stuck up all over his head.

Lexie didn't mince words. "You look like hell."

Realizing his appearance, Will brushed down his hair with shaky hands. "That's right, you like the more put-together brothers."

"Ouch. You *are* in a mood," Lexie replied, wrapping her robe around her.

Will shook his head. Why was he taking his anger out on her? It wasn't her fault Ryan was hospitalized. "I'm sorry, Lex. I'm just tired."

"It's okay." Lexie pulled him inside the apartment and shut the door behind him. Dog-tired, Will barely made it to the couch before bowing his head in his lap.

"Would you like some coffee?" she asked, padding to her kitchen. She didn't wait for an answer. Instead she searched the cabinet for some filters and her Starbucks canister.

Will looked up. Even though sleep-deprived, he still noticed everything about Lexie. From her hair hanging in loose waves down her back to her painted red toenails. And with the moonlight streaming in from the window, Lexie was absolutely the most beautiful woman in the world. Will wanted to kiss her senseless and forget the pain.

"How was your mom after I left?" Lexie asked, pulling out her coffeemaker. Measuring several tablespoons, she dumped the coffee into the filter and turned the machine on to percolate.

"How do you think she is?"

"It's your club. She probably blames you. Even though it's absolutely not your fault." Lexie came forward and settled next to Will on the sofa, folding her knees underneath her.

"I'm glad someone thinks so because I doubt everyone else will."

"It's going to be okay, Will. We'll figure this out in the morning. For now, you need to get some rest. You have a long road ahead of you."

Will put his head down. "You have no idea, Lexie.

The fallout could be massive. I could lose my license. I could lose the club."

Lexie heard the fear. She'd felt it herself because she would be faced with a similar situation in the morning. She had no idea what lay ahead for her career. But, for now, she would put her own needs aside and focus on Will. He had faced betrayal and death tonight. He needed her and she needed him, too.

Reaching out, she pulled him into the safety of her arms. Will held onto her tightly. Eventually she felt tears trickle down her arm, but she still held on. "It's going to be all right," she said soothingly, her voice becoming lower and lower.

The next morning, Will left Lexie's early. She'd been so marvelous last night, coming to the hospital, and of course afterward she known exactly what he needed.

After a long hot shower, he arrived at the hospital only to discover that his mother had beaten him to the punch. Eve was already holding her youngest son's hand and whispering something in his ear, but all conversation ceased as soon as Will walked through the door.

"You're awake," Will said to Ryan.

"Yes. He regained consciousness early this morning," his mother replied haughtily. "I went to look for you, but you were nowhere to be found." Will heard the accusatory tone in her voice and chose to ignore it until his mother flat-out asked him. "Where were you?"

"I had to go out for some fresh air."

"While your brother was on his death bed!"

"Mother, don't be so melodramatic." Will sucked in

his breath. "I believe you were the one who told me not to disturb Ryan until the morning."

"That didn't mean I was giving you an excuse to go out carousing."

"For heaven's sake, Mom." Will clenched his teeth. "My brother was just stabbed. Exactly who would I be carousing with?"

"Oh, I don't know," his mother replied. "Maybe that fashion girl you've been talking to lately."

"Mother, you know her name is Lexie. I thought you liked her."

"I did, I do." Eve shook her head. "But your place was here last night."

"Enough, okay?" Ryan yelled from his hospital bed. "I'm tired of you two fighting. It doesn't help anything. And it most certainly won't change anything." Slowly, Ryan tried to sit upright, but the pain was too intense. Eve jumped up to place pillows behind his back.

"I'm sorry," Will apologized, coming to sit at his brother's side opposite his mother. "How are you feeling?"

"Aside from feeling a little sore, I'm fine, Will," Ryan answered, lowering his head. "Mom, could you give Will and I a moment to talk?"

"Ryan, I don't think now is the time to—" She stopped midsentence at his pleading look. "All right, all right. I'll go grab a cup of coffee."

Eve left the room and several long moments passed before Will or Ryan spoke.

"All I want to know is why?" Will asked finally. "Why did you do this? Why didn't you come to me if you were in trouble? I asked you a million times what was wrong and you lied to me every single time. Told me nothing was wrong. I gave you every opportunity to tell me the truth and you didn't."

"Will, I'm sorry." Ryan hung his head. He knew it was no consolation now, but he was truly sorry for ruining Lexie's fashion show and quite possibly destroying his brother's livelihood.

"I'm not sure what your apologies can do for me now after the morning papers." Will had been heartsick when he saw the front page of the *Chicago Tribune*. The headline read *Fashion show turns deadly*. Though no one had died, that didn't prevent the press from putting a spin on it to sell more newspapers. Will was furious and he couldn't help but take it out on the one person who was the cause of this bad publicity, the one person who could have stopped it from occurring: his baby brother.

"Because of you, Ryan, I have a lot of damage control to do. And at this point, I'm not sure it can be undone, but I'm going to try."

"I'm so sorry, Will."

Will watched the tears run down his face, saw his shoulders shake as he sobbed, and couldn't bear it. Will patted Ryan's shoulder. The boy was only seventeen, but he still should have known better. "It's going to be okay, Ryan. Somehow, someway, I'm going to pull this family out of the fire."

His mother returned with two steaming Styrofoam cups of hot coffee. "I brought one for you," she said, handing the cup to a surprised Will.

Will didn't know if it was a peace offering, but he took it as a gesture of goodwill and let the animosity go. "Thanks, Mom."

Will placed several calls to high-profile public relations agencies. After speaking with a few, only one really suited him: a black-owned agency run by the Chandlers, two sisters.

The two women had successfully turned the tide during the Michael Williams scandal and he was hoping that these two spin doctors could do the same for him. Williams, an alderman for the fifth district, was running for mayor and had been accused of infidelity. Like a moth to a flame, the press had stuck to Williams like glue, determined to show the affair as a lack of morals on Williams's part. The Chandlers had been able to salvage his reputation by placing him at every charity benefit and kids' event in the district. Soon the press was fawning over alderman Williams as a man of great character. Thankfully, the Chandlers agreed to meet with Will and he could only pray that they would consider taking his case.

This morning alone, many of his best clients had canceled their events at the club, all claiming they didn't want to be associated with a business that sold drugs. These very people were Will's bread and butter and helped keep Millennium from being just another supper or dance club. The Chandler sisters were going to have to do some serious spinning. They thankfully agreed to a one o'clock lunch meeting. The two had seen the morning papers, but thought they could assist Will in turning the tide his way. The club meant everything to him. He definitely wouldn't lie down easily. Failure did not sit well with him.

He needed a pick-me-up and knew who could supply it. His lean fingers quickly dialed Lexie's number at work. She answered almost immediately.

"Lexie Thompson."

"Hey, it's me."

"Hey, you." Lexie smiled. It was so good to hear his voice; she was going crazy waiting for a summons for

Lauren, which she knew was sure to come. More than that, she'd been besieged by the press on her way into work that morning, asking what her relationship with Will was. Lexie had pushed past them with a terse "no comment."

"Did you see the papers?"

"I have, Will." And it broke her heart to see her man beat up in the press. The press had taken the opportunity to highlight drugs in the black community and was holding Millennium up to the spotlight.

"Everyone is going to think that I'm a drug dealer and my club is a front for drug dealing."

"No, they won't. At least not those people who love you. They know you're an honest businessman, loyal friend, and devoted brother. They'll know it's all hogwash."

"Wow, that was some impassioned speech."

"I meant every word."

"I appreciate it, but not everyone will share your opinion. They'll believe what they read."

"Then they're idiots," Lexie replied vehemently. She refused to let self-doubt affect one of the most upright men she'd ever known. "Don't get down on yourself, now, do you hear me? You have to stay positive, you have a lot of work ahead."

"How did you know exactly what I needed to hear?"

"ESP." Her other line rang. It was probably Lauren. "Listen, Will, I've gotta go. But we'll talk later." Lexie blew him a kiss.

"Got it."

Seconds later, Lexie replaced the receiver. It was indeed Lauren. It was time to face the music. With wooden legs, Lexie made the long walk to her boss's office. She felt like a dead woman walking.

Lexie suspected that she was about to be told to

pack up her office quickly. Although Lauren knew Sydney was behind the sabotage at the fashion show, Lexie had taken Bentley's reputation in her own hands by premiering her own designs. It was grounds for dismissal.

When she walked in, she was surprised to find Bentley's legal counsel Edward James Martin and assistant vice president, Stuart Young, sitting at the table. Her stomach tied in knots, Lexie marched through the room, unable to get a true read on any of their faces. Lauren looked somber and Stuart stood by the window looking as stalwart as ever. She was really in for it now. If they were trying to scare her, they were doing a good job.

"Lexie, please take a seat." Lauren motioned to the chair in front of her desk. Self-preservation told her it was in her best interest to say as little as possible at the outset. "I'm sure you know why you're here," Lauren began. Lexie held her breath and waited for the inevitable. "Your behavior Friday night was not only careless and reckless, but also could have seriously hurt our business. I received a call from Vera Wang's publicist who was especially insulted that Vera's collection was not displayed as promised. I've had to do a lot of ass kissing this morning. But on the plus side, we know who the saboteur is and we've appropriately tossed Sydney on her rear end. Needless to say, she'll never find another job in the fashion business as long as Bentley's has anything to say about it. But as for you," Lauren paused, "there's no doubt in my mind what action Bentley's should take."

Lexie sighed. Why was the woman dragging it out? *Just fire me and get it over with.*

"But instead of firing you," Stuart piped in, "we've decided to promote you."

"Pardon?" Lexie looked in shock around the room as though everyone they had suddenly sprouted horns. Had she heard correctly?

"Quite frankly, your collection was the most inventive we've seen in years and we'd like to hire you on to design for Bentley's exclusively," Lauren stated.

"Are you serious?"

Bentley's legal counsel, Edwards, gave his two cents. "Yes. Although your behavior was risky, your collection shows great promise. But there can't be any more stunts like the one you pulled at the show. We're still looking at the legal implications of the entire fiasco."

"I'm stunned," Lexie replied with her hand splayed across her chest. Who would ever have imagined that one day she would see her designs grace Bentley's store shelves?

"Well, what do you say?" Lauren asked.

Determinedly, Will walked through the revolving glass door at Bradley Savings & Loan. He could always count on Damon for sound advice, be it financial or personal.

"I need some advice," Will said, walking into Damon's office.

"Well, hello to you, too," Damon said, looking up from his paperwork. "Make yourself at home."

"As a matter of fact, I will." Will headed to Damon's bar and poured himself a glass of water. "Sorry, did I catch you at a bad time?" Will asked, noticing the pile of paperwork on Damon's desk. "It's just that you're the great romantic and all and I need help with Lexie's birthday. She's turning twenty-nine on Friday."

"What about the club? I've seen the papers."

"The club I can't do anything about right now,

but I can focus on the good things in life," Will answered, upbeat.

"See you've learned something from hanging around me."

"What's that?"

"Optimism."

"Say what?"

"After your father died, you blamed the world. You didn't believe in anything. Thought the world was against you. Look how far you've come," Damon said.

"I guess you're right. Now, what about Lexie?" Will asked.

"What about throwing her a little dinner party? You know, invite a few of her closest friends."

"That's a good idea. See, you're useful for something, bro." Will punched Damon in the shoulder.

"Do you have any idea what you're going to get her?"

"I have a few ideas up my sleeve." Will smiled knowingly. He had picked up the perfect platinum and diamond pendant necklace at Tiffany's. He had seen Lexie eyeing it in the mall several weeks earlier. She had *oohed* and *aahed* over it so much, it had been impossible to forget. He'd gotten that and a bottle of her favorite new fragrance Hanae Mori, sold exclusively at Saks and Nordstrom. Jewelry and perfume—Lexie would eat it up with a spoon.

"My, my." Damon laughed, leaning back in his chair. "Am I listening to the same man? Who a mere two months ago spouted that the ideal woman did not exist? Sounds to me like you've found her."

"Could be." Will rubbed his goatee. "I can't deny that since I've been with Lexie, I haven't so much as looked at another woman. Lexie keeps me very satisfied in that department."

"Then Nia and I were right. You guys are well suited."

"Yeah, but keeping a woman like Lexie satisfied could prove exhausting. She's high maintenance, you know?"

"C'mon, Will. Are you saying you're not man enough to handle it? Now that I don't believe."

"She is a challenge."

"Which is exactly what you need. Otherwise you'd get bored."

"Thank you for your input, oh wise one," Will replied.

"Anytime," Damon said. "But why do I have the feeling Lexie's party isn't the only reason you stopped by?"

"You would be correct on that assumption. Listen, man, I've been looking into the stabbing at the club and—"

"Don't go any further." Damon stopped him. "Will, why aren't you letting the police do their job? That's what they get paid for."

"I can't let this rest, Damon. I'm going to find the punk that stabbed my brother and ruined my club's reputation. Do you know that the DuBoises pulled out of the expansion deal?"

Damon's eyes widened. Expanding was crucial to Will's continued success. This was a major setback. He saw hurt and disappointment were evident in Will's expression.

"Yes," Will continued, "they saw the reports and called me up and said they didn't want to get into business with a man that sold drugs. After all the legwork I put into making this deal happen, wooing them. Hell, even Lexie put in her two cents, and now to have it all fall apart . . ." Will slammed his hand on the maple desk.

"I know you don't want to hear this right now, Will,"

Damon squeezed his shoulders, "but there are other investors, and you know my father and I will help you any way we can. I can set up some meetings for you."

"Don't you get it, Damon? I got this deal. I made it happen. These guys came to me based on my reputation. And now it's kaput." He snapped his fingers. "Just like that. I won't come back to you guys on my hands and knees. Bradley Savings & Loan gave me the collateral I needed to start the business. I can't come back to you again. I've played that card already."

"Listen to me." Damon rose and took an authoritative tone like the one he used with his employees at the bank. "You will never use up that card. Do you hear me? You're family. Don't you get that by now? You're my brother."

"Thanks, Damon. I appreciate that." Will accepted a hug, but somehow he would find that thug J.T., and when he did there would be hell to pay.

CHAPTER EIGHTEEN

An emergency summit with her friends was in order. Lexie couldn't believe Bentley's had offered her her life's dream on a silver platter. Could this day really be happening? Her pulse was racing and her heart was pounding like it was ready to leap out of her chest.

Never in her wildest dreams could she have guessed they would make her such an offer. Taking a deep breath, her fingers dialed Nia's office. Nia picked up on the fourth ring, completely out of breath.

"Hello," Nia answered, breathing harshly.

"Girl, it's me."

"They fired you," Nia said, guessing.

"Wrong. They offered me my own collection!" Lexie shouted into the phone.

"Are you kidding?" Nia couldn't believe it. She had to give it to Lexie. Girlfriend had the Midas touch.

"Yes. I'm sure. It's no joke, Nia. Bentley's offered me my own collection at their store."

"And what did you say?"

"I told them I would have to think about it. I don't want to sign some long-term contract and have someone telling me what to do and how to do it.

My designs are just that: mine. You know what I'm saying."

"I've got to hand to you, Lex. You always land on your feet," Nia said with a laugh.

"I guess I do." Lexie chuckled in return. "Listen, girlfriend, I've gotta go. I've got to call everyone and share the good news. Talk to ya later."

After hanging up, Lexie called Sebastian. When she ended the call, she wanted to cry. It all seemed so surreal. She had waited her whole life for this moment and she owed it all to one person. If it hadn't been for Will, she would never have premiered her designs on that stage. Without his absolute faith in her, she would never have taken that leap. Frantically, Lexie rang the club, then realized that she couldn't tell him this news over the phone. This was something she had to do in person. Grabbing her coat and purse, she made a hasty exit from her office.

Twenty minutes later, her silver convertible Audi pulled into a parking space at Millennium. Hopping out of the car, Lexie ran the few steps to the front door. Swinging them open, she rushed inside only to find Will huddled at a booth with two very attractive women.

One was a stunning tawny-colored beauty with long, straight brown hair with blond highlights and hazel eyes. The other woman was equally gorgeous with smooth chestnut-colored skin and curly black hair, half of which was swept into an updo.

Will looked into Lexie's stunned face. Glancing down at his watch, he noticed the hour. It was only ten-thirty. Had they already let her go? he wondered. If so, she would find another job. His woman was talented.

"Babe, is everything okay?" Will asked, standing up.

Excited, Lexie threw caution to the wind and

charged Will, throwing herself in his arms and nearly knocking the wind out of him.

"Easy there, woman." Will laughed, catching his balance before they both tipped over and embarrassed themselves in front of the Chandler sisters. "Where's the fire?"

"Will, you will not believe it!"

"Believe what?" Will asked. It had to be good news because Lexie's eyes were lit up like a Christmas tree.

"Baby, they want my collection!" Lexie replied, clutching Will's sleeves. "Yes! Yes!" Lexie jumped up and down like a five-year-old. "Will, they want me to design exclusively for Bentley's. Can you believe it? All my dreams are coming true."

"That's fantastic, Lex!" Will swung her around. "I'm so proud of you. You deserve it, darling."

"Thank you, sweetie." Calming herself, Lexie remembered the two serious women who'd barely looked up from the paperwork despite her loud outbursts. Lexie kissed Will's cheek. "How's everything here?"

"Not so good." Will exhaled. "We're trying to come up with a plan to save Millennium from all this bad press."

"Is there anything I can do?"

"I don't know. This may be something I have to weather on my own."

"No, you won't." Lexie beamed, throwing off her coat and rolling up her sleeves. "You know what they say, four heads are always better than three. Scoot over."

The chestnut beauty raised an eyebrow at Lexie's commanding voice and was about to make a comment but thought better of it after noticing the serious look on Will's face.

"Have a seat," the sister said.

Lexie turned to find Will staring at her strangely.

Was there lipstick on her teeth or something? She wiped at her teeth with her tongue.

Will on the other hand was a little bit awestruck. All the women he'd ever known, no matter how beautiful or successful, would be hightailing their behinds out the door at the first sign of trouble—but not Lexie. She continued to surprise him more and more each day. Damon was right. He was staring his ideal woman in the face.

After a short pause, he finally found his voice. "Paris, Iman, allow me to introduce my girlfriend, designer Lexie Thompson."

Turning to him, Lexie connected with those sultry midnight eyes and knew she'd fallen hopelessly in love with William Kennedy.

It didn't take long for Lexie to panic over such thoughts. Later that evening, after successful polishing off two bottles of champagne, Lexie and Christian were both lying back on a bed of pillows carelessly thrown across her hardwood living room floor.

"How can it be?" Lexie asked, her speech slightly slurred. "How did that playboy sneak his way into my heart?"

"I don't know, cupcake," Christian answered, equally sloshed. It didn't take much for him; after two glasses he was usually down for the count. "Maybe it was that hot bod of his."

"Mmm . . . nope. I don't think that was it." Lexie shook her head. "Though I admit initially it caught my attention. He's one great package, you know?"

"Ain't that the truth. Girl, if he sealed that up and bottled it, he'd make a fortune."

Lexie burst into a fit of giggles.

"So, now that you know you're head over heels, what pray tell are you going to do with this information?" Christian raised his eyebrows. "Seems to me you should be sharing all this with loverboy."

"I don't know, Chris. It could be way too soon for vows of undying love. It's not like we've made a commitment to each other."

"But you're sleeping together."

"Two people committed to having sex does not a relationship make."

"You mean to tell me the loverboy has not grabbed you by your thong and told you he wants you for his one and only?" Christian snapped his fingers twice.

Lexie shook her head.

"Well, what is he waiting for? Maybe he's not too swift after all. You know what they say about good looks and no brain . . ."

Lexie pinched him. "Chris, don't talk about my man."

"Sorry, darling. It sounds to me like you need to take action. You know, find out where his head is."

"And if it's not where mine is?"

"We'll cross that bridge when we come to it. Until then you need to take baby steps."

"That's what I love about you, Christian." Lexie leaned over to give her best pal a sloppy kiss on the cheek. "You're a comedian."

"And don't you forget it, sweet cheeks."

Two cups of coffee later, Lexie arrived at Will's apartment determined to find out exactly where his head was. Will would be upstairs shortly just as soon he closed the downstairs, so her time was limited.

Preparing the apartment was easy. Soft Will Downing jazz played in the background, large scented jasmine-vanilla candles lit the room, and a cold bottle of Dom

Perignon were all waiting for her man. She hadn't spoken with him since she'd left his meeting with Paris and Iman Chandler earlier. She could only hope they'd come up with some innovative solutions to save the club after she left; she'd had no luck. And while they were working on the business end, she'd take care of him personally and introduce him to an incandescent night of pleasure the likes of which he'd never seen.

Knowing Will had really brought out the best in her. She actually thought of others first before herself. Tonight, for example, she would give herself to him completely, without expecting anything in return. To that end, she'd brought her special sensual kit of feathers, blindfolds, massage oils, and much more.

Staring at herself in the mirror a half hour later, Lexie had to admit that she looked pretty hot in a red, strapless, satin and lace merry widow with matching thong, garter, silky smooth thigh-highs, and tall three-inch sandals. Her freshly washed hair had been teased to perfection until it lay in soft waves around her face. Oh, yes, Will would be very pleased indeed. After gliding on a little lip gloss and spraying Will's favorite scent, Lexie was ready for the evening. Glancing at her watch, she swiftly strode into the kitchen and checked on her fondue. When it was completely melted, she took it and an assortment of fresh strawberries, bananas, and pound cake to the cocktail table. Will would enjoy these before sampling the final dessert: her.

At the sound of footsteps on the stairs, Lexie rushed to the couch to position herself.

When Will walked through the door a few moments later, he was shocked to find Lexie spread out on his couch in one of the sexiest getups he'd seen in years.

"Come here." Lexie motioned with one red-tipped finger. Lashes lowered, she gave him her sultriest gaze.

"What did I do to deserve this?" Will inquired.

"I thought you might need some relaxation after a hard day's work."

Will accepted Lexie's hand as she pulled him down to join her on the couch. "That I could," Will replied.

Resting his hand in her lap, Lexie commanded him to close his eyes while she began a slow massage of his temples. "I want you to take it easy tonight. You're always trying to be so strong. Let me take care of you tonight," Lexie said as she tenderly divested him of all his clothing, leaving him in nothing but a pair of boxer shorts. "Hmmm, now that's more like it."

"Thank you, Lexie," Will replied seriously. "You knew just what I needed."

Lexie could tell he appreciated her thoughtfulness because his expressive eyes spoke volumes even through candlelight. It made her want to absorb him all the more. Twisting her fingers around her his head, Lexie brought his mouth down to hers. Will's kiss was searing and rampant. Fueled by passion, Will sunk his tongue into her mouth and an altogether familiar feeling came over Lexie, evoking a very primitively female moan from her lips.

"Hmmm, you taste so good," he whispered huskily. "I just want to eat you up."

"All in due time." Lexie pulled away to kneel on the floor beside the couch. "But first, I have a special feast for you."

Swirling one ripened strawberry in the hot amaretto white chocolate, Lexie turned around to feed the delicious piece to Will. When chocolate dribbled onto her fingers, Will took the chocolate-covered finger in his mouth and licked it off.

"Hmmmm." Will moaned in delight. "This is so good. Did you make this, baby?"

"Don't start. You know I can't cook, but I can manage to throw a few bars of chocolate in the microwave and melt them."

"Well, you have already melted me."

"Let's take this to the bedroom, then." Rising, Lexie led the way to the master bedroom.

Stunned was the word that came to Will's mind when he walked up the stairs. Sheer scarves were strewn from one bedpost to another, creating a light netting over the bed. Candles of various sizes illuminated the room while the fragrant smell of vanilla and lavender wafted through the air, gently caressing his nose.

Clearly, Lexie had gone through a great deal of trouble for him. First the outfit and then the decorations—Will could truly sense that she cared for him. Who would've ever thought that two self-indulgent people like the two of them could ever find happiness together? But indeed it appeared that somehow they had.

"Do you like?" Lexie asked as she whirled around to give him a better view of her ensemble.

"Like? I love it." Will pulled Lexie toward him, crushing her body against his while his mouth closed over hers in one fell swoop. Lexie barely had a chance to catch her breath before Will began his assault on her senses. His lips and hands were everywhere.

"Slow down, slow down, Will," Lexie whispered, disengaging herself from his strong arms. "We have all night," she added, using his tag line.

Taking his hand, she guided him to his king-size platform bed and threw back the sheer netting. Never taking his eyes off her, Will slid in between the sheets.

"You're going to like what I have in store," Lexie replied, joining him on the bed and turning him onto his stomach.

Seconds later, Will felt warm liquid trickling down his

back, right before Lexie's hands sensually massaged and kneaded his neck, tight shoulder muscles, and tense back. Her hands slowly caressed him, applying pressure where needed.

When she turned him over to face her, there were telltale signs of passion in his dark eyes. Lexie felt herself drowning in those murky depths and had to blink several times to focus on the task at hand. She drizzled oil down the valley of his chest, savoring the moment as her hands caressed the hard muscles of his chest and concave stomach. He looked good enough to eat and boy was she hungry.

Because they had been lovers for months, Lexie knew every sensitive nerve ending. Bending down, she allowed her tongue to travel a leisurely path from the soft, sensitive flesh at the nape of his neck to his shoulders before finally stopping to slowly outline the hardened pebbles of his nipples.

Will emitted a low, guttural moan when she quickly dispensed with his boxers and her hands and tongue found their way to his manhood. Closing her mouth around him, Lexie brought Will to a fevered pitch, forcing him to reach out and tangle his fingers inside Lexie's soft, silken hair. He couldn't endure the exquisite torture anymore. "Enough," he rasped.

Hauling her onto her back, his mouth swooped down to cover hers hungrily. Her calm was shattered when his tongue darted inside her mouth, past her teeth, to connect with her hot, wet tongue. Like a carnivore, he explored the shape and feel of her mouth, suckling and tasting every inch of her honeyed interior.

Will meanwhile attacked her merry widow with a vengeance and ripped at her bustier until her swollen breasts were released from their confined state. High and pert, Will took one hardened peak into his mouth and sucked on it voraciously. He treated the other to a rotating massage between his fingertips before gently sliding her thong down her hips.

His hands slowly massaged her thighs, his gentle caress sending currents of desire straight through her. Lexie cried out when she felt his fingers find her moist cavern and teased the tiny bud at the center of her womanhood.

When his tongue left hers to replace his fingers, Lexie's whole body was galvanized and she whimpered softly in response. Molten hot desire quickly spread through her veins. Her body ached for him to enter deep inside her and cure the thirst that only he could quench.

Lexie roughly pulled him to her and reclaimed his mouth for another drugging kiss. Grasping his buttocks, Lexie ground her hips seductively against his. She found him hot, hard, and ready for her. Will took the cue and picked up the pace and before she knew it, her breathing was coming in quick, uneven gasps.

Will knew it was time. He'd felt her moist heat and knew she was ready for him as he was for her. His whole body was consumed with desire and if he held on any longer he would explode. Leaning over, he grabbed a foil packet from the bed and sheathed himself before he pinned her to the bed, parted her thighs, and sank into her moist heat. Lexie's pliant body lifted to welcome him easily as her tight muscles clinched around his manhood.

Their gazes met through the darkness and a mutual understanding was achieved. Lexie recognized the hunger and intuitively arched to meet his demanding thrusts with her own lusty need. Together they found a tempo and an uncontrollable passion that soared them to new heights. The real world seemed to spin on its axis and before long Lexie was moaning as she reached her plateau.

Will was right behind her, giving a loud shout of satisfaction when pure, explosive pleasure took over his entire body. He collapsed on top of her until she squirmed underneath him and he eased onto his side.

Later, lying naked in the haven of each other's arms, their bodies moist and fully satiated from their lovemaking, Will was confounded by how deeply his feelings ran for Lexie. This vibrant, beautiful woman had touched his soul. He no longer cared about satisfying his own physical desires, only pleasing her. For the first time in his life, he'd discovered what it felt like to truly make love.

CHAPTER NINETEEN

"I heard about what happened," Mina said, sticking her head into Lexie's cubicle several days later. "I can't believe Sydney sabotaged the show just to get your job."

"She sure did," Lexie replied, swiveling around in her chair. "Let my troubles be a lesson to you, Mina, to always stay on top of your game."

"I most certainly will," Mina said. "By the way, congratulations on your promotion."

"Why thank you, Mina," Lexie replied, grinning from ear to ear. "But you know, I haven't accepted it yet."

"I know, but that doesn't mean it's not well-deserved. Anyway, here are those files you were looking for." Mira handed her several manila folders before leaving.

As she walked away, Lexie felt bad about not revealing the promotion to her parents.

But on the other hand, it sure felt good to be vindicated, Lexie thought. It was now public knowledge that Lauren's protégée Sydney Hamilton had intercepted the Vera Wang shipment to make Lexie look bad. Of course, the joke was on Miss Thang because her plan backfired. Sydney's personal effects were being shipped to her this very second.

Lexie smiled smugly. *Serves the witch right!* She was basking in Sydney's demise when Lauren stopped by Lexie's cubicle to apologize again for the gaff.

Dressed conservatively in a smart gray Dior suit and black pumps, Lauren was the epitome of professionalism. Her mousy hair was twisted in a sleek chignon while her nails had the perfect French manicure.

"It's not your fault," Lexie said, whirling around in her chair.

"How could it not be?" Lauren asked, coming to sit in the chair beside her at the desk. "I encouraged the competitiveness between the two of you."

"No, you encouraged us to be better than the rest. You and I both know that's what the fashion biz is all about. And if I'm not ready for the cutthroats of this business, I'd better get out of the game." Lexie smiled at Lauren. She was smart enough not to ruffle Lauren's feathers.

"That's what I love about you," Lauren replied, patting Lexie's shoulder, "your ability to always see the brighter side. And it's what I'm going to miss, too, if you accept the job."

"Pardon?" Lexie asked, raising one finely arched brow. "Why would you miss me? I'm not going anywhere."

"Of course you are. Didn't we tell you? The position we offered is in our flagship store in Paris and we're going to need you there in three weeks," Lauren said, standing to leave.

The moment the words escaped Lauren's lips, Lexie's heart sunk to the floor. *Please, say it ain't so,* Lexie thought.

"No, I hadn't realized that, Lauren," Lexie snapped.

She rose to her feet. "You made no mention of Paris in your initial offer." Was Bentley's trying to get rid of her? Or maybe Lauren needed her out the picture. It didn't do to have your protégée exceed you in power.

"Bentley's would like you to work with several of their couture designers in Paris. And you know as well as I do that Paris is the fashion capital of the world. It would be a great way for you to network with the best in the business. This is a great opportunity, Lexie."

Lexie digested the information before speaking. "I know, Lauren. But my life, my family, my friends . . . they're all here."

"There are planes and telephones in Paris, too," Lauren replied snidely.

"Lauren, I'm still going to have to give this offer some serious thought."

"I suggest you do, Lexie. Opportunities like this only come once in a lifetime," Lauren commented before walking out of the cubicle.

Lexie slunk down into her chair. How was she ever going to broach the subject with Will? They'd spent so much time together lately, they were practically living in each other's apartments. And the thought of her moving thousands of miles across an ocean would not endear her to him.

What was she going to do? When she tried telephoning Nia, all she got was voice mail. Then she remembered that Nia and Damon were meeting with the wedding planner. She lucked out on her next choice.

Sebastian arrived half an hour later, apologizing profusely for being late due to some horrible accident on the Kennedy expressway. He met her at their favorite spot, a small park half a mile from their first home in

Hyde Park. Lexie was on the swing waiting for her brother, desperate to voice her concerns to someone.

"It's okay," Lexie replied. "I wasn't going anywhere."

"So, what's going on?" Sebastian asked, taking the swing next to hers. "You called and demanded I hightail myself in the midst of rush-hour traffic to the suburbs and meet you."

"I have news about the Bentley's job offer," Lexie said. Pushing her feet off the ground, she started to swing.

Sebastian stopped her swing. "Sis, don't tell me they rescinded the offer?"

"No, it's not as horrible as that."

Sebastian punched her shoulder. "Well, what then? You nearly gave me a heart attack."

"Sorry." Lexie lowered her head and sat quietly, staring at the two little children playing on the monkey bars across from them. Why couldn't life be as easy as it was when you were a child?

"Do you know how proud I am of you?" Sebastian smiled jovially. "You're living your dream, but from the way you're acting, it makes me wonder."

Lexie stopped. There was no sense in beating around the bush; she might as well reveal the whole pitiful truth. "The job is in Paris."

"Paris!" Sebastian jumped off the swing. "You can't go to Paris." Sebastian paced in front of her. "What would I do without you?"

"Yes, and they want me to leave in three weeks, right after Nia's wedding."

"Sis, no!" Sebastian whined, stomping his heel.

"I don't know what do, Sebastian." Lexie's voice broke. "Everyone I love is here." Lexie blinked back the tears that threatened to fall down her cheeks.

Kneeling down, Sebastian patted her knee. "Does everyone include Will?"

"I don't know." Lexie lowered her gaze, trying to mask her inner feelings, but her brother knew her too well.

"I think you do. That's why you asked me to meet you. Forget some man. The Lexie I know would be flying off to Paris at the drop of a hat if it meant her designs would be on clothes racks across America. As much as you loved us, the old Lexie would be off with the quickness, sending us a postcard from gay Paree."

"Sebastian!"

"It's the truth and you know it, Lex. The only reason you're doubting yourself is because of Will. You're in love with him. Aren't you? Just admit it."

"If this heart-wrenching drama is love, then you can have it back because it hurts too much," Lexie replied, pulling out a hanky from her purse and dabbing her eyes.

"Stop being a drama queen." Sebastian stood up from the swing to face his older sister and give her a few words of wisdom. "Since you've been with this man, you've changed for the better, Lex."

"So you're saying I was for the worse before?"

"No, but you have grown."

"And now look at me. This job in Paris is the opportunity of a lifetime. How can I pass that up?"

"I don't know. All I can say is go with your gut. It's never steered you wrong. But in the meantime I've got to get you ready—I mean, get you back," Sebastian corrected himself.

"Why?" Lexie asked, bewildered. "I don't have any plans."

"Don't tell me you've forgotten what today is!"

"What?" Lexie looked perplexed. "Look at my face."

Lexie pointed to her tearstained cheek. "Does it look like I've had time to ponder what day it is?"

"It's your birthday, you dope!" Sebastian popped her on the head.

"Oh, my God." Lexie looked at her watch. "I completely forgot. Between the show and the job offer, it completely slipped my mind."

"Well, your boyfriend will kill me if I don't get you back in time."

"Why? What is he planning?" Lexie asked curiously, grabbing her brother by the arm. "You know something, don't you? Give it up, Sebastian."

"I wouldn't dare," Sebastian replied, releasing his arm from her clutches. "Have you seen your boyfriend? He's Mr. Beefcake and I'm not tangling with him. Just have your butt at his apartment at seven, okay?"

Lexie arrived at Will's apartment for an evening of she didn't know what. As usual, Will didn't disappoint. When she arrived, Nia, Damon, Sebastian, Christian, and Mina were all waiting for her.

So he hadn't forgotten her birthday. Lexie smiled. "Thanks, babe," Lexie murmured in a soft, husky whisper. She greeted him with a long, lingering kiss at the doorway before stepping inside. It was so rare that he let anyone into his inner sanctum.

He looked incredibly sexy, wearing faded jeans and a royal-blue shirt. If her friends only knew what an amazing body was hidden underneath that shirt!

"You're most welcome, darling. You sure are looking mighty fine tonight," Will commented, looking over Lexie's ensemble. He could always count on Lexie to make an entrance. Radiant as ever, her hair was loosely secured in place with chopsticks, dangling gold earrings hung from each ear, and ruby-red lipstick accentuated the red-and-gold kimono she wore. And let's not forget the firm, high-perched breasts that called out to everything male in him. Will growled as Lexie passed him by.

Her nipples hardened in response at his dark scrutiny. All it took was one look at her like that and he could send her body into a state of flux.

"Down, boy." Lexie grinned, coming inside the apartment while Will went to the kitchen to serve appetizers and make cocktails.

Christian greeted her with enthusiasm as usual. "Buttercup, you look scrumptious as always." Christian twirled her around. "I just love your style."

"Thank you, darling." Lexie smiled and kissed either cheek. "And you're not looking too bad yourself." Who could miss his daring, loud, pink, fitted capri pants and print pop-over shirt.

"Come on in, sis," Sebastian said, drawing near. "Have a drink. We're here to celebrate the day you made your blessed appearance on God's green earth."

"And what a day it was." Will smiled at Lexie from behind the counter. Lexie didn't miss the look of sheer happiness on Will's face. Was she imagining it? Or did he look content in spite of the club's woes?

"Happy birthday, sweetie," Nia and Damon joined in, giving her bear hugs.

"You guys are all so wonderful." Lexie lips curved into a smile. She was blessed to have such a great support system. It was why the very thought of leaving Chicago filled her with such dread. These people where her lifeline. She wouldn't have a life without them in it.

Lexie looked up and found Will watching her strangely. Did he sense her dilemma?

"Can an old man get some of that loving, too?" a

strong baritone voice asked from behind Sebastian. *Could it be?* Lexie's heart leaped when her father emerged from behind Sebastian with her mother in tow.

Lexie's lips parted in surprise. "Dad."

"Look who I pulled away from the stove." Her father beamed back at her.

"Mom, what a wonderful surprise!" Lexie bestowed a heartfelt smile at Will. She appreciated his inviting her family, especially her mother. Isabel always claimed that her children didn't include her in their lives, but Will had. Lexie knew how much her mother appreciated the thought even if she didn't show it.

"Well, I figured I could spare a few hours." Isabel smiled at her daughter. "I have to tell you, Lexie, I'm really impressed. It's not every day your daughter gets her own clothing line."

"Who told you?" Lexie asked, peering strangely at her mother. She couldn't believe her ears. Was her mother actually proud of her? After all these years of trying to please this woman had she actually given her a compliment? Wonders never ceased. Lexie wanted to touch her mother's forehead and make sure she didn't have a fever.

"I confess, I confess," Sebastian replied, interrupting the moment. "I couldn't resist, Lex. The news was just too juicy to keep quiet."

"Don't get mad with your brother," Isabel said. "You've achieved a great feat."

"Indeed, she has." Will came forward and handed her a glass of wine. "My baby got skills. Everyone, please raise your glasses in a toast to Lexie Rose Thompson." Will smiled down at Lexie. "We're all so proud of you. And we know this'll be the best year for you yet."

"Happy birthday, Lex!" Everyone cheered and clinked glasses.

"Congratulations, Lexie," Damon rushed over to give her a bear hug. "Your own clothing line. That's really impressive. You're moving up in the world, old girl." Damon lightly patted her shoulder.

"I know, I can hardly believe it," Lexie said choking up slightly. It was so amazing having everyone she loved in attendance. She wished she could bottle this moment and keep it with her always.

"To get the evening rolling, ladies and gents, I'll present Lexie with her first birthday gift of the evening." Will crossed the living room to his side coffee table. "Come here, sweetheart." Will extended his hand.

Nia's eyes rose in inquiry, but Lexie shook her head. She had no idea what Will was planning. The evening had been perfect so far. In their short time together, Lexie had learned that first impressions weren't always right. Will may have been a ladies' man, but he was also a kind, generous, loving man with the people he cared about. She was lucky to have him in her life. Her decision to go to Paris would be extremely difficult. But first, she would try to enjoy the rest of her birthday.

Smiling, Lexie walked toward him. She was stunned when Will pulled out a large jewelry box from the drawer. Her breath caught in her throat.

Will was excited. He knew Lexie would love the piece and although his finances were heading down the tubes, there was no way he would take it back. It was his woman's birthday.

Will watched as Lexie's eyes widened in astonishment as she opened the box. Lying on a bed of black velvet lay the diamond pendant necklace from Tiffany's. After several long, tense moments, Will wondered if it was too much, but then Lexie finally managed to utter, "Oh, my God, Will!"

The guests moved in for a closer look.

Will breathed a sigh of relief. He'd made the right choice and Christian's squeal of excitement sealed the deal.

"Will, you are a doll. Lexie, babe, put it on," Christian demanded.

Sebastian moved in closer. "I've got to hand it to you, Will. You've got style. It's not every day a man can render my sister speechless." Sebastian shook his hand.

Tears sprung to Lexie's eyes. The necklace was beautiful, but way too extravagant. Will's business was in dire straits and although she appreciated the sentiment, he couldn't afford it. Once upon a time she would've taken the expensive baubles men threw at her to gain her affection, but Will didn't need to; he already had her heart. She would allow him his pride and accept it now in front of everyone and then later when it was just the two of them, mention that he should take it back.

"It's lovely, Will. Thank you." She kissed him full on the lips.

"You're welcome. Here." He took the box from her hands and removed the necklace. "Let me put it on you." Pushing her hair back, Will placed the necklace on Lexie's slender neck and closed the clasp.

Inhaling, Will breathed in her sweet honeysuckle scent and wished he could ravish her neck and rain kisses upon it. But they had guests. He would follow through on that sentiment later.

Isabel came forward to have a closer look. "Wow, that's some gift," she said. "It looks to be at least a couple of karats. Are you sure you can afford it?"

Will saw Lexie's jaw tighten in response to Lexie's

mother's complete lack of etiquette. Placing a hand on Lexi's arm, Will stopped her from saying something she might regret later. "It's okay," he whispered.

Will displayed his most disarming smile and replied, "Don't worry, Mrs. T, I've got it covered. Despite what you may have heard or read, I'm not in the poorhouse yet."

Wesley chuckled and even Isabel couldn't resist a smile. The boy had a backbone!

"Now, is everyone ready for a delicious meal that will entice your palate?"

"Yes!" the group sang in chorus. Will led the way to his dining room; with Lexie's family, it was sure to be an entertaining evening.

Sebastian took the opportunity to pull Lexie aside. "I take it you haven't told Will about Paris yet?"

Lexie shook her head. "No, I haven't had the chance. How can I tell him now after this?" Lexie fingered the diamond pendant necklace.

"Better it come from you than someone else," Sebastian warned.

After the final guest left, Will whisked Lexie into his arms and crushed her slender body to his. Caressing her delicate jaw with his fingers, he tilted her head back so he could claim her lips. His kisses were urgent and explorative while his hands were slow and thoughtfully as they caressed every inch of her heated flesh. Her hands ventured out and underneath his shirt while his pushed her kimono dress up around her waist. When his long, narrow fingers slipped inside her bikini panties to stroke her intimately, Lexie gasped in sweet agony. The friction sent her into the throes of sensual bliss and caused her to orgasm almost immediately.

Afterward, Lexie lay cuddled in his lap on the couch, sullen and withdrawn, leaving Will to wonder if something was wrong. He'd noticed she was withdrawn during the party and not her usual showstopper self. Cupping her chin, he searched her face. "What's wrong? I noticed you were unusually quiet tonight."

"Was I? I didn't realize. I guess have a lot on my mind."

"Thinking about a new collection?" Lexie shook her head.

"The bachelorette party? The wedding? Okay. I don't know, what is it?" Will asked.

Lexie had to tell him. She'd never been afraid of a confrontation before. She didn't know why now was so hard. Summoning up the courage, Lexie forged ahead.

"Come here, Will." Turning to face him, Lexie looked into his deep set eyes filled with so much passion and lust that she wanted to drown herself in him and forget about all the rest. But the truth would still be there in the morning. "Will, I spoke with Lauren today."

Will flashed his pearly whites at her. "And?"

"She told me that the job offer is in Paris."

"Pardon?" Will couldn't believe his ears. Did she just say Paris? Will slowly removed their intertwined fingers and retreated to the other corner of the couch.

"When did all this happen? And more importantly, how long have you known about this, Lexie?"

"I don't like your tone, Will," Lexie replied, her chest heaving. "I just found out today."

Will shook his head in amazement. Shock and bewilderment may have been on his face, but they belied his inner turmoil. What he was feeling was hurt. In his wildest dreams he'd never imagined that one day he would meet a woman that could fulfill all his needs. A woman that excited him and one he could respect and admire. Yet here she was staring him in the face. He'd been ready to reveal his true feelings, that he was falling in love with her. And now this.

"Well, aren't you going to say anything?"

"I really don't know what to say, Lexie. An hour ago I was the happiest man on the planet. And now my girlfriend is telling me she's about to move to the other side of the world. I knew this was too good to be true." Will rose from the couch and gathered the half-empty wineglasses and decanters scattered across the room from dinner.

Lexie stood up. "I've made no decisions." And that was the truth. Didn't he understand how much he'd come to mean to her? All she had done the last few hours was agonize over telling him the news.

"Oh, c'mon, Lex. We both know what that decision will be. 'Au revoir, Will. Maybe I'll see you the next time I'm in Chi-Town and we can have a great night in the sack,'" Will said, throwing the glasses into the sink. *Cling.* One glass shattered in a million pieces. Uncaring, Will began picking up the shards and throwing them into the trash.

Lexie jumped up. "Are you okay?"

"I'm fine," Will answered with a sudden chill in his tone.

"You know I didn't deserve that." Lexie returned to their previous topic. She couldn't believe how childishly he was behaving.

"No? Then it's probably the reverse," Will continued with heavy sarcasm. "You'll probably forget you ever knew me and treat me like a pebble underneath one of your Manolo Blahniks."

"Why are you acting this way, Will?" Lexie stormed

to the kitchen and faced off with him. "Are you trying to push me away? Because if so, you're off to a rockin' start."

"All right, Lex, I'll bite," Will said, folding his arms across his chest. "Have you thought about what you're going to do?"

"No, Will. I really hadn't gotten that far yet," Lexie said through thinned lips. She was fast becoming very annoyed; she would not let the almighty William Kennedy walk over her. And thank God she had nerves of steel to take the way he was glowering at her from across the room. "I'm still digesting all this, Will. All I knew was that I had to tell you." Lexie walked toward him, trying another approach. "But then Sebastian reminded it was my birthday. And when he told me you had something special planned, I didn't want to spoil the evening. Please don't be this way, it's my birthday." Lexie held out her arms to him. "Can't we just table this discussion? Nothing has to be decided tonight."

Will debated going to her, but in the end his heart won out. He allowed Lexie to take him in her arms and wrap him up in her fragrant comfort, but in the pit of his stomach he knew the happiness he experienced in Lexie's arms would be short-lived.

He'd been completely caught off guard when Paige's husband, Maxwell, had said "you better get used to the red-eye my friend. I hear long distance relationships aren't what they're cracked up to be. Personally, I'm glad I have my woman right by my side." Will had wanted to punch that smug look right off his face.

Will had been silent on the ride home from Maggiano's the following Friday and Lexie knew that the honeymoon was over. The entire week they'd been running on borrowed time, but tonight after the fiasco at the rehearsal dinner, there was no turning back.

"So everyone knows!" Will hissed in the foyer of her apartment building.

"I guess so," Lexie replied as she dug into her purse for her keys. Finding them, she inserted the key into the lock. "The only person I told other than you is Sebastian, he must have let it slip. Seems he's been a blabber mouth lately." Fumbling, Lexie made several attempts but couldn't get the key in the lock.

Grabbing it from her, Will twisted the lock and opened the door. He held the door open and allowed her to precede him. "Well you might as well have taken out in advertisement in the *Chicago Sun Times*." Will shut the door forcefully.

"This isn't Sebastian's fault. He means well." Lexie stood up for her brother. "He's just excited for me because he knows that this has been a lifelong dream."

Annoyed, Will threw his hands up in the air. "There, you see what I'm talking about? The elephant that's been in the room for the last week. You and I both know that you can't walk away from this opportunity. Go to Paris, Lexie. Take the job offer."

Will's callous disregard for her feelings stung. "Is that how you really feel?" Lexie asked, swallowing the sob caught in her throat. "If I go, you'll have no feelings one way or the other?" Her voice cracked slightly.

Will turned and faced the wall before answering. If he told her to stay and she regretted it, he would never forgive himself. So, he had to tell her to go. He couldn't stand in the way of her dream, even it meant he wouldn't have her in his life. If he didn't convince her to go, he'd lose her anyway.

"Lexie, really . . ." Will sighed in frustration. "Why don't we just call this what it was. An enjoyable sexual relationship. You got what you wanted and I got what I wanted. And now we can go our separate ways."

Lexie felt the blow deep within the pit of her stomach. It hurt but she was still standing. "A sexual relationship. Did I mean so little to you?"

"Lexie, what we had has run its course. Now it's time to move on."

"Move on? So you can go back to the hordes of women that frequent your club to get in line for the Will Kennedy train?"

Will watched the light in Lexie's eyes go out and the tenderness in her voice die, but he continued. "Yes, that's right," he replied, attempting smugness. "Many women love the Kennedy train. As you have the last few months."

He hated himself the moment he said the words, but he had to make his act good or she'd never believe him otherwise.

Lexie's hand swung out and connected with his face. The old Lexie, the one who wouldn't stand idly by and be insulted, was back in effect. Clearly she'd had misjudged Will Kennedy. The academy should give him an Oscar for his performance because he had sure convinced her that they were building a relationship. The worst part was that she wasn't even looking for one. Could she really have been so far off the mark?

"You forget who you're dealing with." Lexie wagged a finger in front of Will's face. "I have never let a man defame me and I'm not about to start now. I hope you enjoy your next round of nameless, faceless women because you just missed out on the best thing that's ever happened to you. And I guarantee you're going to regret it."

Pushing past him, Lexie stalked to his bedroom

closet and pulled out her Bentley's overnight bag. While she packed her belongings, she remembered a happier time, such as when he'd first offered her a key to his place and what a big deal that had been. And now none of it seemed to matter; he was tossing her aside in favor of the casual fling.

Lexie fiercely tore her clothes off the hanger and stuffed them into her bag. It didn't take her long to clear out the closet.

Will followed her and stood solemnly watching from the doorway. His heart ached. He desperately wanted to stop her. Tell her he loved her and he never wanted her to leave. But he couldn't. He had to let her go. If he didn't and she stayed, she would resent him for the rest of her life.

With sheer effort, Lexie managed to keep any tears at bay until she finished cleaning out the armoire as well. She would not give him the satisfaction of seeing her cry. She would get over him just as she had done every other loser before him.

When she was done, she threw the bag over her shoulder and pushed past him toward the door, but Will gripped her arm. "Listen, Lex, I'm sorry it had to end like this. I want you to know that I enjoyed every bit of our time together."

"How kind of you, Mr. Kennedy," Lexie said, sneering, buoyed by her pride if nothing else. "I really hope you enjoy your newfound independence. Now drop dead." Lexie stormed out of his apartment.

Frozen in place, Will stared at the door that reverberated after her.

CHAPTER TWENTY

Will was miserable, as he, Ryan, and their mother sat at the dining room table listening to the options Julian Masters laid out. As one of Will's best friends, Julian was serving as Ryan's attorney and, boy, did he need the big guns. After all the bad press, the district attorney suddenly had a tough attitude on drugs and was determined to charge Ryan as an accessory to selling them.

"So basically you're recommending that he plead guilty and make a deal with the DA?" Will asked.

"Yes, in my legal opinion. If he tells the DA all he knows about this J.T. person, he can prevent himself from being sent to a juvenile home or, worse yet, jail. He is seventeen and able to be charged as an adult," Julian replied. "Ryan, I'm sorry to say you're in a lot of hot water."

"Will!" his mother cried. "You can't let this happen. Isn't there something that can be done?"

Ryan was scared. This lawyer Julian didn't pull any punches. But he had to do the right thing. "Mom, it's not Will's fault. I'm the one that got myself into this," Ryan said.

"You hush. You're just a child, what do you know? Will should be handling this. It was his club after all that caused all this trouble."

Ryan was tired of seeing their mother blame Will for everything. It was time he stood up like a man and was accountable for his actions. Will had taught him that. Couldn't she see his brother was a man of integrity?

Will shook his head. It was always the same game. Blame Will. After a restless night of sleep and a splitting headache, he was in no mood for his mother's theatrics.

"Julian, he'll take the offer. Please make the necessary arrangements." Will stood up to leave. He'd had enough family for one day, and without Lexie by his side, his patience was short.

"You have no right to make this decision." His mother's voice began to rise.

"What's done is done, mother. Julian, let me walk you out." He waited for Julian to pack up his briefcase before escorting him to the door.

"Don't worry, Will. I've seen that boy grow up. He's a good kid. I promise I'll take care of him for you." Julian patted him on the shoulder.

"You have to. My family means everything to me," Will replied.

"I know. Listen, I go way back to law school with the assistant district attorney. I'm hoping I can still turn her eye, if you know what I mean. Perhaps she can persuade her boss to change his mind."

"Do what you can," Will said, closing the door. With lead feet, he returned to the dining room to face the wrath of Eve Kennedy.

"Do you have any idea what you've done?" Eve wailed. "Now Ryan's going to have a record. You've ruined his whole future. Is that what you wanted?"

"No, Mom, but it's the only way out of this nightmare."

"He could have gone to court and proved his innocence. And now that's not possible. God, you're just like your father. He always thought he knew what was best, and look where he ended up. Dead. Is that what you want for your brother?"

"You're exaggerating as usual, Mother. And you know what?" Will grabbed his leather jacket off the back of his chair. "I won't stand here and let you bad-mouth my father one more minute. So he made some mistakes. But so have you—you got involved with another loser, but do you see me blaming you, for being a single mother? My father is gone now and I won't let you blame me anymore for his choices. Do you hear me?"

Whipping around, he found Ryan in the corner watching their argument, but Will didn't care. He just wanted out. Minutes later, he slammed the front door. Once he reached his car and got inside, Will banged his fists against the steering wheel. The pent-up anger from losing Lexie and the challenges ahead for Ryan's mistake were eating him inside. But he shouldn't have lashed out at their mother in front of Ryan, even though she deserved it. He had to show Ryan, to respect black women. Will made a mental note to talk to his brother once he had time to cool off.

In the middle of packing up her office, Lexie was startled to find a strange woman at her doorway.

"May I help you?" Lexie asked.

"Are you Lexie Thompson?" the redhead inquired.

"Yes."

The redhead smiled, revealing a large, toothy grin.

"I'm a huge admirer of your work. I saw your designs at Millennium and they were fantastic."

"Thank you. But I'm still not quite sure why you're here," Lexie said, immediately defensive. Since the fashion show, Lexie was very cautious of reporters. She'd had enough of people prying in her affairs, personal or otherwise.

"Forgive me, my name is Natasha Jackson and I'm with *Chicago Magazine.*" Natasha extended her hand.

"Oh, my God!" Lexie beamed, clutching her chest. "It's so great to meet you. I've read several of your articles. Please sit down." Lexie offered Natasha the seat that flanked her desk. "What can I do for you?"

"It's more like what you can do for me," Natasha began. "My magazine would love to do a story on you, a rising designer in the Chicago marketplace. We think you're the next big thing."

"I'm flattered, but—" Lexie paused.

"What's wrong?" Natasha asked. "This would be great exposure for the launch of your collection."

"To tell you the truth, Natasha, I'm not going solo. I'm selling my designs to Bentley's and moving to Paris next week."

"You can't be serious!" Natasha's voice rose. Lexie had clearly stunned her. "Are you absolutely sure about this, Lexie? You don't know me from Adam, and the fashion business can be a huge risk, but you don't need Bentley's."

"What are you talking about?"

"You're a talented rising star. Bentley's is the one that needs you. In today's competitive marketplace, they need a designer like you to infuse their store with new blood, and what better way than to convince you that *you* need *them* to succeed."

A bell went off in Lexie's head. It had never occurred

to her, but now that Natasha mentioned it, maybe it was worth considering starting her own business. She'd only agreed to go to Paris on a trial basis while her attorney reviewed the contract.

"Just consider it before you go signing away your future." Natasha rose. "Here's my business card. I would still love to do that story on you if you're interested."

"Thanks again, Natasha." Lexie shook her hand. "You may have solved all my troubles." Dazed, Lexie went to stand at the window at looked out over State Street. Natasha Jack had just given her the answer to staying in Chicago.

Later that evening while Will was in the midst of making dinner, Julian stopped by with news of Ryan's fate. Julian came dressed in a navy suit and tie with matching blue tie while Will stood casually dressed in gray sweats at the kitchen counter, cutting vegetables for a stir-fry.

"Can I get you a drink?" Will asked, heading to the fridge.

"A beer would be great," Julian replied, taking off his jacket and plopping his briefcase on the coffee table. "I never pictured you a cook, Will."

"I can manage stir-fry," Will answered, pulling out two bottles of beer. Cracking one open, he held it out to Julian before returning to the counter and vegetables. He searched Julian's expression for some indication of how his meeting went with the assistant district attorney, but Will couldn't read it. "So, what's the word?"

"I've secured a meeting with the DA," Julian announced,

"That's fantastic. And quick," Will said. "How'd you manage that?" After adding a touch of peanut oil to the hot wok, Will threw the assorted vegetables inside before glancing back up at Julian.

"I have my ways." Julian smiled. "No, seriously, I spoke with Elizabeth Brackett, the assistant DA, and convinced her that this case was a waste of time. Ryan's a good kid and doesn't belong in jail with juvenile delinquents. She spoke with the DA on our behalf and apparently he agreed not to press charges."

"Then why does he want to meet with us?" Will inquired, stirring around his vegetables with a large wooden spoon. "Why doesn't he just throw the case out?"

Julian shrugged. "I don't know, Will. Maybe he doesn't want to come out of this with egg on his face. He made such a big deal in the press and now he might have to eat those words. Let me see what he wants and I'll let you know."

"No way." Will shook his head. "I'm coming with you."

"I don't think that's a good idea," Julian said, taking a swig of beer.

"Ryan's future and my future depend on this guy. I'm not about to leave that in anyone's hands. Not even you, my friend."

"Understood." Julian realized that Will was in a precarious situation, and wouldn't hold it against him.

"No hard feelings?" Will held out his hand.

"None." Julian shook it and placed the bottle of beer on the counter. "I've got to run; I'm meeting Whitney for dinner. Be at the courthouse at ten A.M. on Wednesday."

"Sure thing."

Will could only hope that the DA was a reasonable man because his livelihood depended on it. Picking up the phone, his first thought was to call Lexie and tell her that the DA wasn't pressing charges, but then he remembered the current status of the relationship.

Hanging up the receiver, Will decided to blow off some steam at the club. Thank God he still had his baby, Will thought, as he started toward his bedroom. At least for now.

After working late finishing up pending projects, Lexie headed to Millennium. She and Will had some serious talking to do. It was high time they cleared the air. After having a few days to think, she decided maybe all the pressure had gotten to him; he'd acted completely out of character. Now that things had settled, maybe there was still hope for the two of them.

Lexie didn't see him immediately when she entered the jam-packed club filled with couples swaying to R. Kelly's stepper's song, "Step in the Name of Love." Pushing through the crowd, Lexie made her way to the bar for a much-needed drink after a hard day's work.

"Hey, Jerome." Lexie smiled at the bartender.

"Lexie, long time no see."

Jerome leaned over to give her a kiss on the cheek. She had always liked him. Unlike some other bartenders who talked too much, Jerome knew when to keep quiet and let you drink in peace.

"I know, I know." Lexie smiled. "Hook me up with a Cosmo, will you?" Lexie gave him a wink.

"Sure thing. I suppose you're looking for the boss man?" Jerome asked as Lexie unsuccessfully tried to look over the crowd.

"Yes, I am. Would you happen to know where I might find him?" Lexie accepted the martini.

"Over in his usual spot, the corner booth."

"Thanks." Taking a sip of her drink, Lexie gave

Jerome a thumbs-up on the drink and slid him a five-
dollar bill. Walking to Will's favorite booth secluded
in the back of the club, Lexie found several women
hugged tight to *her* man, and Will sure didn't seem
to mind. Lexie blinked in disbelief. Was she so easily
forgotten? Anger filled her belly. She thought about
going over and ripping out the weave on all those big-
boobed bimbos, but she had too much class for that.
Will had returned to his old lifestyle, and if that's the
way he wanted it, then so be it. A new life awaited her
in Paris. One that didn't include him.

With a splitting headache after the previous night's
festivities, Will headed to the Chandlers' office on the
South Side the following morning. He wanted to discuss Julian's news with the Chandlers and get their
perspective, as well as advice on how best to proceed.

Without an appointment, Will was kept waiting for
several moments before the receptionist ushered him
into the conference room where the Chandlers sat
waiting for him at a large table. After filling them in
on the status of the case, Paris and Iman thought the
fact that the DA wasn't pressing charges was a positive
indication that the tide was turning in Will's favor.

"You think so?" Will was little skeptical.

"Yes, the DA knows what a good kid Ryan is. But
it's reelection time and with his lackluster track
record on crime, now he has to appear tough on it,"
Iman commented.

Paris continued. "Your story only gave him fuel to
add to the fire. But we can use this to our advantage."

"How so?" Will asked.

"We need positive publicity, right?" Iman asked, rising from her chair as the wheels began to spin in her

head. "Well, what better way to achieve that than to have it come out of the district attorney's own mouth?"

"That's right." Paris took the ball and ran with it. "We said we wanted to have a press conference. Show the public you have nothing to hide. Having the district attorney admit that you're working with him would definitely put a positive spin on the situation and put Millennium back on the map."

"Exactly," Iman said, standing behind her sister. "I think we should have a press conference right after your meeting with the district attorney."

"Well, what do you think?" Paris asked, her eyes bright with excitement.

"I think it's brilliant," Will answered, "But do you think, he'll go for it?"

"Of course," Iman replied. "He'll do it. It's free publicity and he's a politician, isn't he?"

The three of them sat huddled together for several hours, preparing Will's speech for the press conference and discussing further ways to increase his profile in the media. Once they'd come up with a plan and broke for lunch, Will felt decidedly optimistic. Maybe there was hope for him after all.

As he stepped from his Lexus outside the courthouse on Wednesday morning and stared at the facade, Will was amazed at what a dull, dreary building it was. He dreaded going inside. The cold gray exterior and antiquated architecture was extremely depressing. How could the wheels of justice prevail in that gloomy place? As Ryan and his mother exited the vehicle, Will prayed it would.

He was happy the day was finally here. They would meet Julian and together they would go inside and face the district attorney, Ken Warner, and iron out the terms of Ryan's fate. Will hazarded a look at his kid brother and felt sorry for him. Fear was etched across his fate. Will hoped this would be a lesson to him to always tell the truth.

Walking up the courthouse steps, Ryan trembled at Will's side. He was scared out of his mind at the prospect of meeting the district attorney. Julian had told Will that the DA had agreed not to press charges. So why did he want to see him? Had he changed his mind? Was he being sent to juvenile hall or jail? A tear fell from Ryan's eye.

"It's going to be okay," Will said, glancing over at a very-shaken Ryan. Will comforted him with a bear hug. "I'm here and so is Mom and Julian. We're all looking out for you, and with the two of us at your side, you've got nothing to worry about. Isn't that right, Mom?" Will looked over at his mother, who had remained surprisingly quiet during the car ride.

"Of course," Eve replied, solemnly standing by Will's side.

Ryan attempted a halfhearted smile to satisfy them, but inside he feared for his life.

Determinedly, Will and Eve strode through the revolving doors with Ryan by his side. They were stopped in the lobby by security and forced to go through a security check before entering the premises. Once through the checkpoint, they proceeded down the hall toward the district attorney's office. They found Iman and Paris Chandler already waiting in the hallway outside the office with their briefcases in tow.

"What are you guys doing here?" Will queried, checking his watch. "The conference isn't until noon."

"We're your publicists. We wanted to be here to support you," the sisters replied in unison.

Will smiled. This was why he'd selected the Chandlers' firm, because they were known for their commitment and integrity. "Thanks, guys, we really appreciate it. Don't we, Ryan?" Will gave Ryan's shoulders a tight squeeze. But all he received from Ryan was a nod.

"Ready?" Julian asked, peeking his head outside the door. He'd arrived fifteen minutes early, eager to get a feel from Elizabeth on what the DA Warner's mood was. Elizabeth, however, had told Julian that he appeared in good spirits, but that she had no idea what his agenda was. She was surprised he hadn't just handed the case over to her.

"Yes, we're ready," Will said and pushed Ryan toward the door. Will turned and stopped Eve from joining them. "Mom, why don't you stay outside while Julian and I handle this?"

"Why don't you want me in there? Do you plan on striking some kind of deal with him?" Eve inquired suspiciously. She was not ready to hand off her youngest son to the system.

"Of course not, Mother. I want only what's best for Ryan."

Eve clutched Will's arm. "Promise me you'll do nothing to jeopardize his future."

"I promise you, Mom," Will said, helping his mother to the bench outside the DA's office. Glancing over at the Chandlers, Will said, "I'll see you both outside on the courthouse steps for the press conference."

"Sure thing, Will. We'll have everything ready for you," Iman replied as he shut the door behind him.

Five minutes later, Julian, Will, and Ryan were led into the district attorney's private office. Will was surprised to find a short, balding, middle-aged man in an old-fashioned suit and checkered tie. And his office, well, that was nothing much to speak of. It had to be about eleven-by-twelve feet wide with an oak desk, an old shelf full of books, and several overstuffed filing cabinets. Will gathered that public servants didn't receive many perks.

"DA Warner, it's a pleasure." Julian shook his hand.

"Please have a seat." The district attorney pointed to the chairs opposite his large oak desk. Julian, Will, and Ryan all took their seats.

Opening his briefcase, Julian wasted no time pointing out to the district attorney Ryan's clean arrest history and his superior academic record. Suddenly, the DA put his hand up and stopped Julian midmonologue. "I understand all that, Mr. Masters. so let me put your mind at ease. I have no intention of charging your client, Ryan Kennedy, with drug selling." He pointed to Ryan, who was quivering in his chair. "Or imposing a fine on your club, Mr. Kennedy." The DA stared at a shocked Will, who'd sat stalwart the entire time. "Just as long as you do a favor for me," he said, pulling a handkerchief out of his breast pocket and dabbing the sweat from his upper lip.

"And what might that be?" Will asked, speaking up. Was the DA trying to shag him? If so, he was in for a rude awakening. Will would not be blackmailed. He ignored the disdainful looking coming from Julian. "I hope you're not suggesting something illegal."

"Of course not." Mr. Warner appeared shocked by such a suggestion. "As you well know, I'm in the middle of reelection and I need a win desperately. If your brother agrees to help us apprehend J.T. Rodriguez and testify at his trial for the prosecution, then he's a free young man."

Will exhaled, letting out the large breath of air he'd

been holding inside. "All you want is for Ryan to speak the truth on the stand?" he asked.

"That's all I want," DA Warner replied, leaning back in his chair.

Will glanced over at his brother. "Well, I think that's fair. Ryan can attest to the fact that that punk J.T. bullied him into letting him in my club. What do you think, Ryan, can you handle that?"

Overcome with emotion, Ryan's head remained bowed in his lap and he could only nod at his older brother.

"Then let's get out of here," Will said leaping from his chair. He had a press conference to attend. He was ready to shout from the rooftops that his brother was no criminal. "Thank you, sir." Will shook the DA's hand before heading out the door. Afraid to look up for fear his good fortune might not be true, Ryan followed quietly behind him.

Julian, meanwhile, closed his briefcase with a smile. Thankfully, he hadn't even needed it. Ryan was a lucky kid; he'd seen many youths go the other way.

"Good. Then let's consider this matter settled." Pressed for time before his next trial, the district attorney stood up and shook hands with Julian. "You be sure to have your client prepped and ready for trial, ya hear?"

"I most certainly will." Julian was happy that all that was well, had ended well. Before turning to leave, Julian asked for one final favor.

"I only have fifteen minutes."

"I promise this'll be quick," Julian said and closed the door behind him.

Eve was immensely relieved when her sons exited the district attorney's office within ten minutes of their arrival. "Is everything okay?" she asked, looking to Will first and then to Ryan.

"Everything's great, Mom!" Ryan exclaimed, lifting his mother in his arms and swinging her in the air. "Will did it. He got me off. I'm free as a bird." Ryan kissed his mother's face profusely.

"Put me down, boy," Eve Kennedy replied, but she couldn't resist grinning at her eldest son. Will didn't look for Eve to speak the words he saw in her brown eyes; instead he held out his hand to his mother and his brother and together they walked to his press conference.

Before a group of reporters and with Eve, Ryan, and Iman and Paris Chandler behind him, Will gave a statement of the events surrounding the fashion show. Will accepted no questions until the district attorney appeared briefly to corroborate his statement. District attorney Ken Warner was a man of his word and attested to Ryan's innocence in complicity with drug selling and revealed Will's cooperation with the authorities. The press ate it up with a spoon. It didn't take long for them to question what Will's next move would be.

"I have the answer to that," Evan DuBois stated from behind the crowd of reporters. Bulbs flashed in front of Evan's face as he walked toward the podium to face a stunned Will. "Mr. Kennedy will be expanding his nightclub business with a new club called Risqué." Glancing at Will, Evan spoke loudly into the microphone so everyone in the community could hear. "Courtesy of DuBois Investments." The press snapped a photo as Evan shook Will's hand before moving to the side of the podium.

Was it true what they said, that all goods things came to those who wait?

After taking several questions, the Chandlers wrapped up the press conference amidst a flurry of speculation about Will's next project. As the production crew took down the podium, Will wondered if the positive press would be enough to pull Millennium out of its slump.

"Trust us, Will," Paris reassured him, squeezing his shoulder, "we know the media. They can put a good spin on anything, and with the DA behind you, you've got it made."

"Again, ladies, I thank you." Will shook both their hands.

"We were happy to assist you," Iman replied for the both of them. "Remember us the next time you need some good PR." She smiled before she walked away with her sister.

"Well, we're heading home now, Will, to celebrate." Ryan grinned up at his big brother. "Wanna come and join us?" The invitation was an olive branch. Ryan knew he'd hurt his brother; he only hoped that one day Will would forgive him for all the trouble he'd caused.

"I will later on," Will said, giving his baby brother a long hug and a wink before Ryan and Eve left to go home. As they walked away, Will breathed a sigh of relief that the nightmare was finally over. But now he had no one to share his triumph with. Lexie was no longer a part of his life and he had no one to blame but himself.

Dejected, Will walked alone back to his car.

CHAPTER TWENTY-ONE

Will, Julian, Maxwell, Sebastian, Marcus Bradley, and Nia's father, Nathaniel Alexander—hell, even Christian—gathered around Damon to toast his impending marriage to the love of his life, Nia Taylor.

Inconspicuous waiters were sure to keep the liquor flowing while Will's deejay kept the music lively with an assortment of songs, from "Who Let the Dogs Out" to Shaggy's "Hot Shot." Will was determined that his best friend would say good-bye to bachelorhood with a bang.

Will had prepared an evening of fun and debauchery for Damon's bachelor party, but no matter how hard he tried, something felt off. The cigars tasted stale and the cognac tasted dry. Sure, in his capacity as best man he'd done the standard fare of cigars, cognac, brandy, Crown Royal, and the like, but right now Will had no interest. Only one thing was on his mind. His woman, who would soon be heading off to the land of the Eiffel Tower. Not that he'd had much say in the matter.

When she'd told him about Bentley's offer, it felt like someone sucker-punched him. Somehow he'd gotten into his head that they were building something, a foundation. He'd thought nothing but good things were ahead of them; he could never have guessed how wrong he would be. It killed him to convince her to take that position, but what other choice did he have? He wouldn't stand in the way of her dream.

Damon caught him staring off into space and commented on his odd behavior. "You all right?"

"Sure, buddy. Hey, it looks like your glass is empty. What do you want to drink? A Slippery Nipple, Sex on the Beach, or a Purple Hooter? Or how about an Alabama Slammer?"

Damon smiled. "Whoa, there, buddy."

"It's all about you tonight, Damon. Whatever you want is on the menu." Will attempted to be enthusiastic.

"Looks to me like you've got everything covered." Damon inclined his head toward the big blow-up doll, the plasma television screen on stage playing an adult film, and the full-blown buffet with spicy Caribbean skewers, plantains, and jasmine rice.

"Nothing but the best for you, my friend." Will laughed devilishly. Wait until Damon saw the rest.

Several hours and a couple of drinks later, the strippers arrived and pranced around in G-strings and bikini tops, enticing and delighting Damon's friends and colleagues. While they were a hit with the other gentlemen at the party, Damon remained detached, preferring to enjoy the cigars at the bar instead with his soon-to-be father-in-law, while Will's mind was focused on finding that punk J.T.

Just then, Will's cell vibrated on his hip. The screen listed an anonymous call and Will debated on whether to take it. It was his best friend's bachelor party, after all, but it could be news on J.T. and he had to finish this drug business once and for all. He didn't want a cloud over Millennium any longer than necessary.

"I have news of J.T.'s whereabouts," a raspy voice whispered from the other end. "Meet me at the corner of Fifty-Fifth and Halsted." *Click.*

Will hated to leave the party, but he had to.

It was the first solid lead he'd had since he began his own investigation. After interrogating Ryan, he'd discovered that J.T. had been harassing him for weeks and was the cause of that mysterious black eye. At the time, Will suspected foul play, but had let it rest. Maybe if he'd kept a better eye on his little brother, the whole situation could have been circumvented.

Will tried sneaking out of the bachelor party unnoticed, but Damon caught him going out the VIP entrance.

"And where do you think you're going?" Damon asked. "The girls are in there getting buck wild. Come on back in. There is plenty of fun to be had, at least for you. You're still single. Me? I'll watch from a distance. Nia's all the woman I need."

Will paused at the door. "No can do, man. I've got to go."

Damon stared at him suspiciously. "But you're the host."

"I know. You stay." Will pushed Damon inside. "Have fun. I'll be back before you know it." Will turned to walk away, but Damon grabbed him by the arm.

"All of a sudden the best man and host is leaving the party? What's going on, Will?" Damon demanded.

Will stopped midstride. He couldn't lie to his best friend. Damon wouldn't believe him anyway, he knew him too well. So he told the truth. "I've got a lead on that punk J.T.'s whereabouts."

"And you're going follow-up on it alone?" Damon asked. The man had no common sense.

"Yes."

"Not without backup, you aren't," Damon said, tossing his beer bottle in the trash. Together he and Damon snuck out of the party unnoticed.

Shortly thereafter, Will was walking through some darkened, garbage-filled corridor while Damon waited in the passenger seat of his Lexus. The scent of rotten food and dirty diapers overwhelmed Will. It had been a long time since he'd seen this side of town, but he was determined to follow-up on the lead he'd received. The unidentified caller had asked to meet him at this undisclosed location.

Knocking on the door, Will waited for an answer. After looking over his shoulder for several nerve-racking moments, the door finally cracked open.

"Come on in," a masculine voice called out.

Cautiously, Will crept inside the room and searched the darkness for a figure, but couldn't make out anyone. The room smelled pungent and stale. He was starting to get the feeling that this could be a setup when he sensed a presence behind him.

Before he could move, a figure rushed him, tackling him from behind. Seconds later, a fist connected with Will's jaw. First one and then another, followed by a one-two jab to his middle. Will crashed to the floor with a loud thud.

"Yeah, I'm about to mess you up, pretty boy." Will recognized the voice. "So, you been looking for me, have you? Well, you don't know who you've been messing with, but you're about to find out."

It was J.T. and he was laughing. Anger rose inside him. Somehow he found an unknown strength and sought J.T.'s figure through the moonlight. Will grabbed J.T. by the throat and slammed him against the wall, then punched him in the abdomen.

J.T. bowed over in pain, crouching to the floor. Will prepared for battle until he heard the click of the trigger.

"You think you're tough, huh, pretty boy?" J.T. taunted, pulling the weapon out from the back of his pants. "Well, let's see how tough you are with a gun pointed at you."

Will wasn't about to be punked by some criminal. "Why don't you put down the gun and fight me like a real man?"

"How dumb do you think I am?" J.T jeered. Before Will had a chance to react, J.T. smacked the gun across Will's temple. Will collapsed in pain and seconds later the world faded to black.

On the other side of town, Lexie and Paige were putting the final touches on the buffet table for Nia's bachelorette party. Paige had graciously agreed to allow the party to be held at her home in Arlington Heights. The large two-story, five-bedroom home had a spacious living room and adjoining dining room that could easily house the fifteen women who had RSVPed for the night's rousing festivities.

Balloons and streamers filled the room, along with a banner labeled *Ball and Chain*. Lexie had chosen a Hawaiian luau theme for the party, complete with dancers. Well, one in particular. Lexie knew Nia was going to kill her, but she'd hired a fabulous stripper she'd encountered at a previous bachelorette party. She was sure he would get the party started, Lexie thought with a smile.

"That smile looks very devilish," Paige commented. "What have you got in store for us this evening?"

"Oh, a little of this, a little of that," Lexie said with a shrug.

"Are we going to be seeing a little flesh tonight?" asked Paige excitedly. Lexie's face split into a grin.

"Now, what would a bachelorette party be without a little entertainment of the male variety?"

"Lexie, you bad, bad girl."

"That's me."

Once Paige disappeared into the kitchen, the grin Lexie had splashed on her face since the moment she arrived with the balloons and decorations and food was replaced with a frown. As much as she loved her girl, her mind was on another person entirely. For days she'd thought of nothing but Will.

How had this happened? She'd never allowed herself to get attached before. Men pursued her, but only as far as she let them. Will had penetrated her soul and now she kept reliving the horrible fight with him that occurred several days earlier. And they'd said such mean things to one another. Some of which could not be taken back so easily. And then there was the other night at the club with all those hoochie-mamas pawing her man. How had they gotten to this point? Had she driven him back to the arms of all those other women?

"Earth to Lexie." Paige waived her hands in front of Lexie's face.

"Sorry."

"Where was your mind wandering off to? To that new job of yours? Nia told me you got a promotion."

It was the source of all her current woes and the last thing Lexie wanted to talk about. Sure, the reporter had mentioned starting her own design business, but it was a huge risk. If she took Bentley's offer, she'd have it made. She'd be living in the fashion capital of the world, sipping lattes while Bentley's helped her create her own line. Lauren was waiting for a final answer, one she wasn't all that prepared to make. On the one hand, Will, and on the other, the dream of a lifetime. How could she choose?

The doorbell rang, signaling the arrival of her guests. There was no time to worry over the mess her life had become. Plastering her smile back on, Lexie greeted Jordan Bradley, Whitney Travis, and, surprisingly, Carly Matthews.

Lexie was surprised Jordan had deigned to grace them with her presence this evening. Although close to both Lexie and Nia's age, Jordan rarely socialized with them. She wasn't Nia's biggest fan and, from what she'd heard, Damon's sister had practically chained herself to her desk at work. In her opinion, the girl needed to loosen up and have some fun. Lexie could only imagine how she would react if a stripper like Carlos sat in her lap. Grinning, Lexie determined to make it happen. "Hey, Miss Jordan. How's life at Hamilton Morgan and Gilbert?" Lexie inquired.

"Everything is going quite well," Jordan answered. "Thanks for asking. Congrats on that promotion. It's quite a coup for a black woman in today's society."

"Indeed it is. It's not easy, as I'm sure you're aware in the legal field."

"Only the savvy sistas such as ourselves survive."

"Let's toast to that." Lexie reached for two Appletinis and handed one to Jordan. She needed stiff ones to keep her mind unaware of a certain bachelor party on the other side of town. "To the savvy sistas."

Breaking away, Lexie found time to make contact

with Carly, a surprise guest. How had Will's ex gotten an invite? Did they have a party crasher?

"Carly," Lexie greeted her and kissed either cheek. "I'm surprised to see you here."

"Nia invited me," Carly answered, walking over to the punch bowl. Lexie's mouth formed an "O."

Carly explained while filling her cup at the punch bowl. "She and I became great friends while I was dating Will and have kept in touch ever since. She's a really great person, you know."

"I do." Lexie flashed a smile. "And if she invited you, then you're definitely welcome. Please make yourself at home." Lexie had no beef with Carly. She'd handled herself professionally during the show and had never made a play for Will. Lexie respected her for that.

Nia was blissfully happy when she arrived and anxious to open all her bachelorette gifts. Christian appeared several minutes behind her in a desperate panic to get away from "all that testosterone," as he'd called it, and over to the real fun. Before long, the ladies were down to the serious business at hand: food, drinks, games, gifts, and, of course, the stripper. Lexie couldn't wait to see Nia's shocked expression.

The stripper arrived as planned, looking like he'd just stepped out of *Playgirl's* centerfold. Six foot-four with large biceps, six-pack abs, and a deliciously tight bottom, the stripper was the pièce de résistance.

He was quite the private dancer, but Nia took a pass. The surprise out of the bunch was Jordan. When the stripper danced his way in front of the stiff attorney, Jordan stuck several dollars bills in his G-string. The stripper used that as an invitation to back up that tight behind and plant it firmly in the young attorney's lap. With her café-au-lait coloring, Jordan turned several shades of red when Carlos gyrated his bottom against her middle. Before long, the entire group of women was screaming, "Go Jordan! Go Jordan!"

When the stripper released the clip in Jordan's hair, sending a pile of curls raining down her back, Jordan let loose and tried a little dirty dancing of her own. While Nia howled uncontrollably at Jordan's attempt to dance, Lexie disappeared from the group and the loud blaring Cameo music to find a moment of peace and quiet in the kitchen.

Closing the doors behind her, she breathed a sigh of relief. Thankfully it was empty, except for the stack of half-eaten platters sitting on the countertops. The ladies had devoured the feast of hot spinach and artichoke dip, sesame chicken, pot stickers, black-bean quesadillas, and sangria that Lexie and Paige had laid out. The silence gave Lexie a moment to think about Will. She struggled with indecisiveness. Why were life's big decisions never easy?

"There you are!" Nia exclaimed, entering the kitchen. "What are you doing hiding in here?"

Attempting a smile, Lexie swung around to greet her best friend. "No reason. I just came to make some margaritas." Lexie looked around for some margarita mix.

"Now, do you honestly think you can fool me?" Nia asked. She'd noticed that Lexie's smile hadn't quite met her eyes. "You may fool the others, but not me. Why don't you tell me what's bothering you?"

Lexie paced the floor. "It's your night. I don't want to bring you down. Hell, I already borrowed your wedding dress."

Nia laughed. "That you did. And that same dress made you a star. Now sit down. I'm not budging until you start talking." Nia pulled Lexie by the arm and dragged her into a chair nearby.

"You're too good to me," Lexie said when Nia reached inside Paige's refrigerator, grabbed a bottled water, and handed it to her. Lexie took a long swallow.

When she didn't immediately speak, Nia interjected. "Does this have something to do with Will?" When Lexie turned away, Nia knew she'd struck gold.

For the second time in her life, Lexie had experienced true heartache. She loved Will and he had slipped through her fingers. Lexie's head fell to her lap in despair. "It's simple, really. I have a choice to make. I can either stay in Chicago or jet off to Paris. Either way, I lose something that means everything to me."

"I gather Will didn't react well to the news."

"Quite the opposite," Lexie replied sarcastically and took another large gulp of water. "Imagine my surprise when Mr. Smooth was as cool as a cucumber, telling me to go off and fulfill my dream."

"Are you hurt by his reaction?" Nia inquired. Lexie had claimed that she and Will were just a fling; perhaps their casual relationship had turned into something more.

"Yes, but more than that, I'm pissed!" Lexie raised her voice. "Nia, if you could have seen him, he was so cavalier. Acted as if the last three months didn't exist, like they meant nothing to him." Lexie shook her head in disbelief. "Obviously he couldn't wait to get rid of me. I must be a real nuisance." Lexie rose from the kitchen table and paced the ceramic tiled kitchen floors. "Or maybe I got boring in bed and he needed someone new between the sheets."

"Stop for a minute here, Lex." Nia put her hand up and halted Lexie's speech. "Don't you think you're overdramatizing things a bit?"

"No, I don't," Lexie said and punched the table for emphasis. "Ouch." They both laughed when Lexie kissed her sore knuckles. Embarrassed, Lexie took her seat.

"Did you ever think that maybe he's hurting, too? That he told you what he thought you wanted to hear?" Nia asked, turning Lexie's chair to face hers.

"Are you taking his side? I thought you were my friend." Lexie pouted.

"No, I'm not taking his side. I'm just trying to get you to see the big picture before you leap to the wrong judgment. Think about it, Lex." Nia grabbed her Lexie's trembling hands. "If he knows you as well as I do, and cares about you as much as you say, then don't you think he would know how much this opportunity means to you?" Nia paused for effect. "And if so, then he would have to let you go. Otherwise you'd resent him for the rest of your life and that would be much worse."

Lexie thought about Nia's logic. It all seemed to make sense. "Or maybe he's just ready to resume his playboy ways," Lexie said. She'd seen Will the other night at the club and he wasn't having any problems in that department. "How could he do this?" Lexie wondered aloud. "Nia, just the other day he told me this was the longest he's ever been with a woman. Could he really have discarded me like yesterday's trash?"

"Haven't you done the same?" Nia countered. At Lexie's curious expression, Nia continued. "I seem to remember a certain woman casting aside men like they were last season's purse. Why are you so content to believe the worst in him? Maybe you're afraid, too."

"I'm not afraid," Lexie replied a little too quickly for Nia's taste. "If he cares for me, then he wouldn't let me go, plain and simple. It's certainly not easy for me to walk away."

Nia's eyes widened in recognition of what she'd seen

in her own eyes when she was falling in love with Damon. "Oh, my God, Lexie, are you in love with Will?"

Pausing for a moment to catch her breath, Lexie finally nodded the truth. "Shock of all shocks, huh, Nia? I don't know when or how it happened, but somewhere along the way I fell in love with him." Amazed, Lexie shook her head. "I sure as hell wasn't looking for it, but there it is, the whole sad story."

"Lexie, trust me. Love has no rhyme or reason. It just is. Sometimes it sneaks up on you when you least expect it, but if you love Will, you have to fight for what the two of you have."

"How can I when the decks are stacked against us?" Lexie ran her fingers through her hair. "Anyway, if what you say is true, it changes nothing. It still begs the question: do I stay or do I go?"

"Do not call Lexie," Will instructed Damon from his bed in the emergency room. He was fine. All he had was a concussion. There was no reason to bring Lexie into this. It would only cause her undue worry and bring added friction to an already tense situation. What was done was done.

Thank God for Damon; he'd had the good sense to dial 911 and come in after him. He'd prevented J.T. from taking a shot at him by tackling him to the ground. Now Will could sleep again, knowing J.T. was in custody. And after an hour of interrogation, the punk had cracked under pressure and revealed that he set the whole plan in motion to move drugs through Millennium. He also admitted to making that anonymous phone call Will received during the bachelor party.

"And why not?" Damon inquired, rubbing his bald head. Why did Will have to be so stubborn? "She would be worried sick if she heard the news from someone else."

"Why? Because I said so, that's why. She'll worry and there's no need. Let her enjoy her night." Will started to sit up, but when he did all the blood went rushing to his head, forcing him to lie back on the pillows.

"Now you'll know better the next time you go taking matters into your own hands," Damon said. "Listen, I'm going to grab a sandwich and some coffee. I didn't get to eat much at the party."

The moment Damon mentioned the word *party,* Will felt horrible. They were off playing detective when Damon should have been enjoying his last night of bachelorhood.

"Damon, I'm sorry. I ruined your night."

"It's cool. Unlike most, I look forward to the day I make Nia my wife."

"Has anyone ever told you you're a hopeless romantic?" Will smiled.

"On that note . . ." Damon exited, but he didn't go to the cafeteria. Instead he pulled his cell phone from his breast pocket. He didn't care what Will said. He'd seen how much Lexie had changed from a spoiled, carefree spirit to a loyal, caring woman who cared deeply for his best friend. Lexie would want to know.

Lexie answered her cell on the second ring. "Hello?"

"Hey, Lex. It's Damon."

"Hey, big boy. You enjoying your bachelor party? I bet you want to talk to my girl."

"No, Lex. I called to speak to you."

At the strained sound of Damon's voice, Lexie's stomach sunk. "It's Will. Something's happened to him, hasn't it?"

"Oh, my God!" Nia looked up, stunned at Lexie's outburst. "What's wrong? What is it?"

Avoiding answering, Lexie scanned the kitchen for a pen and paper. Finding them on the adjacent coffee table, she scribbled down the hospital information.

"Okay. Thank you for calling me, Damon." Shakily, Lexie closed her cell. "Nia, I've got to go. Will's been hurt."

"Then I'm coming with you," Nia replied. "You're in no condition to drive." They returned to the living room, where Nia gave her apologies and explained what happened.

"I am so sorry, ladies, I thank you dearly for coming," Nia said. "Truly, from the bottom of my heart, I appreciate all the gifts and heartfelt wishes. I loved everything and I'll see you all at the wedding." With a quick wave and a kiss at the remaining women, Nia accepted her coat and purse from Paige and rushed out the door behind Lexie.

CHAPTER TWENTY-TWO

Bursting through the door of the emergency room, Lexie raced down the hall to the admit station. Nia followed, carrying Lexie's coat and purse.

"I'm here to inquire about William Kennedy. He was injured tonight."

"Are you a relative of the patient?"

"No. I'm his girlfriend," Lexie replied shortly.

The nurse searched a pile of files in front of her. "Yes, he's here, but I'm afraid I can't give out any more details on the victim unless you're a member of his immediate family."

"Listen, woman!" Lexie shouted. "The man I love has just been hurt. All I want to know is how he's doing. It's not the Holy Grail."

The nurse and Lexie argued back and forth for several moments about privacy laws, until Nia jabbed Lexie in the arm.

"There's Damon!"

With her heart beating rapidly, Lexie ran toward Damon and clutched his arm. Was that Will's blood? "How is he? Is he okay?" *Oh, please, God, please don't take him away from me.*

"Slow down, Lex." Damon patted her hand. "He's fine. It was just a small bump on the head. He was knocked unconscious for a while, but he's okay. They are keeping him overnight for observation."

"Thank God." Lexie hugged Damon close. "How did this happen?"

Damon pulled her away and led them both toward the waiting room.

"I don't know how much you know, but he's been searching for that thug who stabbed his brother?"

"What? Who in the hell did he think he was, Superman?"

"I don't know, Lex. He got an anonymous tip and went off to meet him. And of course it turned out to be a trap. J.T. was waiting there for him. But Will brought backup."

"Are you hurt?" Nia interrupted, running her hands over Damon's whole body.

"No, baby, I'm fine." Damon halted her hands.

Nia sighed. "Thank God."

"Do you mean to tell me that Will took on a criminal?" Lexie shook her head in amazement. She could strangle him for endangering himself.

Damon shrugged his shoulders in response.

"Well, when can I see him?"

"Soon, real soon, Lexie." Damon tried to soothe her frazzled nerves.

"Why are you stalling, Damon?" Lexie asked with her arms folded across her chest. "He doesn't want to see me, does he?"

Damon nodded. Will was going to be furious that he had called Lexie. He'd been adamant that he didn't want her contacted, but after what Damon had just seen, he had to.

"Well, that's tough. I'm going to see him whether he likes it or not."

"Good for you, Lex. Will needs a firm hand."

"Where is he?" Lexie asked.

"Follow me." With his arms encircling Nia's waist, Damon led Lexie to Will's curtain in the emergency room. Luckily, the strict nurse was distracted by a flurry of new patients.

Damon and Nia stood outside the door, allowing Lexie to be alone with Will.

Gearing up her courage, Lexie swung back the curtain. Will was asleep on a stretcher with some gauze wrapped around his head, but otherwise he appeared healthy. Lexie hoped the experience had sobered him from ever attempting to play hero again.

Coming forward, Lexie stood at his bedside. Staring down at him, he looked so peaceful that Lexie decided to lean down and press her lips softly against his temple, but when she did, his eyes immediately popped open.

"Hey, there," Lexie whispered, pulling herself up.

"Damon called you, didn't he?" Will glowered at her from the bed.

"Of course. You had to know he would. How're you feeling?"

"How do you think? I have a concussion," Will managed to croak out. The moment he uttered the harsh words, Will wished he could take them back, but it was too late. The concern etched on her face turned to sadness.

At the edge in his voice, a cold shiver went down the length of Lexie's spine. Even after a near death experience, nothing had changed between them. Why did she continue to torture herself? Wasn't seeing him at the club with his slew of women enough?

She didn't know what she'd hoped for, but it was definitely not this.

"I had to see for myself that you were okay. We meant something to each other at one time, you know?" Lexie wiped away a fallen tear. "And now that I have, I can go. I hope you have a speedy recovery."

Lexie managed to walk out the door before Will could see her break down and know exactly how much he'd hurt her.

But the hurt in Lexie's eyes was not lost on Will. He called after her, but she'd already fled down the hall.

From the wedding chapel bridal chamber at the New Hope Baptist Church, Lexie helped Nia dress for the biggest, most important day of her life: her wedding.

"You look so beautiful, Nia. Absolutely stunning," Lexie said as she stared at Nia in a Lexie Thompson original. The V-neck, dropped-waist ball gown was made of satin and embellished with pearl beading, while the long cathedral veil and train were embroided with lace. The florist had outdone itself, creating Nia a one-of-a-kind tiara headpiece made of tiger lilies. Open-toed ivory sling-backs finished the look of a woman on her way to meet her destiny. As Nia stood in front of the long pedestal mirror, Lexie's breath was taken away and she withdrew a handkerchief from her purse and dabbed at her eyes.

"Why are you so sentimental all of sudden?" Nia inquired as she fingered her platinum three-stoned, three-and-half-karat, princess-cut, diamond engagement ring.

"Thanks a lot." Lexie sniffed. "It's just that you look absolutely marvelous in the dress that single-handedly launched my design career. And now . . ."

At the thought of Lexie leaving, Nia's eyes welled up. "Stop it, okay? You're reminding me that you're leaving and I can't think about that right now." Nia sighed wistfully. "We've always lived nearby, and now, after all these years, you're leaving!"

"That's life, honey. Eventually one of us had to fly the coop. First me to Paris, and now you to marriage. Can you believe you're marrying the man of your dreams?"

Nia smiled through her tears. "Sometimes I can hardly believe how lucky I am."

"Nia, how did you know when it was right? That Damon was the one?" Lexie asked, fingering Nia's train.

"I think I knew the first moment I met him. I felt an instant connection with him, like we were two halves of the same whole."

"Wow. You have got to use that in your vows."

"I am." Nia laughed. "I've been rehearsing for days. I'm so nervous. Do you see my hand?" Nia displayed her shaking fingers.

"It's okay," Lexie said, holding Nia's cold hands. "You're going to get through this, girl. You and Damon were made for each other. Now, here's something blue." Lexie handed her a blue lace handkerchief.

"Thank you," Nia said, "but don't change the subject."

"I've had it with that man, Nia. After the wedding, I'm off to start a brand-new life in Paris."

"So you're going to leave without telling Will how you feel? Are you sure you're ready to walk away from the best man you've ever known? The man that made your toes tingle and your heart race?"

"Well, when you put it like that, it does make me look kind of foolish, but what other choice do I have? Will has told me in no uncertain terms where he stands. He's made no declarations of love. He hasn't asked me to stay."

"Did you tell him how you feel? Maybe that would've changed things."

"No, I didn't, okay!" Lexie looked away and stared into her freshly cut tiger-lily bouquet gathered together by a band of satin ribbon. "But I suppose you think I should?"

"Only you can answer that, Lexie. All I'm telling you is that it's not every day you find the person you're meant to be with. Do you know how hard it is to find 'the one,' as you put it? You'd better think long and hard before you walk away from him. Now get out there, maid of honor." Nia pushed her toward the door. "I hear the wedding march."

"Okay." Lexie blew her a kiss and exited the bridal chamber.

Nia had made some great points. Of course now she didn't know what to do. She was torn. Should she leave? There was no time to answer that question.

The wedding march was already in full swing, with Damon's little cousins marching up the aisle, sprinkling red rose petals along the white aisle. Standing at the doorway, Lexie's stomach fluttered the moment Will emerged from the back of the church. Since he was the best man, she would not be able to escape him the entire day. He was her escort and would have to walk her down the aisle after the ceremony was over. Luckily she would not have to endure sitting next to him at the reception because she would be sitting next to Nia. But they would have to share a customary dance after the happy couple and their parents.

When she heard her cue, Lexie began a slow ascent up the aisle toward the love of her life and the minister at the opposite end. Forcing her feet to move, she strolled toward them. When she arrived, Lexie breathed a sign of relief. Thank God, she'd made it with no event. Venturing a look over at Will, Lexie found him staring resolutely down the aisle, awaiting Nia's arrival, so she followed suit.

On the other side of the altar, Will was awed by Lexie's beauty. She was a vision as she glided toward him in an ivory halter sheath that revealed her lithe body without being scandalous. Trust Lexie to design a one-of-a-kind piece while the rest of the bridesmaids— Jordan, Paige, and Whitney—wore standard A-line, peach-colored, strapless gowns. The wedding and reception would be difficult. No, make that impossible. It was truly going to be one of the hardest and longest days of his life. Will was not looking forward to what came next.

Lexie meanwhile was welling up with tears. In her peripheral vision she saw Damon beaming, Nia's aunt Olivia crying—hell, even her mother was part of the occasion, offering Olivia a handkerchief. But the only person Lexie could think about was Will. The touch of his hand on hers, the smell of his woodsy cologne . . . it all filled her with longing. For what? Commitment. Marriage. Children. Those had always seemed foreign to her—until now. And now that she had found love, they never seemed further away.

The guests stood to watch Nia glide down the aisle like a fairy princess to meet Prince Charming. Leading her down to the altar was none other than her father.

It wasn't too long ago that Nia had hated her father and refused to have anything to do with him, but look how far she'd come. Who would've ever thought that she'd see this day? Damon looked equally dashing, dressed in a black Armani tuxedo and silver cummer-bund.

Jordan recited one of the couple's favorite poems and Paige and Maxwell sang "Endless Love." Lexie's eyes teared up when Nia and Damon spoke their vows and pledged their undying love and devotion to each other. Anyone watching could see how heartfelt it was and how truly in love they both were. Even Will had felt it; although he'd tried to ignore Lexie, once or twice she had caught him wistfully staring her way. Was he imagining that they too could have this life, just as she was?

Before she knew it, the wedding ceremony was over and the bride and groom were jumping over the broom and heading down the aisle.

Will's heart thumped loudly in his chest as he extended his arm to Lexie. It was a wonder she couldn't hear it.

Putting on her best impression of a happy maid of honor, Lexie accepted Will's outstretched arm as they filed out of the church and into the foyer. Putting one foot in front of the other, they moved smoothly down the aisle as one.

Simone was playing the happy hostess in the receiving line while Marcus and Nia's grandfather, Samuel Taylor, vied for top host position.

Now the real test would come. Lexie would have to stand and smile in front of everyone and pretend her heart wasn't breaking. Luckily she had a little help from the wedding photographer, Sebastian.

He pulled her briefly aside. "How are you holding up?"

"I'm managing."

"Keep it together. I'll try to make these shots as painless as possible. Okay?"

Lexie nodded.

Sebastian placed the bride and groom in several poses before adding Nia and Damon's parents. Her brother took several shots of the bride and groom's party as well as the entire wedding party.

Lexie was happy when it ended and she could remove the fake smile plastered on her face. It killed her standing there watching several ladies flirt with Will, who ate up all the attention. Long live the playboy!

The guests and wedding party arrived before the happy couple at the luxurious Riviera Country Club in Orland Park. The wedding was hailed by the *Chicago Defender* as the premier event of the season, and with society matron Simone Bradley in charge, there was no doubt in Lexie's mind that the wedding reception would be a classy affair.

When Lexie arrived, the club was already in full swing. The Bradleys had spared no expense. It was the wedding of the season. Guests were mingling or strolling about, trying to find their name cards on the round tables strategically placed throughout the large ball room that encircled the huge dance floor.

Beautifully decorated centerpieces adorned each cream-colored tablecloth while crystal wine goblets, fine china, linen napkins, and stainless-steel flatware covered each place setting.

A jazz quartet was settled nicely in the corner, ready to begin their long evening, while the bartender shone up glasses in preparation for an open bar. All the while, a videographer was there to capture the entire event.

Lexie turned when she felt a finger tap her shoulder.

"Hey, Daddy." Lexie leaned in to give her father a peck on the cheek. "Wasn't the wedding beautiful?"

"Yes, Nia was a sight for sore eyes."

"By the way, where's Mom?" Lexie asked, looking over his shoulder.

"Simone stopped us on the way in and asked your mother if she wouldn't mind taking a look at the caterer's progress."

"I don't know, Dad. Maybe that wasn't a wise idea. You know how caterers are about their turf."

"And you know your mother."

Lexie laughed. "I do indeed."

"Ladies and gentlemen." The emcee for the evening interrupted their conversation. "The bride and groom have arrived."

"Gotta go, Dad," Lexie said as she kissed his cheek quickly and rushed to her place at the head table.

At the sound of the trumpet, everyone turned to face the doorway and watch the newlyweds' arrival. "Ladies and gentleman, I give you Mr. and Mrs. Damon Bradley."

Nia walked in, beaming and radiant on Damon's arm. The groom looked equally smitten. The couple took their place at the head table, surrounded by their bridesmaids and groomsmen, while their parents and grandparents sat at a table nearby.

Before long, liveried waiters brought in their first course of house salad with raspberry vinaigrette along with baskets of fresh Italian bread. The second course consisted of either a fourteen-ounce, grilled, center-cut filet mignon with red wine sauce, chicken Wellington, or a herb-crusted Chilean sea bass, along with parmigianá mashed potatoes and fresh seasonal vegetables. Vegetarians were served grilled vegetables with risotto and shiitake mushrooms.

Everything looked delicious, but Lexie could hardly eat a bite as they brought course after course. Her mind would wander to another time when she and Will happily sat sipping café lattes at Starbucks or when they were in the shower making mad, passionate love into the wee morning hours.

Will didn't appear to be having any problems; she'd seen a waiter carry away his empty plates. After the final course was removed, the emcee announced that it was time for the first dance. Damon led Nia to the floor and danced to one of their favorite Kenny Lattimore songs "For You."

She looks so beautiful, Lexie thought. *Maybe one day I'll have that kind of happiness.*

After the first song was over, Nathaniel tapped Damon's shoulder to cut in. Lexie had never seen Nia look so . . . Lexie searched for a word . . . so content. Lexie wondered if she was destined to be alone.

There wasn't time to debate the answer because Will was standing in front of her table, holding out his hand. Her first instinct was to deny him, but Simone would kill her if she didn't follow tradition. Reluctantly, she accepted his hand for what was sure to be their final dance.

From the moment Will's hand touched the small of her back, Lexie was taken back to the times they had danced at his club. Especially that first time when she'd tried pretending she wasn't attracted to him. It had all been a lie. And he'd known it.

As they swayed together to the music, Will's heart beat loudly in his chest. When he rested his head softly against Lexie's hair and inhaled its fragrant scent, Will knew he couldn't continue. If he did, she'd realize he wasn't as over her as he appeared. He had to convince her.

Pulling away, he kissed her right hand and said, "Thanks for the dance."

Still riveted to the spot on the dance floor, Lexie watched as Will had the unmitigated gall to head to another table and ask another woman to dance. The song wasn't even over yet.

And trust Will to find the most gorgeous woman in the room; he selected a gorgeous, curvy woman with long curly hair, fake breasts, and a big behind.

When he returned with the other woman, Lexie put on a stiff upper lip and tapped him on the shoulder. "I don't know why you're behaving like this, Will," she whispered in his ear. "But it's really beyond tacky. You could have least waited until the song ended." Lexie stormed off the dance floor. Will had made his point. They were over.

"I need to talk to you," Damon stated a short while later, grabbing Will by the elbow and shoving him into the groom's chambers. Although the place smelled of the bride's father's cigars, it was the only quiet place Damon could think of, and Damon needed to change into his honeymoon clothes.

"You and Nia getting ready to head out?" Will inquired, gulping the last of his champagne. A little bit drunk, he stumbled into the lounge chair in the corner of the room.

Damon snatched the plastic flute out of his hand. "Are you sure that's how you want to play this?" he asked, tossing the flute into the garbage.

"What do you mean?" Will replied, tucking his shirt back into his tuxedo pants. When had that come undone? he wondered. Probably when he was dancing around with the buxom babe in the red party dress.

"I mean parading all these women in front of Lexie in an attempt to make her jealous. Do you have any idea what you're doing? You can only push women so far before they push back. Especially Lexie."

"I know what I'm doing," Will said and attempted to stand up.

"Famous last words." Disgusted by his friend's behavior, Damon turned away and began removing his tuxedo, starting with his boutonniere.

"You don't understand, Damon." Will's voice slurred. "I have to appear like I'm having the time of my life so Lexie will get on that plane and fulfill her dream, when in fact I could care less about any of those women."

"Then why do this?" Damon whirled around and shook Will's shoulders. "Tell her how you truly feel, man. It could make all the difference." Damon let Will go and finished dressing.

"Easy for you to say. You're a happily married man now." Will grinned.

"Yes, I am. Which is why I can tell you to stop wasting time. Life is too short," Damon said, putting on his sports coat. "Now listen, I want you to go grab hold of that woman and make her yours. Do you hear me?"

Will wished it were that simple.

"I'm going to round up Nia now and get this honeymoon started." Damon grinned mischievously. "I'll see you when I get back." The men shook hands and Damon left in search of his new bride.

"You aimed that bouquet directly at me," Lexie accused Nia as she helped Nia into a casual cream-colored pantsuit back in the bridal chamber.

The tiny room left little space for Nia to get ready, but because this was Simone Bradley's favorite church, Nia had agreed to have the wedding there even though the small, perfunctory room barely held her and Lexie. *The angels ought to clone that girl,* Lexie thought, *Nia hasn't complained once about the tiny bathroom, closet, and makeup desk.* All she'd commented on was that the chamber housed every bride's essential ingredient on her wedding day, a floor mirror.

"And your point? Maybe it'll throw some good luck your way in the romance department. Take my word for it, you're next, kiddo," Nia said as she nervously tried buttoning her suit jacket.

"I sure hope so," Lexie said. At Nia's nervous fingers, Lexie asserted herself. "Here, let me." She slapped Nia's hand away and buttoned the jacket for her. "Whoever it is will have to drag me kicking and screaming to the altar." They both stopped what they were doing to imagine the thought and burst out laughing.

"I am going to miss you so much, girlfriend." Nia hugged Lexie fiercely once she was finished dressing.

"Me, too." Lexie squeezed her hard before finally letting go. "We've come a long way, you and I, from college students to career women and now a wife. I'm so proud of you, Nia. Look how far you've come. You look absolutely fabulous in that cream Dolce & Gabbana suit and every bit the society maven." Lexie laughed.

"Oh, stop." Nia sniffed. "You know I learned from the best!" Nia's eyes began to mist. "So, we'll see each other soon?"

"Absolutely. You and Damon will come visit me in Paris and have a second honeymoon." Lexie perked up. "Imagine how much fun we'll have shopping in all the couture houses now that you've married into money." Lexie tickled Nia's side.

Nia leaned in to give Lexie a quick kiss. "Call me if you need anything, okay?"

Knock. Knock. Damon peeked his head inside. "You ready?"

"Give me one minute, sweetheart."

"All right," Damon replied, closing the door.

Nia turned around and gripped Lexie by shoulders. "Okay, this is it." She breathed a long, audible sigh. "Before I leave, I want you to know how incredibly proud I am of your accomplishment, Lex. I know that you're going to be a great success. And if you never listen to any of my advice, please listen to this one: I know Will is behaving like an ass, but trust me, he loves you. He's just scared. When you find love like what you have with Will, you've got to hold on to it for all it's worth and never let go."

Nia closed the door behind her, leaving Lexie to wonder if she was making the right choice.

Her mood, however, veered sharply from sadness to anger when she exited the chamber and found Will with yet another woman draped over him. Her face grew hot with humiliation. How dare he behave as if what they shared never existed? She'd really had enough. Making her way through the reception, Lexie found her purse.

"Where you going, sis?" Sebastian asked as he followed her to the exit.

"Home. And as soon as I can the first plane, to Paris."

Sebastian instantly knew the source of his sister's dismay. His eyes found Will's across the room, and if looks could kill, Will would be dead in an instant.

"Don't worry, little brother. I have my black book." Lexie tapped her purse. "And trust me, all I have to do is pull out any one of those numbers and I'll have a man so fast, Will's head will spin."

"You'll return to your old ways, I suppose?" Sebastian asked tartly.

"Not at all. I'm open to another relationship. It just won't be with Mr. Kennedy. Gotta go." Lexie gave him a quick peck before rushing out.

CHAPTER TWENTY-THREE

Alone in his apartment the following afternoon, Will sat at his laptop and was buoyed by the club's receipt results. Business was indeed picking up. He breathed an instant sigh of relief. For a minute there he was scared the Kennedys wouldn't come through, but after the press conference, business had improved. Paris and Iman Chandler said it would be a slow progression, but things were definitely on the upswing.

Glancing at the clock, Will noticed the time and date. Today was the day Lexie flew off to Paris to begin her new life. He hadn't known, but apparently she'd stopped by the club a few days ago. And he would never have known if the usually close-lipped Jerome hadn't finally spoken up. Lexie must have weaved a magic spell on him, too. Had she come to say she'd decided not to go to Paris? Of course, now he would never know.

The damage was already done. He'd already behaved like a fool at the wedding, hamming it up with any number of available and willing females, all in attempt to make her jealous. And he had succeeded. She'd left the reception early right after catching Nia's bouquet.

Was it a sign? Because if so, he'd messed it up royally and he had only himself to blame.

By now she was probably on a plane somewhere over the Atlantic. Or maybe not. Maybe he could convince her to stay with three words. It wouldn't solve their problems, but it could change things. Maybe he should call and at least say good-bye and wish her a happy life.

He quickly dialed her direct line at Bentley's. Another feminine voice answered.

"Lexie Thompson, please."

"I'm sorry, sir, Lexie has transferred to our Paris office. Would you like me to give you her number there?"

"Uh, no." Will was heartbroken. "Um, do you know when she left?"

"If I'm not mistaken, her plane is set to depart at five P.M. today," the receptionist responded.

"Thank you." Will hung up the line. He was too late.

Buzz. Buzz. Will glanced down at the phone and saw Jerome buzzing him from downstairs.

"What is it, Jerome? Didn't I tell you I didn't want to be disturbed?" Will barked.

"Yes, I know, but—"

"But what? I said no calls—"

"Boss," Jerome stopped him midsentence. "A Mrs. Thompson is here to see you. She says it urgent and she would not be denied."

Will smiled. Isabel Thompson was here to see him. There was about to be hell to pay. "Thanks, Jerome. I'll be down in a minute."

"That would be wise," Jerome advised. "She said she doesn't like to be kept waiting."

Rolling his eyes, Will put on his mental armor and exited the apartment. Entering the club, he found Isabel seated at the bar, sipping a fruit juice.

"Surprised to see me?" Isabel asked sardonically.

"I must admit that I am, Mrs. Thompson. You do realize that Lexie and I are no longer seeing each other."

"Which is precisely why I'm here, to prevent this travesty from happening," Isabel stated unceremoniously.

"I doubt you can stop it, Isabel. I called the office earlier to wish her the best and she's already gone."

"She's not gone yet, Will. My husband and I are on our way to see her now and say our good-byes."

"So she's still here?" Will asked.

"Yes, haven't you heard a word I've said?" Isabel finished her drink and stood. Opening her purse, she slid a few dollars toward Jerome. "Listen, Will . . ."

He took a step backward, even though she was only five-feet, he assumed Isabel Thompson could pack a powerful wallop.

"I don't know what happened between the two of you, but what I do know is that my daughter happens to love you and you'd be a fool to let her go. You have one final chance to correct your mistake, Will. "I'm inviting you to her loft with the rest of the family. I suggest you take me up on the offer."

"Mrs. Thompson . . ."

Isabel dismissed him with a wave of her hand. "We're beyond formalities. Call me Isabel."

Will rubbed his head in frustration. "Isabel, I'm not sure I can keep her here. I've said some things I may not be able to take back."

"Listen, Will," Isabel pointed her finger in his face, "I don't want my daughter traipsing about in some foreign country where the people eat snails. My daughter belongs here in Chicago. And my money is on you to convince her of that fact. Now, she may be stubborn, but I have faith you'll win her over." Isabel looked at her watch. "The time is twelve-thirty. Be there at one-thirty or you'll regret it for the rest of your life. Good day."

Will watched Isabel march out the door. Now that was a woman he feared!

After she left, he debated all of five seconds before running up to his loft and searching for the keys to his other car, a Corvette. He would need speed if he wanted to reach the North Side to—as Damon once said—fight for his woman. Once he found the keys, he bolted out the door.

"Not you, too, Chris," Lexie said, when his eyes broke out in tears at her loft the afternoon of her departure. Lexie patted his hand to soothe him.

"How will I survive without you?" Christian asked, placing his other hand on his head with a dramatic flourish.

"Don't despair. It's going to be okay. Don't worry, you'll visit me all the time. Just you wait and see. It's going to be fabulous. Me and you, we're going to rock Paris."

"Of course we will, darling, please forgive me." Christian wiped away tears from his cheek with the back of his hand. "It's just that . . ." Christian walked away, unable to finish his sentence.

"Personally, I think all of you are overreacting." Isabel put in her two cents as she taped up several boxes to ship across the Atlantic. "Paris is an eight-hour plane ride away. She's not going to Asia or Africa, for goodness's sake."

"How can I be overreacting when my one and only baby girl is moving all the way to Paris?" Her father's voice broke. Always the sentimental one, she could always count on her father to make her feel special.

"Come here, Dad." Lexie planted a huge kiss on his cheek. "But for once I'm going to have to agree with Mother."

"Say it ain't so!" Sebastian laughed. "After twenty-nine years, you two actually agree on something. And all it took was you leaving the country."

"Oh, shut up, Sebastian. You're going to miss not having someone to harass."

"They do have phones for that, you know," Sebastian said, joking.

Lexie ignored her younger brother's sarcastic comment and hugged her father. "I love you, Daddy, with all my heart." With his face in her hands, Lexie kissed either cheek. "And I'll be back soon. I promise."

Lexie spun and found several sad faces, and she knew she had to end the misery. "Okay, guys, we should say our final good-byes. The limo will be here any minute and I need to give the place a final once-over. Now, all of you come here and give me a big hug."

One by one, they each took their turn. Her mother's was short and sweet, just as Lexie expected.

Her brother was all smiles as he gave her a long squeeze. "I know it's going to be hard doing without all my amazing wit and my inventive cooking, but you'll be fine in gay Paree." Lexie's eyes began to water. She and Sebastian shared such a great bond; she would miss him terribly.

"Don't get all teary-eyed on me. It's all good, sis. I'll see you soon," Sebastian said, walking away. When he gave her a final look and Lexie caught the tear in his eye, she felt ill to her stomach.

Fortitude, Lexie whispered to herself. *Fortitude.* But once Christian came and stood in front of her, her fortitude turned to mush. He was the worst, holding a tissue and dabbing at already swollen red eyes. "You stop this, okay?" Lexie said, shaking his shoulders. "Look at you. If the Fab Five ever saw you with puffy eyes, you'd be devastated. Give me a kiss."

"I'll do you one better." He gave her a hug the size of Texas. *"Au revoir."* And with a kiss on the cheek, he rushed out the door before she could say good-bye.

"From the day you were born. I always knew you were an angel. So you go out and become the star you were always meant to be." Her father squeezed her tightly before letting go. "Bye, pumpkin."

"Oh, Dad," Lexie cried.

"C'mon, Wesley." Isabel stepped forward and grabbed her emotional husband by the arm. She'd had enough of this crying fest. Her daughter sure knew how to be dramatic. "I'm taking your father home. You call us when you land, okay?" Yet Isabel hoped it wouldn't be necessary. If Will listened to her advice, he would be here any minute.

"Bye, Mom."

Isabel nodded at Lexie before closing the door. She didn't have to speak; Lexie knew she cared and would call her the second she landed in Paris.

Once they were all gone, Lexie walked around her loft for one final look. Her new apartment in Paris came fully furnished, so all her furniture would remain in Chicago.

Suddenly she realized her new hideaway would seem cold without her African masks, design easels, or Sebastian's photographs.

The only things she was taking were her clothes, shoes, CD's, and a few other odds and ends.

Glancing down at her watch, Lexie noticed it read one-thirty. Where was her limo? She didn't want to miss her flight.

Knock, knock, knock.

Lexie shrugged on her motorcycle jacket that matched her leisure T-shirt and Levi's jeans and prepared for her long journey. *That must be driver,* thought Lexie, and swung open the door. She was astonished to find Will leaning up against the doorway. For a moment, neither spoke. Will wanted to reach out, but Lexie stared at him in amazement. They both started talking at the same time.

"What are you doing here?" Lexie said.

"I'm here to win you back," he said simultaneously, a little too matter-of-factly, in Lexie's opinion.

Needing to face her on equal footing, Will stood up straight.

Shock turned quickly into fury for Lexie. "*Excuse me,* what makes you think that's even possible?"

"May I come in?" Will asked, out of breath. He had sprinted up the stairs, taking two at a time, hoping he hadn't missed her. His car was still parked haphazardly on the street.

He'd come to beg her to take him back. He was prepared to tell her that he'd stuck his foot in his mouth, and ask her to stay in Chicago and try to make a go of it.

Lexie considered slamming the door in his face, but she couldn't resist hearing what he had to say.

Will forged ahead and walked inside. Walking to the window, he stared below and saw her limo driver waving, but ignored him. "Before we met each other, we were used to keeping people at a distance, but then we let each other in. Hell, I'm amazed we lasted as long as we did, but we did and that's because you let me see the real you, Lexie. I got to see into your soul and see what a truly wonderful person you are, and I'm the better for it."

"And look at where it got me." Lexie laughed deri-

sively. Will had hurt her badly and she wasn't going to
let him get away with it a second time. "You're de-
luded. And I don't have time for this. My driver will
be here any minute."

Will heard the harsh tone in Lexie's voice, but it
wasn't going to scare him. He was here to reveal his
true feelings and nothing was going to stand in his
way, not even the lady herself.

"I was a fool to let you go, Lex. I should have asked
you to stay. Don't you see? I only wanted what was best
for you. And I thought that by giving you your freedom, I would save you from a lifetime of resentment.
I couldn't stand it if you grew to resent me. That I
couldn't bear. So if it meant giving you up, then that's
what I was going to do. But I want you to know how
very proud I was—no, *am*—of you. You've accom-
plished a great feat. You're living your dream. I didn't
want to stand in the way of that."

Lexie's cell phone rang. It was the limo company. "I
don't have time for this, Will. It's a little late in the
game. The limo is waiting downstairs. I've got to go or
I'll miss my flight." Lexie didn't want to hear his re-
grets. It was too late. She tried to push past him, but
Will stood firmly in her path.

"Not until you hear what I have to say. And if you
want to leave after that, I won't stop you. Fair
enough?"

"Fine." Folding her hands over her chest, Lexie
took a seat on her couch. "I'm listening."

Swiftly, Will moved to kneel at Lexie's feet. "Don't
worry, princess, I'm not about to beg, at least not yet."

Lexie tried to avoid smiling at his cute jokes.

"Lex." He grasped her petite hands in his large ones.

Looking at his watch, he didn't have much time to
convince her not to leave. He didn't have time for

long explanations. He had to cut to the heart of the matter. "Babe, it's plain and simple. I love you, Lexie Rose Thompson."

Lexie's bottom jaw dropped. When Will had said he wanted to talk to her, Lexie assumed she'd hear some last-minute apologies, but definitely not this. His admission of love stunned her. She was at a loss for words and Will took her shock as an opportunity to continue speaking.

"I was afraid to admit it. I've never been in love before, but for the first time in my life I was faced with this foreign emotion and it scared me. Made me push you away when all I wanted to do was draw you near. Lexie. . . ." Will rose from the floor and came to sit beside her on the couch. He tried clutching her hand with both of his, but Lexie snatched it away. "I don't want to lose you. You mean everything to me. You're as tantamount to me as breathing. Without you, I can't go on. Please don't go to Paris. Please stay and share a life with me. I know we can have a great life together if you're willing to take a leap of faith."

"You're asking an awful lot of me, aren't you, Will?" Lexie asked, standing abruptly and facing the window. She saw the driver waving frantically below, but ignored him. "You've treated me horribly, Will. Tossed me aside like I meant nothing, and now you're asking for a second chance?"

"Yes, I am. I know it's bad timing. I should have revealed my true feelings sooner, but I wasn't the only one not being completely honest."

"What?" Lexie turned on her heel. "So now this is all my fault?"

"No, but why don't you tell me how you feel, Lex? Why don't you admit the truth?" Will hurled back at her.

"The truth? You want to know the truth now? When I'm ready to walk out of your life forever? That sure is convenient, Will. The truth is I do love you, Will. I love you so much I can't even think straight. Sometimes you're all I think about, dream about. But I won't be dismissed. I came to you at the club and in the hospital and you asked me to go." Lexie's voice broke. "So, I'm giving you your wish." Lexie rushed to her purse and threw it over her shoulder. "And now it's time for me to go."

"Please don't go, Lexie." Will wasn't going to let another moment slip through his fingers. He rushed to her and pulled her into his arms. "I am so sorry for all I put you through, that I put us both through that kind of misery. Can you ever forgive me?"

Tilting her chin upward and wiping her eyes, Lexie forged on. "Do you think you can just snap your fingers and all the pain from the last couple of weeks will just dissipate into the thin air? Will, it's not that easy," Lexie said, withdrawing from him.

"I never thought it was. But, Lexie, you're the best thing that's ever come into my life. God, for years I thought I wasn't worthy, that I didn't measure up, but you've changed me. When I'm with you, I'm a whole man. Free to love and be loved."

"I . . ." Lexie shook her head. "Plans have been made. What do you want me to do?"

"Plans change," Will stated. "And we adapt. Listen, Lexie, love is a gamble and I guess you have to decide if you're willing to take that risk with me. Will you do it? Will you take a gamble on us?"

Will looked deep into her brown eyes and gently wiped away a tear from her cheek. He prayed she would follow her heart.

"Damn you." Lexie hit Will hard on the shoulder.

"Ouch!"

"Damn you." Lexie hit him again.

"Does this mean you're not leaving?" Will asked, holding his breath.

There was a pregnant pause in which Lexie shook her tresses and fought with herself before finally uttering, "You know I can't leave." Grabbing his face in her hands, Lexie pressed her lips hard against his. Will opened his mouth to her invading tongue and Lexie darted inside, drinking in the warm interior of his sweet, sweet mouth. When they finally separated, Lexie let him have it.

"Why did you let things get this far? We could have lost each other forever."

"Then I would have hopped a plane across an ocean to the City of Lights."

"You're mad. Do you know that?" Lexie cried as tears fell down her cheeks in earnest. "And that's why I adore you."

"Oh, God, Lex. I love you so much." Will rained kisses all over her face and neck. When he finally let up, Will shared his great news about Risqué.

"You mean to tell me that Risqué is back on?" Lexie's eyes widened in astonishment. "That's fantastic news!" Lexie swung her arms around his neck. "Risqué is going to rock this town."

"You'd better believe it." Will smiled.

Several hours later, snuggled in the comfort of each other's arms and languid from a splendiferous night of lovemaking, Lexie started to inform Will of Natasha's idea. But, with a finger over her lips, he stopped her. "I know I'm asking you to give up a lot for me, Lexie. I hope I'm worth it."

"Don't doubt yourself, Will. Don't you ever wonder

why I came to the club that night?" she asked, resting her head on her elbow.

"I assumed it was to convince me to stop being so bullheaded," Will answered, looking into her beautiful face.

Lexie chuckled. "That was part of it. But the truth is I came to tell you that I had an idea on how I could still live my dream without ever leaving your side."

Intrigued, Will sat up. When he did, the covers slid down and revealed his muscular thighs and trim waist. Lexie tried refocusing. "And?"

"Oh, yes," Lexie continued. "A reporter suggested I open my own line."

"Isn't that what Bentley's was offering?" Will asked.

"Yes, but to be sold exclusively to their stores. If I open my own line independently, I would have autonomy and could sell to any store. It's a lot of work and a huge gamble, but the payoffs could be huge. And if all those reviews were right, then it's worth a shot, don't you think?"

"Honey, I think it's a great idea." Will gave Lexie a firm squeeze. "If you need any advice, I'm always here for you. You know how I feel about supporting and promoting black entrepreneurs. And after the success I've had with salvaging Millennium, I'd be more than happy to lend a hand."

And, boy, would she need it. The thought of going into business terrified Lexie. She had seen the trials and tribulations a small business owner could go through, but if anyone could do it, she could.

Yet one final question disturbed her and she couldn't resist interrogating Will. "Will, how did you know I was still in Chicago?"

"Umm, I don't know." Avoiding her eyes, Will looked up at a speck on the ceiling.

"Hmmm, you wouldn't by chance have heard it from my mother, would you?" Lexie said, tickling him at his side until he turned to face her.

Laughing uncontrollably, Will finally gave up. "Okay, okay, I give up. Isabel came to see me and told me I would be a fool if I let you go to Paris."

Lexie snapped her fingers. "I knew it. The woman was too cool when I saying my good-byes. She just couldn't resist meddling in my love life."

"Well, this time," Will playfully kissed the sides of her mouth, "it worked out in our favor."

"It sure did," Lexie said, throwing Will down on the bed. Within seconds, her nightie was lying in a puddle on the floor. "Hmmm, remind me to thank her later." Lexie turned off the lights.

"I will, I will," Will murmured as Lexie placed a tantalizingly sweet kiss on his warm, inviting lips.

Dear Reader,

I hope you enjoyed reading *Dare to Love*, a connecting tale using characters that I grew to love in *One Magic Moment*. Breathing new life into Lexie and Will while still being true to the first book was a challenge, but one I tremendously enjoyed.

It was especially thrilling to write Lexie, a completely different character from my naïve first heroine, Nia. Feisty and vibrant, Lexie started the novel as the sexy friend we all love to hate, but over the course of the book, she grew from a vamp into a courageous woman risking it all for love and success. And, as you well know, Will's no angel, but maybe a leap of faith is all that's required to have a happy ending.

If you're wondering if the Taylor/Bradley saga is over, never fear. A third installment of their stories will continue with brilliant photographer Sebastian Thompson and art seller Leah Gideon.

More information about me is available on my Website at www.yahrahstjohn.com. Please feel free to drop me a note at yahrah@yahrahstjohn.com or via regular mail: Yahrah St. John, P.O. Box 770305, Orlando, Florida 32837.

Best Wishes,

Yahrah St. John

About the Author

Yahrah St. John lives in Orlando but was born in the Windy City, Chicago. A graduate of Hyde Park Career Academy, she earned a bachelor of arts degree in English from Northwestern University. Presently, she works as an assistant property manager for a commercial real estate company.

A member of Romance Writers of America, St. John is an avid reader with a passion for the arts, cooking, travel and adventure sports, but her true passion remains writing. Yahrah first began writing at the age of twelve and since that time has written over twenty short stories. Currently, she is hard at work on her third novel.

SIZZLING ROMANCE BY
Rochelle Alers